TORN APART

TORN APART

SHARON SALA

THORNDIKE
CHIVERS

This Large Print edition is published by Thorndike Press, Waterville, Maine, USA and by BBC Audiobooks Ltd, Bath, England.
Thorndike Press, a part of Gale, Cengage Learning.
A Storm Front Novel #2.
The moral right of the author has been asserted.

The text of this Large Print edition is unabridged.
Other aspects of the book may vary from the original edition.
Set in 16 pt. Plantin.

LIBRARY OF CONGRESS CATALOGING-IN-PUBLICATION DATA
Sala, Sharon.

Sala, Sharon.
    Torn apart / by Sharon Sala. — Large print ed.
      p. cm. — (A storm front novel ; no. 2) (Thorndike Press large print basic)
    ISBN-13: 978-1-4104-2892-9
    ISBN-10: 1-4104-2892-3
    1. Missing children—Fiction. 2. Kidnapping—Fiction. 3. Louisiana—Fiction. 4. Domestic fiction. 5. Large type books. I. Title.
    PS3569.A4565T67 2010
    813'.54—dc22
                          2010023613

BRITISH LIBRARY CATALOGUING-IN-PUBLICATION DATA AVAILABLE
Published in 2010 in the U.S. by arrangement with Harlequin Books S. A.
Published in 2011 in the U.K. by arrangement with Harlequin Enterprises II B.V.

U.K. Hardcover: 978 1 408 49295 6 (Chivers Large Print)
U.K. Softcover: 978 1 408 49296 3 (Camden Large Print)

Printed in the United States of America
1 2 3 4 5 6 7 14 13 12 11 10

Every day, every minute,
in a thousand homes and
cities around the world,
children are being molested.

They are at the mercy
of their predators,
who stalk them like prey; they are
overwhelmed by what is happening,
too frightened and intimidated
to fight back.

And every night, thousands of
children like the
little boy in my story suffer silently
under fear of death.

God will take care of the predators.

It is up to us to speak for their victims.

In my small way, by telling this story,
I am shouting aloud for the world to
pay attention —
for people not to look away.

For everyone who ever
suffered in silence
and for all the children who
never made it home —
this book is for you.

ONE

Bordelaise, Louisiana, May

Moonlight coming through the thin veil of curtains cast a pale yellow glow on the sweat-slicked bodies of the couple in the four-poster bed.

The woman's long dark hair spilled across the pillow beneath her head, while the man's hair, still damp from an earlier shower, glistened in the moonlight.

Her legs were locked around his waist.

His hands were braced on either side of her body.

The intensity of their lovemaking was, as always, made all the sweeter because their time together was so brief. But the briefness of their interlude was not because this was a secretive affair. J.R. and Katie Earle were married, and to each other. It was his job that kept them apart.

A single bead of sweat ran from J.R.'s hair and down the middle of his back, but he didn't feel it. The only thing on his mind was how good it felt to be making slow, sweet love to Katie.

Their bodies rocked in perfect rhythm — the kind that true partners know — meeting each other thrust for thrust as the heat between them grew. Like dancers caught in the spotlight of moonglow, their bodies moved in graceful passion.

It wasn't until Katie began to moan and her body began to tremble that J.R. lost his own control. He gave up and gave in, spilling his seed deep inside her in wave after wave of helpless ecstasy.

Katie was still shaking from the rocket ride of her climax when J.R. buried his face against the side of her neck and then covered her face with kisses.

"Ah, God . . . Katie . . . so good. So good. You don't know how I miss you when I'm gone."

Katie shuddered on a sigh as she wrapped her arms around his neck.

"I love you so much," she said softly.

J.R.'s heart skipped. That was a vow that never got old.

"I love you, too, baby," he said softly, then pulled her to him and closed his eyes.

Like all married couples, their lives weren't

perfect. Katie would have been happier if J.R.'s job didn't take him away from home, if they could be together every night, like most of the other families in Bordelaise. It wasn't the best of situations, but his job was too good to give up, and until now, they'd had no other options.

What Katie didn't know was that this weekend, J.R. had come with a secret. Macklan Brothers Oil had just given him a promotion that would mean he'd be home every night. All they had to do was move to New Orleans and their lives would be perfect.

But there was a kink yet to be ironed out. J.R. knew how attached his wife was to this town and this house, and how fragile she had been emotionally since her parents' deaths.

Katie's parents had lived in Bordelaise all their lives until J.R. and Katie got married. That was when they'd deeded their little house to the newlyweds as a wedding present and moved to New Orleans, and that was where they were living when their grandson, Bobby, was born. Just before his second birthday, Hurricane Katrina hit. Communication ground to a halt. Cell phones didn't work. People who'd been evacuated became separated from their families. Hundreds upon hundreds of people were unaccounted for. And Katie's parents were among them.

The days of not knowing had turned into weeks of pure misery before their bodies were finally found, floating in what had once been the attic of their home.

If it hadn't been for J.R. and the knowledge that she had to stay strong for the child who needed her, Katie would have lost her mind.

They'd gotten through the tragedy together, even though there were still times when the knowledge of how her parents had died threatened to overwhelm her. But the familiarity of Bordelaise, and the comfort of living in her childhood home, had been a buffer against the pain.

J.R. knew she hated being apart from him as much as he did her, but he was afraid to tell her about the promotion, and uncertain how she was going to feel about moving to the city of her nightmares.

It was that very fear that had kept him from blurting out his news the moment he'd walked in, and it was still that fear that kept him silent as they fell asleep in each other's arms.

On the other side of town, the window-unit

10

air conditioner on the south wall of Newton Collins's trailer house vibrated noisily as it wheezed out intermittent puffs of cool air. The living room where Newt was sitting was dark, as were most of the other homes in Bordelaise. But that was as it should be, considering it was after midnight. The only other sound in the room was the steady slapping sound of flesh against flesh as Newt pumped his erection with rock-solid rhythm.

His lips were slack, his gaze locked on the flickering light of his computer screen, which showed the innocent faces of the pretty little boys cavorting on a trampoline. That the little boys were nude was just icing on the cake.

Outside, a passing car suddenly backfired, jarring Newt's concentration. Afraid he would lose his erection, he tugged harder, which distracted his vibe even more. Despite his best efforts, his cock finally went limp. He groaned, then cursed. Now he either spent a night with frustrated dreams, or got up and did something about it.

Even though he was reluctant to leave the comfort of his trailer for the muggy heat of a Louisiana night, he could no more control the urge for satisfaction than he could understand why only pretty little boys got

11

him off.

He dragged himself up from his recliner and began to dress. One positive note about being forty-seven years old and attracted only to little boys was that he didn't need to worry much about his appearance. Women would have been put off by his paunch, narrow-set green eyes and brown, thinning hair. He knew his chin was receding and his nose was too large for his face, but he didn't care. He had no interest in attracting women. They didn't attract him. Why bother to fight it?

By the time he was reaching for his shoes, he was already getting amped just thinking about what came next. He palmed his car keys and headed out the door.

There was an all-night quick stop near the middle of town, and from there it was only two blocks to J.R. and Katie Earle's house. However, he had no interest in the couple who lived there, other than to make sure they didn't know about his midnight runs. For Newt, it was their seven-year-old little boy, Bobby, who was the draw.

But he had to be careful to just look and not touch. He had done time in the California justice system for child molestation, but after leaving the state a few years earlier, he had managed to slip under the radar by keeping his hands to and on himself. His job as a bus mechanic for the Bordelaise School District was the perfect environment for a man with his particular tastes. He was getting paid for a specific skill with engines, with an added bonus of free looks at an endless array of little boys in the school right next door.

Once outside, he broke into an instant sweat from the heat and humidity, and promised himself that when he got to Pinky's Get and Go, he'd buy himself a good, cold Pepsi, and maybe a Snickers bar to go with it. Nothing wrong with adding a little caffeine to the titillation he was seeking.

He got into his truck and started the engine, then quickly switched on the air-conditioning as he drove out of Walker's Trailer Park. Just thinking about Bobby Earle upped his pulse.

When he got to Pinky's, he parked off to the side of the building, away from the single streetlight, and walked inside. As usual, Pinky Barton was behind the counter.

Pinky owned the store and worked the night shift. His wife, Tina, worked the day shift. They attributed their forty-year marriage to the fact that the only time they crossed paths was coming and going from

13

the store.

"How's it going?" Pinky asked, as Newt walked inside.

"Good enough. Couldn't sleep, though," Newt said, as he took a cold bottle of Pepsi from the cooler. He stopped on the way back to the checkout counter and grabbed a can of Vienna sausages.

"Yeah, I hear ya," Pinky said. "Damn heat and humidity. Ain't good for nothin' but skeeters and gators."

Newt didn't have an argument for that.

The yellow tint of neon lights behind the counter reflected off Pinky's bald head as Newt set his cold pop and canned meat on the counter.

"Add a candy bar to that," Newt said, as he flipped a ten-dollar bill onto the counter, chose a Snickers off the shelf beside the register, tore the end off the wrapper and took a big bite while he waited for his change.

"Take it easy," Pinky said, as Newt stuffed the change in his pocket and headed for the door.

"You, too," Newt said, and walked back toward his truck.

But he didn't get in. He cast a quick glance around the area, making sure none of the local cop cars were cruising nearby,

14

then disappeared into the shadows. By the time he got to the street where the Earles lived, he'd finished his candy and was downing the last of his pop. He paused on the sidewalk, giving the neighborhood the once-over. All the house lights were out except for a second-story window down the block.

Newt knew who lived there and that the presence of an upstairs light posed no threat. That was Carlton Weaver's house. Old Carl was a widower with a penchant for women with big boobs. If the light was on, that meant Carl was still up watching the Playboy Channel, which meant he wouldn't give a shit about what was going on outside his house.

Newt glanced up and down the empty streets one last time, then took it as a sign it was time to make his move into the alley that ran behind the Earles' white frame house.

A few yards down, he tossed the empty pop bottle and candy wrapper into a trash can, then popped the top on the can of Vienna sausages. He knew the scent was going to reach the dog in the next backyard before he did, just like he also knew that the routine he'd fostered would keep Old Sounder from barking.

15

Sure enough, as he moved toward the back of the fence, he heard the dog whine in anticipation.

"Hey, boy," he whispered, then paused long enough to dump the meat into the yard.

The old hunting dog was still licking his lips when Newt lifted the lid on the garbage can to dispose of the tin, then ducked behind a hedge and into the Earles' backyard.

Their one-story house was dark except for a dim yellow light coming from the bedroom window on the south side. His heartbeat accelerated, knowing that butter-yellow glow came from a teddy bear night-light in Bobby's room. He would not have been interested in the fact that J.R. had been making love to his wife in the bedroom on the other side of the house, or that he was being watched by a pair of barn owls up in the tree above his head. His entire focus was on getting to that window.

He could hear the steady hum of the air-conditioning unit near the back door, as well as the familiar night sounds of singing crickets and tree frogs. By the time he got to Bobby's window, he had the beginnings of another erection. Hoping that the shade had not been pulled, he stepped behind a pair of lush pink azalea bushes in full bloom and peered into the window, then ran his hand down the front of his pants.

Ahh.

The sheers were pulled back and the shade was more than halfway up, giving Newt an unobstructed view into the room. He could see the little boy's dark, tousled hair against the white of the pillowcase, and one bare arm sticking out from under the covers. He smiled, seeing the brown, floppy teddy bear Bobby clutched beneath his arm. Newt once had one just like that, which strengthened his connection to the child even more.

Anxious to get down to business, he began masturbating, using the fantasy connection to the child as his high.

When the climax came upon him, he groaned and slumped forward — farther than he'd meant to, hitting his shoulder against the side of the house so hard that it rattled the window.

"Shit, shit, shit," he muttered, as he frantically pushed himself back from the wall, then looked up.

To his shock, Bobby Earle was sitting up in bed and staring at him through the curtains with a wide-eyed, panicked expression on his face.

Newt didn't know that to Bobby, the face appeared to be that of a monster — a monster that was surely coming through his window. For a few frantic seconds they stared at each other. The frightened tears running down Bobby's face gave Newt a new kind of high, but when he saw the little boy's mouth suddenly open wide, he knew enough to run before the scream that came afterward. And he did run.

Out of the yard.

Down the alley.

Out onto the sidewalk.

Down the street to his truck, which was still parked in the shadows at Pinky's Get and Go.

By the time he got back to the trailer park, he was fairly confident he'd gotten away without being seen. He crawled into bed and quickly fell asleep, unconcerned about the chaos he'd created.

"Mommmeee! Mommmeee. Help! Help!"

Katie was awake and running out of the bedroom almost before her eyes were open. The screams coming from her son's bedroom had nearly stopped her heart. J.R. was right behind her, scared half out of his mind. They burst into Bobby's room within seconds of each other.

J.R. turned on the light just as Bobby came up from his bed and leaped into Katie's arms. Katie staggered from the impact, and they would have tumbled to the floor together if J.R. hadn't caught them.

"We're here, honey . . . we're here," Katie soothed, as Bobby's arms snaked around her neck, his little hands fisted in the tangled length of her hair. She turned around and sat down on the side of the bed with him still in her lap. "What's wrong? Did you have a bad dream?" she asked.

"No! No!" he sobbed, burying his face against her neck. "The monster! The monster! He was coming in my window to get me!"

J.R. looked toward the window and frowned. It sounded like a bad dream, but Bobby'd had bad dreams before without this kind of frantic reaction.

Like J.R., Katie glanced toward the window. She didn't see any shadows, or anything that would have made him think of monsters. All she saw was darkness between the sheers on either side of the window. It was then she realized they hadn't drawn the shades.

"I'm sure you were just dreaming," she crooned, rocking him where they sat.

But Bobby wasn't having any of it.

19

"No, Mama, no," he sobbed. "I saw him. I heard him. He was coming in my window!"

J.R. frowned. Heard him?

"What did you hear, son?"

"A thump. A really loud thump. It woke me up. When I looked at the window, the monster was looking in at me."

Katie gasped and looked up at her husband, but he was already ahead of her.

"I'll be right back," he said, and left the room on the run.

Katie heard the sound of his footsteps as he ran through the house, heard him open a drawer in the kitchen where the flashlight was kept and then the slam of the back door as he went out. She didn't think he would find anything, but it was better to be safe than sorry.

"Daddy's going to look," she said softly. "Everything's going to be all right, okay? You know Mama and Daddy won't let anyone or anything hurt you ever . . . right?"

Bobby nodded, but he wasn't turning her loose, and he wasn't lying down. Not until Daddy came back with word that the monster was gone.

J.R. cleared the back porch steps in two leaps and began circling the house. The grass was damp against his feet as he ran through the shadows. The hum of the air conditioner was almost drowned out by the thunder of his own heartbeat. He didn't even notice that the yard had gone silent, that the crickets and tree frogs had stopped their midnight chorus.

He reached the south side of the house within seconds. Light spilled out from Bobby's window onto the lawn in an oblong patch. He swung the flashlight along the line of the house, looking behind bushes and trees, before moving closer to Bobby's window.

He paused between the azaleas and swept the flashlight beam along the ground. He couldn't discern actual footprints, although the grass beneath the window appeared to have been flattened. Then the beam of light caught on something shiny on the side of the house. He frowned, then moved closer.

A few drops of a viscous-looking liquid were running down the side of the house, a snail's trail, he thought. And when he squatted down to shine the light beneath the azaleas and saw two fat slugs beneath the farthest bush, he considered the mystery solved.

J.R. stood, then looked into his son's room. From where he was standing, he had a very clear view of his son and the bed.

He swung the flashlight around the yard again but saw nothing out of place. Even if someone had been in the yard, he was obviously long gone. The fact that he hadn't heard the neighbor's dog barking alleviated even more concern. If there *had* been a prowler or a Peeping Tom in the area, the dog would have freaked. Old Sounder barked at everything.

He walked to the back of the yard, then swung the flashlight up and down the alley, which set off the neighbor's dog, just as he'd known it would. He saw nothing and no one. Then he switched off the flashlight and waited in the dark, looking to see if someone came out of hiding.

But nothing happened. Still uneasy that he was missing something important, he went back and circled the entire house twice, but found nothing amiss. Finally he went back inside, locking the kitchen door behind him, then headed to Bobby's room.

Katie and Bobby were still sitting on the side of the bed. The matching expressions on their faces made him sick. He couldn't help but wonder how many times Katie dealt with things like this on her own when he was gone. It made him even more anxious to get his family moved.

"All's well," he said quickly, then sat down beside them and gave them both a hug. "I promise, buddy," he added, when Bobby frowned. "I went all the way around the house twice, and I looked up and down the alley. Old Sounder wasn't even barking until I got to the end of the yard, and we all know how he likes to bark, right?"

Bobby sniffled, but nodded. Daddy was right about that. Old Sounder barked at everything. So maybe Mama was right, too. Maybe it was just a bad dream. Still, when he crawled out of Mama's lap and back into bed, he was nervous.

Katie saw him glancing toward the window.

"Would it make you feel better if we pulled the shades?" she asked.

He grabbed his teddy bear and tucked it beneath his chin as he nodded.

J.R. quickly pulled the shade, then repositioned the curtains.

"Okay, buddy?"

"Okay, Daddy," Bobby said, but his shaky voice and teary eyes tore at J.R.'s conscience.

"Would you feel better if Daddy and I lay down with you until you fell back to sleep?" Katie asked.

It was all the little boy needed to hear.

"Yes, please," he said, and scooted into the middle of the bed with an expectant expression on his face.

J.R. turned out the lights and climbed in on one side of the bed as Katie lay down on the other. They heard Bobby sigh, watched as he pulled the teddy up against his cheek and closed his eyes.

Katie's heart swelled as she watched father and son settling down together. Bobby was his father in miniature — from the angles in their faces and the slight clefts in their chins, to the dark hair and brown eyes. These were the two most important people in her life. Impulsively, she reached across Bobby and clasped J.R.'s hand.

"I'm so glad you're home," she said softly.

"Me, too," he whispered.

But J.R. couldn't sleep. The secret ate at him as painfully as the fear that kept him from revealing it. So he watched as his family fell back to sleep, leaving him and the teddy bear night-light on guard duty.

The rest of the night passed without incident, and it wasn't until they were getting dressed for church the next morning that J.R. got up the nerve to tell her about the job and the need to move.

Katie had chosen a yellow-and-white polka-dot sundress with a matching white jacket to wear to church. It was bright and sunny outside, and her clothing reflected both the weather and her mood. Getting ready for church with J.R. was one of her favorite things to do.

She loved to watch him shave, scraping away the black-as-sin whiskers. She also loved to watch him get dressed. Despite the fact that they'd been married almost eleven years, she still got turned on by his strong, muscular frame.

When she caught him watching her as they dressed, she thought nothing of it. They loved each other. She was glad he liked to watch her the way she liked to watch him. It wasn't until she was brushing her hair at the vanity, and he walked up behind her and put his hands on her shoulders, that she realized he had something besides sex on his mind.

"Katie . . . honey, you look beautiful already. Come sit down on the bed with me a minute. I have a surprise."

She smiled as she laid down the hairbrush.

"Goody. I love surprises."

J.R. smiled back, but inside his gut was in knots. Something told him this news wasn't going to be as exciting to her as it had been to him.

Katie sat, then turned to face J.R. It wasn't until he took her hands in his and took a deep, shaky breath that she began to worry.

"What? Is something wrong?"

"No, no. To the contrary," he said, and gave her hands a quick squeeze. "I got a promotion."

Katie squealed, then threw her arms around his neck and hugged him.

"Oh, honey . . . that's wonderful! I'm so proud of you. Congratulations!"

J.R. hugged her back. "Thanks, sweetheart. You make me proud, too. All the time. You take care of this house and our son for days on end on your own, and don't think I don't appreciate the sacrifices you make. That's why this promotion is such good news."

"What do you mean?" Katie asked.

"The promotion also means no more traveling from rig to rig all over the country as a troubleshooter. I'll have an office and a regular quitting time. No more motels. No more lonely nights and restaurant food. I can share the burden of raising Bobby with you, and he can grow up knowing we're with him, under the same roof, every night."

Katie nodded, but something wasn't adding up.

"Um, honey . . . how will that work? I

mean, is Macklan Brothers going to open an office here in Bordelaise? It's pretty small and too far inland, I would think."

"No, the office is in New Orleans," J.R. said. "I've already done a little preliminary scouting around for housing, but of course I wouldn't dream of deciding on anything until you were along to help decide."

Katie's smile froze. He saw her eyes widen as all the color bled from her face.

"New Orleans? You want us to move to New Orleans?"

J.R. cupped her face with his hand. "It's a beautiful city. The area I've been looking at has some grand old houses just begging for a swing in the backyard and a little boy to climb up and down those big live oaks."

Katie could feel tears pooling in her eyes, but she couldn't stop the flood of emotions. Her voice was shaking as she asked, "But, J.R. What if we moved there and then Macklan Brothers decided to send you off again, anyway? That would leave Bobby and me alone there. What if —"

J.R. frowned. "I'm not going to be sent away, and the city wouldn't be strange for long. You make friends easily. So does Bobby. Please, Katie. I'm the one who spends almost every night alone, away from you and my son. I'm the one who's missing out on so much . . . so much. This is the first real opportunity we've been given to be together."

"But Mom and Dad . . ."

J.R. gritted his teeth. "Your parents are dead, just like mine. But it wasn't New Orleans's fault that your parents died. There was a hurricane. We live through them here, too. And it wasn't my parents' fault that there was a drunk driver on the road. If I let myself fall into your way of thinking, I'd never leave the house again for fear of getting hit by a drunk driver, right?"

Katie knew he was right, but she couldn't get past the horror of how her parents had died.

"But the levees aren't safe and —"

Before she could finish, she saw J.R.'s expression flatten.

He turned her loose and stood abruptly, then glanced at his watch.

"We're going to be late for church. We'll talk about it more later. I'll go check and see if Bobby is finished dressing. We'll be waiting for you in the car."

She knew as he was walking out of the bedroom that she'd hurt him. But he didn't understand. She couldn't take the chance of leaving the safety of Bordelaise. Not for New Orleans, anyway. Why, oh, why, did it have to be New Orleans?

Suddenly the day that had been so hopeful had turned sour. She got up, retrieved her purse and headed for the front door. Maybe a Sunday sermon would help.

The sermon didn't help, and neither Katie nor J.R. knew how to cope with the sudden chill in their relationship.

When Bobby went outside to play after dinner, J.R. stayed in the kitchen to help Katie clean up.

Her shoulders were stiff with tension. She felt guilty for being the holdout, but she couldn't wrap her mind around moving from Bordelaise. Everything here was familiar. Everything here was surely safer. She couldn't bring herself to look at J.R. and see the disappointment on his face. She knew she was at fault, but didn't have the guts to do anything about it.

J.R. dried dishes without comment, though from time to time he cast a nervous glance at her changing expressions. It was as if he could see what was going through her mind, he thought. Fear. Doubt. Shame. Frustration.

But she had to understand. He was missing out on helping Bobby grow up. Being a weekend husband and father wasn't how he'd envisioned his life. He didn't begrudge the years he'd had to spend away, but he wasn't going to turn his back on the opportunity to have it all, like every other man with a family.

Finally he couldn't stand her silence anymore.

"Katie, can we talk about this again?"

She turned, her hands still dripping with soap and water, her expression frantic. "What's there to talk about? You've already decided!"

The words were little more than a verbal slap in the face.

"That's not true," he said. "I've been given a chance at a life with you and Bobby, and I don't understand why that's not important to you."

Katie's heart sank. "It *is* important. But —"

J.R. flinched. "There isn't a 'but' in that statement, Katie. Either it is or it isn't."

Her heart was pounding so hard she couldn't think.

"I need time," she said.

J.R. shrugged. "Fine."

He laid the dish towel down on the counter and started outside.

"Where are you going?" she asked.

"Outside to play with my son. I have to leave in a couple of hours and won't see him — or you — again for another five days."

Tears blurred Katie's vision as the door slammed behind him.

This was all her fault, and she knew it. But he had to understand. She couldn't take their son to a city as unsafe as New Orleans. She couldn't put him in that kind of danger.

She walked to the window overlooking the backyard, and then watched as J.R. picked up a baseball bat, then leaned over Bobby's shoulders as he showed him the proper way to grip it.

Their profiles were almost identical. In the years to come, when their son was grown, she knew he would be nothing short of a clone of J. R. Earle.

She didn't know what to do. She didn't want to move to New Orleans, but she also didn't want Bobby to miss these father-son moments. Time was something a person could never get back.

She turned away from the window with tears running down her cheeks, heartsick and guilty.

And later that night, for the first time in their married lives, J.R. left Bordelaise without kissing her goodbye.

Two

J.R.'s anger at his situation was evident everywhere, from the tension in his face to the length of his stride. This wasn't supposed to be happening anymore.

He had been sent to a Macklan offshore rig to fix a mess and had been stranded here for more than twenty-four hours. What had started out as a day trip to rig number seven in the Gulf of Mexico was turning into a nightmare.

Tropical Storm Bonnie, which had been out in the ocean for several days, had just been upgraded to a hurricane and was headed in their general direction. The National Weather Center was announcing the possibility that the storm could turn toward Houston once it neared land, rather than the coast of New Orleans, which had been the first prediction. Even though the hurricane would most likely veer west, that

32

wasn't going to stop gale-force winds from hitting the rig, or protect the inland cities from hurricane-related storms.

But the weather wasn't his biggest issue. He was stuck on this rig because a crew chief named Stanton Blalock couldn't leave booze and drugs alone. Blalock had worked his Wednesday shift higher than a kite and, as a result, had gotten careless. It had almost cost a welder his life.

Brent Macklan had been responsible for finding a new troubleshooter to fill the job J.R. had previously handled, and while he'd finally hired someone, the guy was en route from the Middle East and had yet to reach the States.

So when the news of the accident reached Macklan Brothers management, J.R. had been pulled off his job at headquarters, and dispatched to the rig to fire Blalock and escort him off.

No big deal. It wasn't anything J.R. hadn't done before, and it was only for the day. He'd flown out to the rig on the chopper that was going to transport the injured man ashore, then come back for J.R. and Blalock. But they were still over water when J.R. got a second call. The arrival of the new crew chief who was going to take Blalock's place had been delayed. That left the rig minus both a crew chief and a welder.

J.R. had been ordered to stay until the new crew chief's arrival. According to the info, it would take a couple of days to get him here, which meant J.R. was going to have to renege on his weekend with Bobby, which also meant he had to call Katie.

Thus the reason he was pacing.

Just hearing her voice made him hurt in so many ways he couldn't name. Knowing it was his fault they were no longer together didn't make the situation between them any easier. When she'd first refused to discuss the move again, he'd felt rejected on every level. Days had turned into weeks, weeks into a month, and she still wouldn't budge.

Then, out of a sense of desperation, he had gotten an idea. He was going to find and buy their new house on his own, then present her with what he considered a "way out." She could at least come and see it. Maybe spend a few nights there with him and see how she liked it.

But the whole thing had backfired. Instead of feeling curious about what he'd bought, she'd panicked and balked even more. The fight that ensued had been startlingly ugly, and they hadn't spoken more than a few words at a time to each other since.

Now he lived alone in New Orleans Monday through Friday, then made the drive to Bordelaise to get his son. They drove back to New Orleans together to spend the weekends at the new house, leaving Katie alone in the town she refused to leave.

He was still reeling from the fact that she'd chosen to stay behind and separate their family. And now here he was, stranded on this damned rig because of Stanton Blalock, and about to miss his weekend with Bobby. Even worse, if the hurricane shifted direction, the rig would be evacuated, which meant, as acting crew chief, he would have to stay even longer and coordinate that, as well.

After a last rueful glance at the darkening skies, he pulled his cell phone out of his pocket and gave Katie a call.

Katie was doing laundry, making sure Bobby had all the clean clothes he would need when J.R. came to pick him up. She was still reeling from the fact that her cowardice had separated her from the only man she'd ever loved.

The news had rocked Bordelaise. J.R. and Katie Earle had been the perfect couple, or so it had seemed, so when the split happened, everyone thought J.R. must have been cheating.

To Katie's shame, she'd let them think it, unable to admit it was all her fault — that she was too big a coward to follow her man and his work, and that she'd willingly broken up their family rather than move to New Orleans. She felt even more guilty that J.R. knew of the gossip but had kept her secret at the expense of his own reputation.

Now so much time had passed that they'd lost the ability to communicate. Katie dwelled daily on how much she was hurting him. She was a coward, and she knew it — so much so that she could hardly bear to look at herself in the mirror.

Just as she dumped the last load of clothes into the dryer, the phone began to ring. When she saw the caller ID, her heart skipped a beat.

J.R.!

The image of him naked and aroused flashed through her mind as she picked up the phone. It had been a long time — a very long time — since they'd made love anywhere but her dreams. She didn't know her voice was shaking as she answered. All she knew was that she ached for the feel of his arms around her. She combed her fingers through her long, dark hair as if he would be able to see its disarray, then picked up the phone.

"Hello?"

"Katie, it's me. Listen . . . there's a situation on the job."

Katie bit her lip. No hello. No how have you been? Just information.

"Are you okay? Are you hurt?"

J.R. heard the anxiety in her voice and wanted to cry. Instead, he pinched the bridge of his nose and cleared his throat.

"No, no, nothing like that. I'm just stuck out on a rig for a couple of days until the new crew chief flies in, which means I can't come get Bobby tonight."

"Oh. Okay, I'll tell him," she said.

"Make sure you explain how sorry I am, and that as soon as I get free I'll come see him."

"I will."

"Okay. Great."

Don't hang up! Don't hang up! Talk to me. Tell me you don't hate me anymore. Tell me you're coming home. Katie's fingers curled around the receiver so tight they went numb as she willed him to keep talking.

Talk to me, baby. Tell me you miss me. Tell me this is all a mistake. Tell me you'll come to New Orleans. J.R.'s stomach was in knots, willing her to keep talking.

But their thoughts never became words, and the silence lengthened.

J.R. was the first to give in.

"Call if you need anything," he said.

"Take care of yourself," Katie countered.

"You, too," J.R. said, and disconnected before his voice started shaking.

The sudden silence in Katie's ear was brutal. He might as well have slapped her in the face.

She hung up the phone. As she turned, she caught a glimpse of herself in the mirror on the other side of the room. The reflection was startling. Her hair hung limply around her face. The blue in her eyes looked gray, and her face seemed flat and expressionless. Even her lips appeared thinner — even hard. She touched the side of her face, felt the tension in the muscles and took a deep, cleansing breath, trying to make herself relax, but it didn't work.

Too disgusted to look any longer, she turned away. But she couldn't forget what she had seen. The truth was, she looked as sad as she felt.

And that was that, she thought, as she gazed around the room. At least she hadn't been wallowing in self-pity.

Everything in the house was clean and orderly.

Everything was in its place.

She took another deep breath, then exhaled on a sob.

Everything was in its place except the people.

Unable to ignore the emptiness of her life, she dropped into a kitchen chair, laid her head on the table and sobbed.

It had been two days since Mama had told him that Daddy wasn't coming this weekend.

At first he had been disappointed, but by the time Sunday morning rolled around, he was excited about the prospects of going to church with Mama like he used to, and then to the monthly dinner at the church after the services.

He hadn't been to church with Mama since Daddy went to work in New Orleans, so he'd missed his regular Sunday school class and his teacher, Mrs. Bates.

He'd also missed playing with his friends, especially Holly Maxwell. He liked Holly. She was fun. Most girls didn't want to run or get dirty. Holly didn't care if she got dirty, and she could outrun almost everyone in their Sunday school class but him.

He was supposed to be getting ready for church, but he was playing Mario Kart on his DS instead of getting dressed and didn't want to stop. He'd managed to get on his blue jeans and socks, but the red-and-blue-striped shirt Mama had laid out for him to put on was still on the bed beside him.

He glanced up at the door, then back at the game, telling himself he would finish dressing in a minute. The only witness to his dawdling at the moment was Oliver, his favorite sleeping companion, and from the permanent smile on Oliver's face, he didn't seem to mind the delay at all.

Katie was secretly excited to have Bobby for the weekend and refused to feel guilty that J.R. was missing out. After her break-down, she'd consoled herself with the fact that she'd been right about Macklan Brothers. They had given him a promotion, only to fall back into their old ways and send him off on a job. If she had moved to New Orleans, then she and Bobby would be there alone this weekend.

She knew it made no sense, but it didn't seem to matter that they were always alone in Bordelaise. Bordelaise was home. Bordelaise was safe. Bordelaise was not the city from hell.

She glanced at the clock as she put down her hairbrush. It was almost time for them to leave for church. She eyed her reflection one last time, trying to ignore the tiny frown

40

lines between her eyebrows and at the corners of her eyes. They hadn't been there three months ago and were the outward signs of sleepless nights spent in regret for what she'd done.

Convinced she could no more hide the lines than she could wish away the mess her life was in, she tossed the makeup sponge in the trash. Makeup couldn't fix what was wrong with her life. That was up to her.

She glanced at the clock, slipped into white, low-heeled shoes, then smoothed her hands down the front of her white eyelet blouse, tucking it a little tighter down into the waistband of her pink linen slacks, then grabbed the matching jacket. Time to head out the door for church or she and Bobby were going to be late.

"Bobby! Are you ready?" she called.

"Almost!" he yelled, and tossed the DS aside and grabbed for his shirt.

She glanced out the window, then decided to put her umbrella in her purse, since there was a possibility of thundershowers later in the day. The eye of Hurricane Bonnie was headed for Houston, which meant it would miss Louisiana. That was good news. But the storm's by-products could not be ignored. Strong thunderstorms would develop, along with stronger winds inland, but

41

they should be home long before that happened.

Since they lived only two blocks from church, they often walked, especially in warm weather. She decided to walk again today, knowing it would be a good way for Bobby to use up some of his energy before they got there, where the rule of thumb was to be quiet. He was a good boy, but quiet wasn't always on the top of his list.

Katie walked down the hall to Bobby's room, then paused in the doorway. He was sitting on his bed, playing one of his computer games.

"Bobby, you're still in your sock feet. Where are your good shoes?"

He laid down the DS and pointed toward the shiny brown loafers.

"But, Mama, if I wear those shoes, they're gonna stick on the slide."

She smiled. He had a valid point. The gym set at their church was an amazing assortment of swings, ladders, slides and tunnels, and he loved to play on it.

"Okay . . . but make sure you wear the tennis shoes you wear to school, not the ones you wear when Daddy takes you fishing."

His smile, so like his father's, pierced her heart as he bounded off the bed.

"Yes, ma'am," he said, and raced to the closet.

"I'm going to the kitchen to get the cake. I'll meet you at the front door," Katie warned.

"I'll hurry," Bobby said, and dived into the back of his closet in search of the shoes in question.

A few minutes later they were on the sidewalk, heading along the shady path on their way to church. The weather was warm and muggy — typical Louisiana weather for this time of year. Katie was carrying the cake she'd made for the dinner — a three-layer coconut with creamy orange filling — in her best Tupperware cake carrier.

She couldn't help smiling at she watched Bobby bouncing along beside her, then in front of her, then off to the side to investigate interesting rocks and flowers in the yards they passed. It was like walking with a puppy off a leash.

"Look, Mama!" Bobby cried, as he pointed to a large rosebush blooming in a neighbor's yard. "We've got a rosebush with flowers that color at our house in New Orleans, only bigger."

Katie's smile slid sideways as a bit of her good mood disappeared. She couldn't stop the twinge of envy, knowing he had already adjusted to the fact that his parents lived in different houses. It reminded her of a dream she'd had Friday night after J.R.'s call.

In the dream, her mother had come and crawled in bed with her, and told her not to be afraid. Then she kept telling her to go, go, go. She didn't need to wonder where it was her mother wanted her to go, or why she'd had the dream. The guilt she'd lived with was overwhelming. But the dream had set the wheels in motion.

She was beginning to realize she was the only one who could fix the break in her marriage, and was going to tell J.R., when she saw him again, that if he didn't mind, she would like to see the new house. It couldn't hurt to visit. If she was still afraid, she could always come home. She just hoped to God J.R. still wanted her there.

Bobby skipped a few yards ahead of her and pointed to another yard.

"Look, Mama. Wisteria. Your favorite. Daddy planted some of that for you last month."

"They *are* beautiful," Katie said, as her conscience kicked again.

J.R. was always thinking of her. Why hadn't she been able to do the same for him? Just like that, another bit of her good mood was gone.

Bobby didn't notice the shift in her emotions. He was too preoccupied with sharing his news.

"Yeah. And Daddy's going to buy me a puppy. I have always wanted a puppy, haven't I, Mama?"

Katie bit her lip to keep from crying. "Yes, you sure have."

"It would be good to have a dog. He would keep me safe from monsters and stuff," Bobby said, and then squatted down to examine a line of ants crossing the sidewalk a few yards ahead of her.

Katie frowned. It was the first time he'd mentioned monsters since the night he'd had that nightmare. She shifted the cake carrier to a more comfortable position, then clasped his hand as he moved back into step beside her.

"Bobby?"

"Hmm?"

"Do you still have bad dreams about monsters?"

He frowned. "Sometimes."

"Do you have them at Daddy's house?"

"The monster doesn't live in New Orleans. The monster lives here."

Katie's stomach knotted. Lord! She'd had no idea he'd been living with this fear. This was terrible! Now she felt guiltier than ever.

They paused at the intersection as a late-model blue truck drove past, then they crossed together onto the church grounds.

"Here we are," she said brightly, as they started up the walk. "Remember. We're staying for dinner after the services."

"I know," Bobby said. "That means I get to play on the slide after dinner."

"You sure do," she said, and then smiled at the elderly man who greeted them as they entered the church.

"Mornin', Miz Earle . . . Bobby. . . . Ya'll come on in outta that heat."

Katie smiled. "Good morning, Mr. Franklin. How have you been?"

"Can't complain," he said, then pointed to the cake carrier. "That wouldn't happen to be coconut cake, now, would it?"

She grinned. It was her specialty. "You know it is," she said.

"Mmm-hmm . . . I'll be havin' me a piece of that for dessert," he said. "See you later."

She nodded, then walked Bobby down the hall to his classroom before dropping the cake off in the kitchen.

A short while later she slipped into a seat beside a friend and picked up a songbook. Opal Passmore, the church organist, played the first stanza of the song — a signal that the services were about to begin. People began ending their conversations and hurrying to their seats while the thick walls of the old church masked the sound of the rising wind.

As he drove past the intersection by the Methodist Church, Newt Collins could not have stopped his treacherous thoughts any more than he could have stopped breathing.

Oh, Lordy . . . would you looky here! There's pretty little Bobby Earle standing on the street corner with his mama, and doesn't he look cute? Blue jeans, and a red-and-blue-striped shirt, with his hair all combed and parted on the side. Pretty as a picture.

Newt was so excited he circled the block one more time in hopes of a second glimpse. But by the time he drove around again, they'd gone inside.

It hadn't taken long for news to get around Bordelaise that the Earles were separated. But for Newt, the downside of that had been that the kid was no longer in town on the weekends. Newt didn't know what had changed that had put him here today and didn't care. So instead of going straight home as he'd planned, he drove past Pinky's Get and Go, grabbed a cold Pepsi and a Snickers bar, and headed back toward the church.

The kids sometimes played out on the church playground after services. Might as well find a shade tree to park under to enjoy his snack. And if he happened to be parked near that playground when the kids came out, well, it was a free country. A man should be able to enjoy a snack wherever and whenever he so chose. Even when the wind began to pick up a bit, it didn't concern him. The day was hot as hell. A good breeze was a welcome relief.

J.R. was at the helipad, waiting for the second helicopter to arrive. The hurricane had not shifted course, which meant the rig had to be evacuated. One chopper had already come and gone, taking the crew from day shift and their chief, Charlie Watts. J.R. had stayed behind with the men from the night shift.

The wind was rising hourly, and he was starting to worry. If the chopper didn't come soon, they would be stranded, and he was sick and tired of playing nursemaid to Stanton Blalock and doing his work while the other man lay in his bunk or hung out in the mess room, eating and playing cards.

Blalock felt no shame for what he'd done and blamed the accident that had sent the welder to the hospital on faulty equipment. Even worse, a few of his buddies had chosen to back up the lies, which was causing a division in the ranks. There were the "feel sorry for Blalock" crowd, and the "feed Blalock to the fishes" crowd. A time or two, it had taken all of J.R.'s people skills to keep the two factions from an all-out brawl. All he wanted was to get the sorry bastard to dry land, and then get in his truck and go home.

The wind was stronger than ever now, which tied the knot in his belly even tighter. In the back of his mind, he already knew the chopper pilot wouldn't fly in this weather, but until he got the news firsthand, he could still hope.

Just as he started to turn around, Blalock walked up behind him and punched him on the shoulder.

"Hey, Earle! What's up with the ride? When are we gettin' off this damned barge?"

J.R. gritted his teeth, resisting the urge to punch Blalock back, only harder — and in the face.

"We'll leave when the chopper gets here, and then only if it gets in far enough ahead of the storm," J.R. snapped; then his eyes narrowed as he looked at Blalock's face.

The son of a bitch was high again. But

how? J.R. had dumped what he thought was Blalock's stash. Obviously he hadn't found everything. Blalock's pupils were dilated, and his body was tense.

"Damn it, Blalock! You're high again. What the hell's the matter with you?"

"I'm not," Stanton muttered.

"And I'm not stupid! Just get the hell out of my sight."

The other man was cursing beneath his breath as he stumbled back toward his sleeping quarters.

Suddenly a strong gust of wind swept across the landing pad — strong enough that Stanton grabbed hold of a railing to steady his footing, while J.R. ducked his head and leaned into the wind. Stanton cursed.

"Hey, Earle! I'm goin' to the head!" Stanton yelled. "If the chopper gets here before I get back, don't leave without me."

Like that would happen, J.R. thought, and glanced back at Stanton as he walked away, just to make sure he was going where he said he was.

At that moment it dawned on him that this was Sunday. His gut knotted. Katie and Bobby would be in church. He couldn't help but picture her sitting alone on the pew where they used to sit together, then wondered who, if anyone, sat beside her now.

It was difficult to accept that he'd been the one who'd chosen to separate the family. He'd been so sure she would come around. It was ironic that he'd finally gotten the job of his dreams and a house to come home to every night, and he was still alone.

Suddenly his hard hat flew off his head. He turned to grab it, but he was too late as it went rolling along the landing pad, then banged against the railing. He glanced up at the sky again, then ran to retrieve his hat. Once he caught it, he headed for the office on the run. Inside, he reached for his cell phone. He had a feeling the pilot and chopper had already been diverted, but he needed to confirm. He punched in the numbers to the home office, then waited for an answer.

"Macklan Brothers. How may I help you?"

"Angela, it's J.R. I'm still out on the rig. What's the status of the chopper?"

"Hang on a sec and let me check."

The receptionist put him on hold, but only for a few moments, and then his boss came on the line.

"J.R. You still there?" Brent Macklan asked.

He sighed. Where else would he be? The

51

gulf made a damned good moat.

"Yeah. What's up?"

"The pilot who was en route to pick you up has gone off the radar. They think he went down in the gulf. I'm sorry as I can be, but I don't dare try to get another chopper out in this weather."

"Oh, my God," J.R. mumbled. "Was McCoy the pilot?"

"Yes."

J.R. felt sick. He and Hank McCoy had gone to work for Macklan Brothers the same year.

"I am so sorry to hear that," he said.

"How's the weather out there?" Brent asked.

"Steadily worsening. What's the latest weather report?"

"The hurricane is still on the same path, which means y'all need to get below deck and stay there."

"What about New Orleans and the surrounding area?"

"They're predicting severe thunderstorms."

"Did they say anything about the area around Baton Rouge?" he asked, thinking of Bobby and Katie.

"It's pretty much the same all over the state. Severe thunderstorms, strong winds, possibility of tornadoes and hail. The usual."

"Okay, thanks. Keep me posted. As soon as the weather clears, give me a call."

"Will do," Brent said.

J.R. disconnected, then headed for the stairs leading below deck. The remaining crew wasn't going to be happy about the news, but then, neither was he.

The kitchen area of the Bordelaise Methodist Church was buzzing like a hive of bees. Some were cleaning up after the dinner and boxing up food to be taken to some of the congregation's shut-ins, while others were sweeping the floors and putting up folding chairs.

The children, accompanied by their Sunday school teacher, Penny Bates, were outside on the playground. Every so often the sound of their laughter could be heard inside the kitchen, where they were barely aware that the wind had begun to rise.

Katie was drying the last of the coffee cups when a high-pitched shriek came from outside and the pastor came rushing into the kitchen with a panicked expression on his face.

"They're blowing the tornado siren!" he shouted. "Everyone get to the inside hallway!"

53

"The children!" Katie gasped, and headed for the door, only to meet them spilling into the hallway. The siren's steady scream of warning only added to their panic.

Katie was scanning the faces, looking for Bobby, when his little friend, Holly Maxwell, suddenly tripped and fell right in front of her. Before Katie could get to her, another child accidentally stepped on Holly's hand.

The pain of squashed fingers, coupled with fear of the impending storm, drove Holly to let out a scream that made every mother in the church come running. Katie snatched Holly up just as her mother, Frances, arrived, then quickly handed her over.

"Holly fell, then someone stepped on her fingers," Katie said.

"Oh, poor baby," Frances soothed, then gave the little fingers a quick glance before lifting them to her lips. "There, Mama kissed them all better," she murmured, and hurried away, anxious to get to the inside hallway, which was the only accessible place of safety.

Once again Katie's attention shifted. She still needed to find Bobby, but when she turned back toward the door, the last of the children had already run past and were flying down the hallway.

Penny Bates was just coming inside.

"Bobby! Where's Bobby?" Katie cried.

"The children are all inside," Penny said, and hurried after them.

Katie turned and ran, flying through the dining area, then through the church foyer toward the wide inner hallway where everyone was gathering. Families had already reconnected and were crouching down together against the walls.

Children were crying, adults were praying, while white-faced parents sheltered the littlest ones with their own bodies.

Katie paused, scanning the long length of the hall, expecting at any moment to spy Bobby's dark head, or his red-and-blue-striped shirt.

Only he was nowhere in sight.

Nervously, she began going from group to group, calling Bobby's name. By the time she'd reached the end of the hall, she was in a panic.

"Bobby! Bobby Earle!" she screamed, then spun and started running back up the hall, praying she'd overlooked him the first time around, or that he'd been in the bathroom.

"I can't find Bobby! Please! Has anyone seen Bobby? Has anyone seen my son?"

Parents started searching within the crowd, but no stray child emerged.

Katie's heart skipped a beat. He must still be outside! Without hesitation, she bolted.

The pastor realized her intent and tried to grab her as she ran past.

"No! Wait! Mrs. Earle . . . stop! Stop!" he cried, but Katie wasn't stopping for anyone.

She was all the way through the foyer and into the dining area when the glass began shattering in all the windows.

Before she could react, the pastor tackled her from behind and pushed her to the floor. Suddenly the roof was gone, the air was full of spinning debris and the roar above was like the sound of a freight train bearing down on them.

"Let me go!" she shouted. "Bobby! *Bobby!*"

She screamed his name until her voice became lost in the roar of wind above their heads.

THREE

After the chaos, the silence that followed was shocking. The fact that Katie wasn't screaming anymore seemed at odds with her earlier panic. When the pastor helped her to her feet and began asking her if she was hurt, the blank look on her face made his heart skip a beat.

"Katie . . . Katie, dear . . . ?"

Katie was shaking so hard she could hardly stand, but she had to keep moving. There was blood on her face and glass in her hair, but she didn't know it. Her mind had gone into lockdown. Her only thought was getting to her son. She pushed the pastor away and began climbing through the debris.

"Wait! Katie! Katie! Come back!" he cried, but she kept on going.

He was torn between the need to see to the rest of his congregation and the urge to follow her. Then Penny Bates came running into the room and took the decision out of his hands.

"Pastor William! Oh, thank God, you're all right! Where's Katie Earle? Did you find Bobby?"

"No, we didn't. Katie went that way. I couldn't stop her," he said, pointing to where a wall had once stood, then looked over his shoulder. "Is anyone hurt?"

"Not severely . . . maybe a few cuts from flying glass," she said, then started weeping. "Oh, oh, I just don't understand how this happened. I looked behind me before I came in the church. There was no one there. I swear. I was sure he'd come inside with the others."

Her face filled with guilt and panic, she hurried after Katie, leaving him to deal with the congregation.

The quiet within which Katie was moving was at odds with what she was feeling. Inside, she was still screaming. There was a knot in her stomach, and her heart was pounding so hard she thought she would faint. All she could think was to get outside. Then she would surely find Bobby. He had to be all right. She wouldn't let herself believe that God would take her mother and father in such a brutal manner, then take her little boy, too.

A slim figure in pink and white, she moved quickly through the rubble, stumbling past upended furniture, stepping on broken crockery that had been so carefully washed and dried only minutes earlier. She didn't feel pain from the cuts on her face, didn't notice that her fingernails were broken and bleeding from clawing the floor as she'd tried to crawl out from under the man who'd been holding her down.

With her gaze fixed on a gaping hole in what had once been the east wall, she ducked under part of the collapsed ceiling, then crawled over shattered lumber, making her way out of the church.

She kept telling herself that she would surely find Bobby hiding in the long red tunnel at one end of the play gym. He'd hidden there once before, when he'd accidentally torn his shirt and thought she would be angry. When the tornado siren had begun to blow, he must have panicked. He could have crawled inside the tunnel rather than run into the church, thinking he would be safe. That was why Penny Bates hadn't seen him. He had to be okay.

Moments later she emerged from what was left of the church, then stopped as if she'd hit a brick wall. There was so much debris outside, she was completely disoriented. Three cars from the church parking lot were right in front of her, but upside down. Broken pieces of wood from demolished houses had been driven into the ground like stakes. Power lines and the poles between which they'd been strung lay scattered on the ground like a giant's version of pickup sticks. A portion of someone's roof was just to her right, and the ground was littered with everything from people's clothing to dishes, toys and lamp shades.

Sparks from the hot wires had already started a fire near a pile of debris, sending a thin spiral of smoke up into the air. But no matter how hard she looked, she couldn't find a trace of any play gym, or the long red metal tunnel. There were no swings or ladders, no big yellow slide, anywhere in sight.

Then a quick thought occurred to her and brought a huge sense of relief.

"I've come out on the wrong side of the church," she muttered, and began circling the building, but there were no visible landmarks left by which she could orient herself.

Suddenly someone shouted from across the street. She spun too quickly toward the sound, which made her stumble and fall to her knees. That was when she saw the founders' plaque.

"Sweet Jesus," she whispered, as her stomach rolled.

The plaque had been embedded in the wall of the church, just to the right of the front door, more than one hundred years ago, which meant this was the front of the building.

In a panic, she pushed herself up from the ground and shoved the hair from her eyes as a new wave of horror swept through her. If this was the front of the church, then where she'd come out had been the back of the church, which meant all the playground equipment that should have been there was gone.

Too shocked to cry, she started running, but when she rounded the church again, there was no denying the stark and horrifying reality.

The play gym was gone. No yellow slide. No red tunnel. No swings or ladders.

"No, no, no," she moaned, and then put both hands over her mouth to keep from screaming. Then she took a deep breath and began calling his name.

"Bobbeee! Bobbeee! Bobbeee Earle!"

In the distance, the squeal of a siren was the only answer to her call.

Overhead, the faint rumble of passing

thunder rolled across the sky.

All she could think was, *This can't be happening!*

Then something fell behind her with a loud, abrupt crash. She spun, just as a car fell off of the chain-link fence where it had landed and into a neighboring yard.

"Oh, Lord, Lord . . . help me," she whispered, staring in disbelief at the chaos as she began turning in a slow, steady circle.

The houses that had stood across the street were gone, and the houses behind the church were nothing but huge piles of debris. In the next block, she saw something yellow wrapped around a telephone pole, and she gasped.

The slide!

Her belly rolled. Please, God. Please, God . . . no.

She began running down the street toward the slide, calling her son's name aloud.

"Bobbeee . . . Bobbeee . . . Bobbeee!"

That was where Penny Bates found her.

Penny's salt-and-pepper hair was wet and matted, and her clothes were stained with a mixture of dirt and blood. When she spotted Katie stumbling down the block, she started running. When she finally caught up with her, she grabbed her by the arm and turned her around.

"Katie! I've been looking everywhere for you," she said, but Katie didn't seem to know Penny was even there. She just kept muttering beneath her breath and began walking in circles.

Penny wanted to weep. Instead, she grabbed Katie by the shoulders.

"Katie! Look at me!"

Katie's eyes didn't focus. In fact, it was as if she just looked right through her.

Penny shivered. "Oh, Katie . . . Katie, talk to me, honey."

"Bobby's gone," Katie whispered, and then clapped her hands over her mouth as if she'd said a vile thing.

Penny moaned, then pulled Katie into her arms. "Honey . . . I don't know what happened, but I swear to God I didn't run off and leave him. When I looked behind me, there was no one there."

Katie was shaking so hard, she thought she might come undone. She didn't know what to do next. There had to be an answer. He couldn't be dead. The moment the word went through her mind, her system revolted. She turned around and threw up.

She didn't even notice Penny holding her upright, or realize that the older woman was sobbing hysterically.

When the spasm finally passed, Katie staggered backward, then covered her face with both hands.

That was when another thought occurred. What if, when the siren began blowing, Bobby had gotten scared and run home?

"Oh, my God," Katie muttered, as she turned to face Penny. "Home . . . home . . . maybe he went home."

The expression on Katie's face was frightening. Penny put her arm around Katie's shoulders.

"Katie, sweetheart . . . I don't think —"

Penny didn't have time to finish.

Once again Katie's reaction was frantic as she pulled out of Penny's grasp and started running back up the street, dodging downed power lines, crushed cars and uprooted trees.

The thunder of her heartbeat was so loud in her ears she didn't hear the growing number of sirens, as police cars, fire trucks and ambulances were dispatched all over town.

She was oblivious to the people emerging from storm cellars or climbing over debris to get out of their shattered houses. All she knew was that Bobby was lost and she had to find him.

But when she got to the block where their

house should have been, she stopped short.

"No, no, no. This isn't right. This can't be right." Every house on the block had been leveled.

She ran to the spot where the house had once stood, and began climbing over wreckage and calling Bobby's name. A mattress was overturned and leaning against what was left of a tree. She could see something brown that looked like hair sticking out from beneath it. Her heart stopped.

"No. No. Please, God, no," she whispered, as she started toward it.

It wasn't until she got closer that she realized it wasn't Bobby's hair she was seeing. It was Oliver, the teddy bear he slept with each night.

She shoved the mattress aside, then picked up the bear. It was wet and matted with dirt, but she didn't care. It was a link to Bobby. Clutching it to her chest, she looked up, then started calling his name again.

"Bobbeee! Bobbeee! Bobbeee Earle!"

She shouted until her voice was hoarse and her vision was so blurred she couldn't see. Her heart was beating fast — too fast. It was difficult to breathe, but she couldn't stop searching. She kept muttering to herself and walking in circles with the bear hugged beneath her chin.

■ ■ ■ ■

On the chief's instructions, all the available deputies, both volunteer and official, had been dispatched to survey the damage done to Bordelaise.

Deputy Lee Tullius had just radioed in about the church being hit when he saw a woman running down the street and recognized her as Katie Earle. After what had just happened, anyone running in such a frantic manner had to mean trouble.

He'd hit the brakes and backed up, then turned the corner to follow her. Within moments, he realized all the houses on both sides of this block were gone, including the one where Katie lived. His heart sank.

"Oh, Lord," Lee said, then stomped the brakes and shoved the cruiser in Park.

Just as he opened the door, he heard her crying and screaming out a name. When he heard the word *Bobby,* his stomach turned at the thought that she might have lost her son.

Bordelaise had been hit hard, and they were just beginning to realize the depth of devastation. They already knew the nursing home had been damaged, and the jail had been hit bad, the storm taking the roof and the four prisoners who had been incarcerated. Many homes had been damaged, and many others, like the ones on this block, were simply gone. But a missing kid was far worse than losing prisoners or buildings. He slammed the door shut and started after her, shouting.

"Katie! Katie Earle!"

By the time Lee got to her, she was walking in circles and mumbling. He reached for her arm.

At the touch, she flinched, then stared at him with a vacant expression.

"Bobby?"

Lee took her by her shoulders. "No, it's me, Lee."

Recognition flickered across her face. "Lee. I found Oliver, but I can't find Bobby."

"Who's Oliver?" he asked.

She held up the bear.

Shit. Lee's stomach flipped.

"Talk to me, Katie. Where were you when it hit?"

"We were at church and . . ." She shook her head, unable to finish the sentence that would give life to the awful truth.

"Talk to me, Katie. What's wrong? Did he run away from you? Did the tornado siren scare him? What?"

67

Katie shuddered. She meant to explain, but when she opened her mouth, nothing came out but a moan.

In her mind, she was seeing her precious little boy, in his red-and-blue-striped shirt, being sucked up into the storm, picturing his tiny, lifeless body buried somewhere in the citywide debris. And for the first time accepting the horror that had been in the back of her mind all along — the knowledge that if she'd just moved to New Orleans when J.R. wanted her to, this wouldn't be happening.

"Help me, Katie. I can't help you until I know what's wrong."

Again she started to explain, but the sound morphed into a gut-wrenching sob, and once the floodgates of despair had been opened, there was no holding back. Suddenly she arched her back, lifted her face to the heavens and screamed, and once she started screaming, she couldn't stop.

Lee reacted instinctively, grabbing her to keep her from falling. He wrapped his arms around her and held on, pressing her face against his chest, afraid that if he let her go she would be torn apart — as torn and broken as Bordelaise.

The sounds of her screams carried up and down the streets, mingling with faint cries

for help and the sirens blasting from every
direction, and masking the thud of footsteps
as Penny Bates came hurrying toward them.

"Oh, Lord, help us, Lee," Penny gasped,
as she threw her arms around them both.

She hadn't moved so fast in years. Her
lungs were burning, and there was a stitch
in her side that might never go away. Then
she saw the look on Lee's face and reached
for Katie. "Here, give her to me," she said,
and took Katie, who was still holding the
wet, bedraggled bear, into her arms.

Penny's jaw clenched as she clutched
Katie's trembling body. Not until Katie's
screams had dissolved into deep, gut-
wrenching sobs, did Lee ask the question.

"Penny. My God . . . what happened?"

Penny's lips were trembling, but she
wouldn't cry. Not again. The horror of her
guilt was upon her.

"We were at church. The children were
outside playing, and I . . . I was with them
when the siren began to blow. We immediately ran inside. I thought Bobby was
with the others, but then we couldn't find
him. I looked behind me before I went in.
No one was left on the playground, I swear."
Her voice broke, then she took a deep
breath. "I don't . . . I didn't . . . I . . ." She
closed her eyes. When she opened them

again, the sympathy on Lee's face was too painful to bear.

She looked down at Katie, and at that moment, if God had offered, she would gladly have traded her life for that of Katie's son. Bobby had been left in her care, and she'd failed. And because she'd failed, a precious little boy was gone. She didn't know how she was going to live with this guilt and not go mad.

"Get her in the patrol car," Lee ordered. "I'll take her to the hospital."

"I'm coming with her," Penny said.

By the time they drove up to the emergency entrance, Katie was eerily silent. Penny found the blank expression on her face more chilling than her grief had been. She feared life had dealt Katie Earle one blow too many. Tears were drying on Katie's face, but mentally she appeared to have checked out. When they began working on her in the E.R., cutting the clothes from her body to make sure she had no internal injuries, getting an X-ray to check the wounds on her head, they tried to take the bear. But no matter how hard they attempted to remove the toy from her arms, Katie would not let go.

Finally Penny leaned down and whispered in Katie's ear.

70

"Give him to me, Katie. Give him to me. I'll take care of him. I promise."

The blank look was still on Katie's face, but her grip loosened. Penny took the bear, then turned and walked out into the hallway, leaving the doctors and nurses to their task. She had her own job to do, and while she'd failed the first time in keeping Bobby Earle safe, she would not fail again.

She found an empty chair and sat down, the muddy little bear now sitting in her lap. It was missing one black button eye, and one ear was hanging on by only a few soggy threads.

"I'll fix you," she said softly, then closed her eyes and began to pray.

While Katie's world had unraveled, Newt Collins was riding a high. He'd still been across the street from the church when the tornado sirens had gone off. Despite his fixation with the children, his first reaction had been a kick of panic. Tornadoes. Damn, but he hated storms.

When the kids began screaming and running toward the church, he tossed his Pepsi can and candy wrapper out the window and started his truck. All he could think of was to get home, back to his trailer and the community storm cellar at the park.

He was about to drive away when he saw Bobby Earle come crawling out of the long red tunnel. There was a look of confusion his face as he stood. At that point, everything Newt was thinking ground to a halt.

The kid was alone on the playground and seemed uncertain as to what he was supposed to do. The first thought in Newt's mind was to warn him. He slammed the truck in Park and jumped out. He started to call out to Mrs. Bates, to alert her that the kid had been left behind.

But when he slammed the door, Bobby turned and looked him square in the face. Newt felt the boy's panic before he even opened his mouth, and then he realized the kid was afraid, but not of the storm — of him.

Bobby and Holly had been playing in the tunnel, crawling through it on their hands and knees. The noise of their giggles echoed inside the metal tube, along with the thumps and bumps of their shoes as they crawled. So when the siren first began to blow, Bobby hadn't even heard it. All he knew was that Holly turned a corner in front of him and disappeared. By the time he got closer to the opening, he could hear the noise the siren was making. It was so startling that at first he was afraid to come out. Then, when he finally crawled out and saw everyone running toward the church, he realized he was supposed to go in.

Then he heard the familiar sound of a car door slam and turned around. He felt a moment of confusion, and then panicked recognition.

It was the monster from his nightmares come to life.

He started to run, but he tripped and fell, landing belly first and so hard that he lost his breath. At that point he couldn't get up and he couldn't run, and the monster was almost upon him.

Newt saw the panic sweep across the kid's face and knew he'd been made. Before he thought about the consequences, he raced over and swept Bobby up in his arms, then began running back toward his truck.

"It's okay, Bobby! It's okay! You know me," he kept saying as he sprinted across the grass toward the street.

Just as he shoved the boy into the front seat, Bobby caught his first breath.

"Mama! Mama! I want my mama!" Bobby cried, and started trying to climb out of the truck.

Newt slammed the door shut, then grabbed Bobby's arm and yanked him flat.

73

"Be still! Don't you hear that siren? We have to get to shelter or we're gonna blow away!" he yelled, then put the truck in gear and stomped on the accelerator.

The tires spun on the pavement, then caught, and within seconds the blue truck was gone.

Newt was breaking every speed limit, taking the corners on two wheels. His heart was hammering. Adrenaline rushed through his body at such a rate he was almost floating on the high. He hadn't intended to snatch the kid, but now that he had, he was going to make the most of it. As soon as this storm passed, they would be out of here, and no one would be the wiser.

A strong gust of wind broadsided the truck, and for a moment Newt thought they were going to roll. But when he turned another corner, the wind was suddenly behind him. All the while he was driving, the kid continued to fight him, crying and kicking and hitting at him as hard as he could hit.

Finally the driveway to the trailer park came into view. Newt skidded around the turn and screeched to a stop in front of his trailer just as a limb broke off from the tree across the drive and came flying toward him. It hit the back end of his truck with a

74

solid thump. The back glass cracked.

Bobby grabbed the other door and tried to get out, still screaming, "Mama! Mama!"

"Mama's not here," Newt said, and grabbed Bobby's waist and yanked him back inside, then out the driver's door.

The wind was up to a roar and blowing so hard Newt could barely walk as he pulled the boy along.

"Mama! I want my mama!" Bobby cried.

"Shut the fuck up!" Newt shouted, but his voice was carried away by the wind.

Now that he had the kid, taking shelter in the community cellar was out of the question. Newt tightened his grip and started running for the trailer, up the steps and then across the small porch to the front door. Something slammed against the side of the trailer, and it occurred to him that he shouldn't be going inside something so flimsy in such a storm. But his actions had limited his choices. He reached for the doorknob, then found the wind pushing against the storm door was so strong that he couldn't open it with just one hand, no matter how many times he tried. If he turned the kid loose, he would run, and if they stayed out here, they were both likely to die from flying debris.

No sooner had he thought it than there

75

was a loud ripping sound. He spun just as a live oak was torn free from its roots and fell toward them, completely blocking in his truck.

At that moment Bobby realized he had more to fear from the storm than the monster. When he dropped to his knees and rolled up in a ball, it was all the break Newt needed. He grabbed the doorknob with both hands and gave it a yank. The wind caught the door as it was opening and slammed it against the side of the trailer, shattering the Plexiglas windows on impact.

"Son of a bitch!" Newt cried, and then reached for the knob of the inner door.

Going inside was far easier. Once he'd turned the key in the lock, releasing the catch, and grabbed the knob, the force of the wind slammed the door inward. Newt snatched up the kid and all but rolled him inside, then followed just as a neighbor's plastic lawn chair came sailing through the air. It took every ounce of strength he had to push the door shut.

Once again, man and child locked gazes.

Newt wondering if they would live long enough to play his little games.

Bobby wondering if the monster was going to hurt him.

Then something slammed against the

door, and the staring match ended. Newt spun toward the sound, expecting at any moment to see the door caving in. The wind outside had morphed into a roar that sounded like a train coming through a tunnel. The trailer house was shuddering, and it occurred to Newt that they might not live through this.

Then he turned around and realized the kid was nowhere in sight. His pulse rocketed. He began running down the little hallway toward the back door, thinking the boy had gotten out through the back. But the door was still locked from the inside, so though the kid was nowhere to be seen, he had to be inside somewhere.

Newt ducked into the bedroom long enough to assure himself the boy wasn't in there, either, than ran back toward the living room. As he did, he noticed one end of the sofa had been angled toward the middle of the room. Then he saw the kid's shoes and realized Bobby Earle had already taken cover. He dropped to his hands and knees and was crawling behind the sofa as a long, earsplitting shriek of wind filled the room. He threw himself on top of the kid just as the world exploded.

The tornado had passed. The trailer house

was still standing, due only to the number of trees that had fallen down around it. It was quite literally still upright only because of fallen debris.

Bobby's heart was pounding. He would have cried out, but the weight on his back was so heavy there was no air left in his lungs. Just as spots began dancing before his eyes and his view of the floor was turning black, the weight lifted.

He began gasping and choking, drawing much needed oxygen into his lungs as he was dragged up and backward.

"You okay, kid? That was some big wind, wasn't it?" Newt asked, as he began brushing dirt and dust off Bobby's clothes.

Bobby nodded, but something about the way the man kept touching him as he brushed off the dirt set off warning bells. He kept hearing his mama and daddy's warnings: Never talk to a stranger. Never let a stranger touch you in private places.

Wary, he took a couple of steps backward, just out of reach.

Newt was wise to the ruse and followed, until he had Bobby pinned against the wall.

Bobby panicked. He'd been right. The monster was going to hurt him. He knew strangers weren't supposed to do this, but the man was rubbing his chest. Instinctively, he felt threatened and pushed at the thick, fat fingers.

"You're a stranger, so you're not supposed to touch me," Bobby said.

Newt smiled. He'd heard that before.

"But I'm not a stranger. I'm Mr. Newt. . . . I fix the buses at your school. Surely you've seen me there."

Bobby frowned. He'd seen the man before, but not at school. He'd seen him outside his window.

"I don't ride the bus," he whispered.

Newt patted him on the shoulder. "I know that. You live two blocks from Pinky's Get and Go. There's a big dog in the neighbor's yard behind your house named Old Sounder."

Bobby's panic began to recede, just as Newt had known it would. It had been a calculated move on his part. Repeating familiar names made him seem less of a stranger.

"Are you gonna take me home now?" Bobby asked.

Newt frowned. "Not now, kid. That big tree fell down behind the truck, remember? I can't move it until the tree gets cut up. How about I fix you something to eat, okay?"

Tears welled and spilled, silently running

down Bobby's cheeks.

"Oh . . . hey, hey. None of that," Newt said, and took a step backward. He wanted this to work the easy way. He didn't want to have to force him. Everything was better when he taught them how to play. He pointed to the cuts on Bobby's hands and arms, obviously from the fight they'd had trying to get inside the trailer.

"Let's get the blood all washed off and see if I can find some Band-Aids, okay?"

It wasn't okay, but Bobby didn't know what to do about it.

"Mama can doctor me when you take me home," he said.

"Not now," Newt said. "Not now."

He had taken Bobby firmly by the arm and started toward the bathroom when suddenly he heard footsteps running up the porch, and then a loud knocking on the door. He saw relief roll across Bobby Earle's face and knew he had only moments to silence the boy before he gave them away.

"Don't!" he growled, as he grabbed the kid up in his arms and pressed a hand across his mouth.

"Hey, Newt! It's me, Sam! Are you okay?"

Newt rolled his eyes. It was his landlord, Sam Walker. He couldn't get the bastard to fix a damn thing on this piece-of-shit trailer,

80

but now he came knocking?

"Yeah. I'm okay!" he yelled.

"Are you sure?"

"I'm sure. I was in the middle of a bath when the storm hit. I'm not dressed."

Bobby was kicking and squirming in his arms. All of a sudden Newt felt pain in the palm of his hand and realized the kid had just bitten him. He yanked him hard up against his chest, then whispered hot, angry words into his ear.

"You little bastard! Do that again and you're gonna be sorry!"

Just then Sam yelled again. "Get dressed and get out here on the double! Bordelaise took a direct hit from a tornado. They're gonna need every able-bodied man for rescue."

Newt cursed silently. Just once, why couldn't things go his way?

"Yeah, sure . . . give me a few minutes to get dressed and I'll be out."

"We're gathering down at the office. When you're dressed, come on over. You'll have to ride with me. Your truck is blocked in by debris."

"Yeah, okay!" Newt yelled. "Be there in a few!"

He listened to Sam's receding footsteps. When he was certain they were alone again,

81

he stomped toward the bedroom with Bobby still in his arms, then threw him down on the bed and pointed a finger right in the kid's face.

"Don't move, or I swear to God, you'll be sorry."

Bobby shrank against the headboard, then pulled his knees up beneath his chin, ducked his head and began to sob.

Ignoring the sound, Newt went into his closet and started digging through clothes and boxes until he found a small coil of nylon rope and a roll of duct tape.

Then he backed out and paused, as if assessing the situation.

As if sensing the man's gaze on him, Bobby Earle lifted his head.

Newt shrugged. "I'm sorry, kid, but I'm gonna have to tie you up until I get back. It's for your own good. Can't have you running around outside with all the storm debris. You might get hurt."

"I want to go home. Mama is looking for me."

The kid's voice was shaking and there were tears on his face, which was just the way Newt liked it. Right now his dick was so hard it hurt. Damn Sam Walker to hell and back for messing up his plans.

"If I see her, I'll tell her where you are,"

Newt muttered, and kept working without looking down, tying the child's arms and legs to the bedposts until he was spread-eagled in the middle of the bed.

Then he grabbed the duct tape, tore off a strip and plastered it across the kid's mouth. Now, if any more busybodies came by, at least he couldn't cry out.

"I'll be back," Newt said. "You just take yourself a nap. I'll fix us some food when I get back."

He pocketed his house keys and headed out of the trailer on the run, taking care to lock the door behind him.

Bobby flinched at the sound of the slamming door and then began struggling against the ropes, trying to pull himself free. He pulled and bucked until he could no longer stand the pain of the nylon cord cutting into his flesh.

Tears were running down his face. His heart was pounding so hard it was difficult to breathe. He knew his wrists were bleeding from the ropes, and from the way his ankles felt, they must be, too.

He moaned helplessly as he looked up at the ceiling. A cockroach was crawling out of the light fixture. Others were crawling on the walls. The whole place smelled like the bathroom at Pinky's Get and Go. Outside, he could hear people talking and cars honking, and somewhere far off in the distance, sirens were sounding.

At that point he closed his eyes and thought of Daddy. Daddy would come and find him, and find Mama, too, and then everything would be all right. But just in case, he thought he might better ask God for help.

God, it's me. Bobby Earle. Make the bad man go away. Help my mama and daddy find me. Amen.

Oddly enough, the silent prayer seemed to calm him, and as time passed, Bobby began to relax. Despite his discomfort and pain, he finally fell asleep.

FOUR

Bordelaise was in chaos. Downtown had taken a direct hit. The department store was a ruin, a florist shop decimated, the barber shop leveled. The back of the jail, as well as part of the roof, was gone, as were the four prisoners who had been incarcerated. The only positive aspect was that it happened on Sunday morning.

Because of that, every downtown business had been closed, and most of the residents had either been at home, out of town or in church. The siren had given all of them enough warning to take cover. Less than an hour earlier, police chief Hershel Porter had learned that Frank and Maggie North and their grown daughter, Carolina, who lived outside of Bordelaise, had all perished as a result of the storm. Besides an elderly man who had died from a heart attack during the evacuation from the damaged nursing home, those were the only known fatalities.

There were some injuries, but few were severe. The worst of the disaster was to the community itself. Already people who owned chain saws, pickups and dump trucks were gathering in preparation for a citywide recovery effort.

He had just asked one of his deputies to put together a couple of search parties for the missing prisoners, while leaning toward the likelihood that they were most likely dead. With the electric and phone lines down, the police and rescue workers were having to use old-fashioned, handheld radios, and distance was a deterrent to communication.

But the place was in shambles, and he needed all the help he could get. For the past hour he'd been on his two-way, calling for Lee Tullius, one of his deputies. But no matter how many times he paged him, Lee had yet to answer. Frustrated, the chief scanned the crowd and spotted Carter, another deputy, near an ambulance.

"Carter! Have you seen Lee?"

Carter shook his head, then suddenly pointed.

Hershel turned around just as Lee pulled up. He headed toward him at a lope. "Where the hell have you been? I've been calling for you on the handheld for nearly an hour!"

Hershel yelled.

Lee got out of the cruiser, then stopped and leaned against the fender without answering. His face was pale and his chin was trembling, as if he was struggling not to give way to emotion.

It didn't take Hershel long to realize something bad had happened. There were tears in Lee's eyes, which was something Hershel couldn't ever remember seeing. He put a hand on Lee's shoulder.

"Sorry I yelled, son. Talk to me."

"I took Katie Earle to the hospital."

Hershel sighed. "Damn. Is she hurt bad?"

"Other than a few cuts, no."

He frowned. "Then what —"

"Her little boy, Bobby. He was out on the church playground when the tornado hit. Somehow they missed getting him inside, and they're assuming the tornado got him. I found her on the block where her house used to be and —"

Lee stopped in midsentence and looked down at his boots, trying to regain some emotional control.

Hershel waited. He couldn't bring himself to talk for fear his own voice would break. He could handle dead prisoners, even the whole North family, but not a kid. Please, God, not a kid.

Lee cleared his throat, then looked up. "And she was screaming. She kept screaming and screaming and . . . Lord have mercy, Chief, but I'll hear that sound for the rest of my life."

Hershel was suddenly sick to his stomach, and his vision blurred. He yanked his hat off his head and shoved a hand through his hair.

"Damn it! Poor Katie. Katrina took her parents, now a hurricane-spawned tornado takes her boy? What kind of karma is that? Damn, damn, damn." At that point, it occurred to him that the Earle family was separated. "What about J.R.! Has anybody notified J.R.?"

Lee shrugged. "I don't know. Penny Bates is with Katie at the hospital, but when I left, Katie wasn't talking. No idea if anyone called J.R."

"All right. I'll look into it, and again . . . really sorry I snapped."

"No problem, Chief. It's been a hell of a day."

"Yeah, and it ain't over yet," Hershel said. "Go help Carter. I've got him organizing a search. You grew up in the bayou. Maybe you can give them some pointers on places to avoid. I don't want any of my people winding up gator food just looking for dead prisoners."

"Yes, sir," Lee said, and headed across the square, dodging debris as he went.

Hershel's hands were shaking as he turned around and surveyed the scene before him. His house and his family had been spared, which was more than a lot of the citizens of Bordelaise could claim. He just wanted to go home and hug his wife, but he didn't have the luxury. With the power out, the phone system down and the local hospital overwhelmed with storm-related injuries, he might not be going home for days. He took a deep breath, jammed his hat a little tighter on his head and waved down an approaching ambulance.

Newt had a cut on his arm and a blister on his hands, and his belly had been growling for hours. Even though the downtown businesses had been closed when the tornado hit, the rescue crew he was working with had been ordered to go from building to building, making sure no one was inside. They'd worked their way up one side of the street and then down the other without finding any victims before they were sent to Chambers Lumberyard.

The owner had donated all the nails, hammers, plywood and lumber it would take to board up broken windows in the town, and they needed helpers to load up the trucks.

It was getting late, and he hadn't eaten since his candy bar and Pepsi that morning, but his hunger for food took second place to the other hunger he had yet to feed. He kept thinking of the boy tied spread-eagle in his bed, planning what they would do together and how they would do it, and getting excited all over again. He was shoving a stack of two-by-fours onto the flatbed of a truck when someone yelled at him.

"Hey, Newt! I need you for a minute. Would you and Warren come here and give us a hand?"

Warren Boyd was president of the local bank. Newt had smirked to himself several times during the day at how inept Warren was at physical labor. When Newt heard the request, he groaned. Once again, he was going to wind up carrying more than his share of the load.

Preoccupied with his thoughts of Bobby, Newt stepped without looking where he was going and bumped into a jumble of overturned shelves. Caught off guard, he began to stumble and, before he could catch himself, did a belly flop into a huge puddle that had gathered beneath the shelving.

"Son of a bitch!" He groaned, wrinkling

his nose at the smell as he pushed himself up onto his hands and knees.

"You okay, buddy?" Warren asked, as he grabbed Newt's arms and hauled him to his feet.

"Other than the smell of whatever this is, I think so," Newt said.

But he'd spoken too soon. Within seconds, his face began to burn, and then his hands, and finally the skin beneath his clothes. Too his horror, his skin was rapidly turning a fiery red.

"What's wrong?" Warren asked.

Newt was pulling at his shirt and scrubbing his hands across his chest.

"What did I fall in? I'm burning!" Newt cried, and began shedding his clothes in an effort to get the saturated fabric away from his skin.

Warren looked back at the puddle, then at the shattered plastic jugs nearby. He picked one up, quickly scanning the label, then gasped.

"Hey, Newt. That stuff you fell in . . . it's some kind of chemical that removes lacquer and stain from wood."

By now Newt was nearly nude and shrieking as he ran toward the street.

"Help, help! Someone hose me down! I'm on fire!"

His cries for help alerted a contingent of volunteer firemen who were putting out an electrical fire across the street. One of them heard Newt and pivoted with his hose on full blast, catching Newt in the flow.

The force of the water knocked Newt off his feet and rolled him across the ground.

Warren came running out of the lumber-yard with an empty jug in his hand as a paramedic named Darrell jumped from the back of an ambulance.

"What's wrong with him?" Darrell asked.

Warren handed him the jug. "He fell in a puddle of this stuff."

Darrell quickly scanned the label, then waved off the fireman before dropping to his knees beside Newt.

Newt was soaked and trembling from both shock and pain, and gasping for breath.

"It's Newt Collins, right?" Darrell asked.

Momentarily unable to speak, Newt just nodded.

Warren felt compelled to answer. "Yes, his name is Newt. He's the bus mechanic for the school."

Then Newt groaned. "It's burning. . . . My skin is burning."

Darrell glanced up at Warren. "See that ambulance across the street?"

Warren nodded.

"Go tell the driver to bring me a gurney. We need to transport him to the hospital ASAP."

Newt panicked. He couldn't go to the hospital. What would happen to the kid? It would be just like his landlord to get all nosy and go inside the trailer while he was gone. Lord, oh, Lord, that couldn't happen.

"No. I don't wanna go to no hospital," Newt said, and then moaned. "Can't you just give me some pain pills and some burn ointment?"

Warren frowned. "Those are chemical burns, Newt. They need —"

"Damn it! I'm not going to the hospital!" Newt shouted, then crawled to his feet.

He was sick to his stomach and shivering from the pain. Water droplets hung on his pale, hairy body like dew on grass, while the burned parts of his skin continued to worsen.

"Yes, you are," Darrell said. "Warren, go get that gurney . . . now."

Warren took off across the street as Newt continued to moan and cry. By the time the gurney arrived, the burns were blistering. At that point he quit arguing.

They loaded him into the back of the ambulance, where Darrell covered him with a sheet, then began to start an IV.

"Just hang tight. We'll be there in no time."
For Newt, it couldn't be soon enough.

Bobby Earle was dreaming. In the dream, a dark, snakelike funnel came out of the clouds and dropped all the way to the ground. It was tearing roofs off of houses and trees out of the ground. And all the while it was happening, he and Mama were running, trying to get away. Suddenly he fell, and before she could help him up he was torn from her grasp. He was screaming her name as she disappeared from sight. And the moment she disappeared, he woke up.

The shock of the dream, coupled with the reality of his situation, was too much. He looked up at the ceiling as his eyes filled with tears. The cockroaches were still criss-crossing the surface like speeding cars on an expressway.

Suddenly one large roach just let go and dropped from the ceiling onto the bed. Horrified, Bobby shrieked and began kicking and bucking, arching his back in a frantic effort to get it away.

The cockroach skittered away as a feeble, high-pitched sound came out through Bobby's nose. The frayed strands of nylon rope with which he'd been tied dug even deeper into his already abraded wrists and ankles. He immediately froze, willing the pain to stop.

His mind was racing, thinking of how worried Mama must be, and of his little room with the race-car bedspread and the pale green curtains at the windows. He thought of his teddy bear, Oliver, and of the chocolate cake he'd had for dessert at the church. He thought of his room at Daddy's new house, and the puppy they were going to get. What if Mr. Newt never took him home? Who would sleep with Oliver? Would Daddy still get that puppy, even if Bobby didn't live there anymore?

The trauma of his situation was setting in. The pain in his wrists and ankles was almost unbearable. The tape across his mouth stung his skin, and the smell of this house was making him sick.

Suddenly he caught movement from the corner of his eye and turned his head toward the light coming from the only window in the room. The blinds were partially opened, just enough that Bobby could see the limbs of a tree smashed against the window. Through them, he could see a small gray squirrel scampering about, obviously as displaced as Bobby. The little squirrel stopped, and for a moment their gazes locked. He held his breath, afraid if he moved the squirrel would disappear.

But the little squirrel stayed, and slowly Bobby began to relax. Time stilled as critter and child had their moment of communication. Then a sudden sound beneath the tree startled the squirrel, which quickly disappeared. In that moment, a part of Bobby's consciousness let go of reality, and he became that little squirrel — running away, as fast and as far as he could go.

Newt was lying on a bed in the E.R., sheltered behind a curtain while the chaos in the emergency room continued to swell. He could hear doors slamming, people crying, others groaning. Someone called out for a wheelchair. The woman on the other side of his curtain was praying aloud.

His body had gone into shock from the pain of the burns, and he couldn't stop trembling, even though the two nurses who were sluicing his body with a sterile solution were being as gentle as they could be.

"God, oh, God . . . give me something for this pain," Newt kept begging, but the nurses didn't waver.

"Doctor will be here soon," one said. "Just hang in there, Mr. Collins. We're almost done."

"Oh, Lord!" Newt cried out, sputtering and spewing, and batting his eyes madly as they began sluicing them, as well.

He hadn't known the true extent of his problem until they had cut off his underwear. Seeing his penis and testicles as swollen and blistered as the rest of his skin, he soon realized there wasn't going to be any playing going on with Bobby Earle, not until all that healed.

Just when he thought he couldn't take it anymore, the curtains parted and a doctor walked in.

"Hello, Mr. Collins. I'm Dr. Luke. I hear you've suffered some chemical burns. Can you tell me what happened?"

Newt groaned. "I was helping at the lumberyard. I fell in a pool of solvent that was meant to remove lacquer and wood stains from furniture."

"And it appears you're quite sensitive to the compounds that were in it," Luke said, as he began his examination.

"I need something for the pain," Newt begged.

"Let's see about your eyes," the doctor said, then grunted with satisfaction as he checked them. "Is your vision blurred at all?" he asked.

"No, no. I can see fine," Newt muttered.

"It's just the pain. Oh, God, Doc . . . it's killing me."

"Mmm-hmm," Dr. Luke muttered. "They seem to be okay, which is good news."

"Yeah," Newt said. "Good news. What about the pain?"

The doctor scanned the chart, then looked up. "You have no allergies listed, I see."

"I'm not allergic to anything," Newt said, and then shuddered as another wave of pain swept through him. "Please, Doc . . . this is killing me. It feels like my skin is on fire."

Dr. Luke gave one of the nurses an order, then moved to pat Newt's shoulder, stopping as he thought better of touching his patient's ravaged skin.

"I'm prescribing you some codeine. You'll feel relief shortly."

"Thanks," Newt said, but he was thinking about Bobby Earle when he added, "how long will it take for all this to heal?"

Dr. Luke frowned. "I'd say weeks, possibly a month. Chemical burns are tricky. And there's always the threat of infection. You'll have to be supercareful and conscious of cleanliness during the healing process."

Newt tried to remember the last time the trailer had been cleaned and couldn't. This could be a problem.

"How much longer will this take?" he

asked. "I need to get home."

Luke's frown deepened. "Oh, no. You'll need to stay in the hospital, at least for a few days."

Newt shook his head. "Can't. Just give me some medicine and some pain pills. I'm going home."

"Mr. Collins, use your head. The town is without power. You will not have water or electricity for God knows how many days. I do not advise it."

"I don't care," Newt said. "I've got things to take care of at home. As soon as you're done here, I'm leaving."

Dr. Luke frowned. He had a room full of patients yet to be seen, and more were bound to be coming as the day wore on. He couldn't make the man stay, and chances were he would be back on his own, anyway — in worse shape from infection than he was right now.

"It's your funeral," he said shortly, wrote briefly on Newt's chart and left without a goodbye.

Newt frowned. So be it. It wasn't like he could explain that he'd just kidnapped a seven-year-old kid and left him tied to his bed.

A short while later Newt was sitting on the

side of the bed with a sheet wrapped around his torso, waiting for a nurse to return with his meds and instructions. Part of his clothing had been left behind at the lumberyard. The rest of it had been cut off his body when he'd arrived at the hospital. When he got to go home, he was going to be leaving in the sheet.

Thanks to the shot he'd been given, the pain was easing, and he told himself that this was the worst he was going to feel.

As he waited, the curtains between his bed and the next suddenly parted on a breeze. He couldn't see who the patient in the bed was, but he recognized the woman beside it.

Penny Bates.

When Penny suddenly stepped aside for an approaching nurse, Newt got his first good look at the patient, then grunted in shock.

What were the odds that he would wind up in the bed beside the mother of the kid he'd snatched? For a moment he was flooded with both panic and guilt, thinking that if Katie Earle saw him, she would know what he'd done.

Then he took a closer look. There was blood all over her clothes, and she was covered in tiny scratches. When he got to her face, he suddenly shuddered. Except for the fact that her eyes were open, he might have thought she was dead. He wondered what had happened to her and if she was going to die, then realized what a stroke of luck it would be if she did. When Penny began speaking to the nurse, he tuned in to the conversation.

"Have you been able to contact Katie's husband?" Penny asked.

"No," the nurse answered. "The hospital is running on generator power, and both the cell towers and landlines are still down. We're exploring other avenues, but for now, we've done all we can do."

Penny looked at Katie. "What about Katie? What's wrong with her?"

"From all she's gone through, I'd say shock. Emotional trauma is a strange thing. Losing a child in such a violent and sudden manner is devastating." Then she lowered her voice. "Have they found his body yet?"

Penny shook her head. "At least, I don't think so." She looked away and started to weep, unaware that the man in the next bed was far too interested in their business.

But Newt was more than interested. He was ecstatic. They thought the kid had blown away! That meant the only ongoing search for Bobby Earle was looking for a body. The urgency he'd felt to get the kid and get away had just been alleviated. Now he had time to heal. As soon as he was back on his feet, they would be free to leave without fear of pursuit. This had to be a sign!

At that point the nurse readjusted the curtain, and Newt's glimpse into Katie Earle's nightmare ended. A few moments later his own nurse came back and handed him a sheet of paper and a small sack.

"Okay, Mr. Collins. These are your instructions, and these are the pills to keep down infection and pain. Since you're refusing hospitalization, you're advised to come back to the E.R. every day for evaluation."

"If I can," Newt said, holding up his bandaged hands. "I'm not exactly able to drive."

"Ask for help," she said shortly. "There are all kinds of people in Bordelaise who will be glad to give you a ride."

"Oh, yeah, right," Newt said, suddenly remembering he needed to be careful not to raise questions or give anyone cause to come to him.

He winced as he picked up the sack of meds, then slid off the bed, careful not to let the sheet come loose. It was the only thing between him and immodesty.

"See you tomorrow," the nurse said, as Newt began hobbling toward the door.

He paused, then looked back toward the cubicle where Katie Earle was lying. Satisfied that she no longer presented a threat, he walked out of the hospital, stopped by a Red Cross station to get some sandwiches and bottled water, then caught a ride home. By the time he let himself into the trailer house, the codeine shot was beginning to wear off and he'd come to the conclusion that this wasn't going to be such a smooth ride, after all.

FIVE

The front door creaked when it opened. It was a sound Bobby had heard plenty of times in his life. Things squeaked. No big deal. But nothing he'd ever experienced before had prepared him to be kidnapped, gagged and tied to a bed. So when the door suddenly squeaked, then slammed, his heart echoed the sound by slamming against his rib cage.

The man must be back! Maybe now he would untie him and take him home to Mama.

But when no one called out and no one showed up in the doorway, uncertainty turned to anxiety. Then he heard a shuffling sound and the rustle of what sounded like paper being torn. He didn't know he was holding his breath until a low, angry growl echoed throughout the house.

His seven-year-old imagination immediately thought a wild animal had gotten in, and he began to scream. The fact that no one could hear him made his panic even worse.

Every step Newt took was agony. He wanted to cry but settled for a low, heartfelt sigh as he shuffled across the room to the kitchen table. He leaned over to let go of his packages, and as he did, a swift pain shot up his arm.

He gasped, then groaned. A large blister between his wrist and elbow had stuck to the sack, and when he'd put it down, it had ripped the skin right off his arm.

When he began to hear a wild, frantic thumping, followed by a thin, high-pitched squeal, his first thought was, What the hell? Then he remembered the kid.

Without thinking, he dropped the sheet and began shuffling toward the bedroom, unconcerned about how the appearance of a nude, fat, full-grown male with too much body hair, and skin as red and blistered as a freshly boiled lobster, would affect the boy.

By the time he got to the bedroom, his pain was beginning to increase even faster than before. Then he saw the raw skin and blood on Bobby Earle's wrists and ankles, the panic on his face, and knew a moment of regret. It wasn't supposed to be happening like this.

"Hey, hey, kid . . . it's me, Uncle Newt. Calm down, okay? No one's gonna hurt you."

But Bobby Earle had moved past reason. Newt Collins's appearance was terrifying, and he couldn't hear anything Newt was saying for the screams inside his head.

Newt scooted onto the side of the bed, wanting to make things right. He needed to untie the kid to calm him down, and he needed to calm him down before he removed the duct tape from his mouth. But Newt's bandaged hands were clumsy, and getting a firm grip on anything, especially a kid who was thrashing around, was almost impossible.

As he fumbled with the knots in the rope, he felt blisters beginning to pop. He needed Bobby to lie still, to stop bouncing and kicking.

"Easy, kid . . . easy. If you'll just lie still for a — Wait! No! Hey . . . look, I'm trying to . . . Shit, kid! I'm trying to untie you! Lie still!"

Finally all he could think to do was to cut off the ropes.

He abandoned the bedroom and headed for the kitchen. Once there, he began digging through the drawers, trying to remember where he'd put his one and only decent knife, then found it beneath an oven mitt.

As he started back to the bedroom, he paused and picked up the sheet he'd dropped earlier. Although it was a case of too little, too late, he wrapped it toga-style around himself and headed down the hall.

Bobby Earle was so out of his depth, he was on the verge of a mental meltdown. His heart was racing.

Every muscle in his body was trembling.

His clothes were drenched with sweat and sticking to his body. He had no understanding of why this had happened, or how his happy life had turned into a living nightmare. All he knew was that the monster from his dreams was real, and he'd taken him away from Mama and Daddy and tied him to his bed.

Even worse, when the monster had finally come back, he'd come without clothes. At that point Bobby had seen for himself just how monstrous his captor was, with his skin red and blistered and rotting off his body. Bobby was afraid that if the monster got too close, he might catch whatever was wrong with him, like he'd caught the chicken pox from Connor White.

When he heard footsteps coming down

the narrow hallway again, his body tensed. Then his heart began hammering — hammering so fast it was hard to breathe. With his gaze locked on the door, the only person he knew who could hear him was God, and he began to pray.

God, it's me, Bobby. I need help! The monster came and took me away. I don't know where I am, but there's a little gray squirrel who does. If You ask him, he can show You.

Before he could say amen, Newt Collins appeared in the doorway. Bobby registered two facts. He'd covered himself up, and he was carrying a knife. A big knife! Just like the kind Daddy used to cut the heads off catfish. Was the monster going to cut him up, just like Daddy cut up fish?

It was, for Bobby Earle, the last straw in a day filled with terror. The room began to spin, and then everything went black.

Newt's emotions were mixed as he headed down the hall. The silence from the bedroom was heartening. At least the kid had finally stopped thrashing around. Now if he could just cut off the ropes without further injury, they could start their relationship over on a happier note.

He paused as he reached the doorway, unable to ignore the spurt of lust at what a picture the kid made, tied to his bed as if just waiting to play games.

But when he saw the kid's gaze lock onto the knife, he realized he'd made yet another mistake.

Oh, crap!

Before he could open his mouth, Bobby Earle's eyes rolled back in his head and he fainted.

"Well, hell," Newt muttered, then looked on the bright side. "At least the little bastard won't be kicking."

He eased himself down on the side of the bed and gripped the knife firmly. Ignoring the pain, he began sawing through the nylon in short, jerky motions, until finally the ropes were off.

One problem solved, but now he had another. The rope had caused some serious abrasions on the kid's wrists and ankles. They needed some doctoring, but it wasn't like he could take the boy to the doctor. Then he remembered the stuff they'd given him at the hospital.

Moaning and cursing with every step, he managed to get back to the kitchen, where he dug through the sack of medicines and pulled out a tube of antiseptic cream.

By the time Newt finished smearing the

stuff on Bobby's wounds, he was in so much pain he was shaking. He needed to lie down, but had to make sure the kid didn't make a run for it when he fell asleep.

After a fruitless search through the closet for yet another means of restraint, he moved to the single dresser and began digging through the drawers. There had to be something that would work to tie him up but wouldn't cause any more damage.

Then he came across a stash of women's panty hose and paused. The grin that spread over his face was nothing short of evil as he closed his eyes, recalling another time and another kid — a skinny little towhead with big blue eyes who'd also cried for his mama. It had taken finesse, but time had worked out the snags in what had become a long and productive relationship.

He chose a pair in a shade of taupe and retied Bobby's wrists to the bed, opting to leave his legs free.

By the time Newt was through, he was covered in sweat and cursing with every breath. He popped a couple of pain pills, smeared some antibiotic ointment onto his burns and then dropped the sheet and eased himself down on the other side of the bed. He looked down at his raw, blistered penis, gave the kid a regretful glance, then closed his eyes and prayed for oblivion to take away his pain.

Penny hadn't left Katie's side since they'd arrived at the hospital. Still clutching the dirty bear, she had no idea if her house was standing or if her cat, Milford, was still alive, as she sat in Katie's dimly lit hospital room and watched her sleep at last, thanks to the sedative the doctor had prescribed. The guilt of what had happened was so horrifying, she felt as if she deserved to lose everything, too — like Katie Earle.

She'd cried until she couldn't cry anymore and prayed to God for things she knew weren't going to happen. The only thing she had left was her faith, and it was wavering.

At one point, when the nurses ran her out of the room, her thoughts shifted to the search parties. She kept wondering if the hospital had been able to contact J. R. Earle and tried not to think about where they might find Bobby's body, or what condition it might be in. She wanted to remember a happy, dark-haired little boy with brown eyes who insisted on sitting by his little friend, Holly, and who had colored his picture of Jesus in red, white and blue.

As she paced the halls, waiting to be allowed back inside, she noticed how much

111

quieter it was here than it had been in E.R. It should have given her a peaceful vibe, but all it reminded her of was a funeral.

When she was finally allowed back inside the room, Penny resumed her watch, like an on-duty sentry. A short while later, she heard a page go out for Dr. Luke and wondered who else's life was coming apart.

A short while later a nurse entered the room carrying a syringe full of something that she promptly shot into Katie's IV.

"Any change?" Penny asked.

The nurse glanced at the machines, noting the vitals, then shook her head. "These things take time."

Penny's gaze shifted to Katie's pale face, and she shuddered. "Has anyone been able to contact her husband?"

"Not to my knowledge," the nurse said, and adjusted the drip in the IV.

"Why not? We know he's in New Orleans. Surely the police there can locate him through the company he works for."

The nurse shrugged. "All I know is that Hurricane Bonnie is playing havoc there, as well. The entire coastline has been inundated with storms."

"Lord, Lord," Penny muttered, and reached for Katie's hand. "She's in bad shape. She needs J.R."

"I'll let you know if we hear anything," the nurse said, then gave Penny a rueful smile and left.

Penny blinked away the tears, then swept a strand of hair away from Katie's eyes.

"I'm here, honey. Whenever you're ready, you come on back to us, you hear?"

She paused, waiting to see if Katie would come to herself and talk back, but it didn't happen. Because there was nothing more she could do for Katie Earle, she bowed her head and prayed for Bobby.

Bordelaise was a city in crisis. The electricity was still out in many places, even though crews were working around the clock, trying to restore power. Inside the houses that had escaped damage, the night air was hot and muggy, making sleep an impossibility.

For the residents who'd lost everything in the storm, the temporary shelter that had been set up at the high school gymnasium was even hotter. The body heat of the hundreds of displaced residents lying side by side on cots and pallets on the hardwood floors only increased their misery.

Outside, Chief Porter and his deputies cruised the debris-strewn streets, hoping their constant presence would discourage any looters, although they'd commented to one another more than once that they had no place left to lock anyone up, should the need arise.

The search parties had been called off for the night and would resume at daybreak. Until then, there was nothing more anyone could do.

For Frances and Tommy Maxwell, life was a little calmer. After the storm had passed, leaving their little family still intact, they counted their blessings as they headed for home. Even their car, which had been parked in the church parking lot, had escaped serious damage.

Tommy was a farmer at heart but a welder by trade, and they were anxious as to what they would find when they got home. Upon arrival, they were relieved to discover that the tornado had completely missed them.

Frances saw the relief on her husband's face. He and Holly were her world, and she couldn't imagine what it would be like right now to be in Katie Earle's shoes. Tommy wasn't Hollywood handsome, but she loved his green eyes and big smile. He took care of them and loved them, and it was all a woman could want.

But their relief was short-lived. No sooner had they walked into their house than they realized their troubles weren't quite over.

Their daughter, Holly, had run to her room to see if her dolly had escaped the storm, but she'd no sooner gotten out of their sight before they heard her shriek.

Shocked, they looked at each other, then bolted down the hall to find Holly standing in the middle of her room with her dolly at her feet. She was clutching her hand against her chest and screaming at the top of her lungs.

"Holly! Holly! What on earth?" Frances said, as she knelt at her little girl's feet.

"My hand! Dolly hurt it when I tried to pick her up!" she wailed.

Tommy squatted down beside her. "Is that the hand that got stepped on at the church?" he asked.

"Yeeesss!" Holly wailed, and when he tried to examine it, she screamed again.

"What do you think?" Frances asked.

After a more thorough examination of her tiny hand and her shrieks of pain when anything was touched, Tommy made the decision.

"I think we better have a doctor look at it."

"Noooo!" Holly wailed. "I don't want to go to the doctor!"

"I know, but you have to," Tommy said,

then picked her up and carried her back to their car, with Frances right behind him.

When Tommy carried her into the emergency room, they were met by chaos.

An elderly man was sitting in a chair in the hallway, holding a blood-soaked towel to his head. A young woman in red shorts and a gray tank top sat next to him, holding a sleeping baby in her arms. Blood was seeping through a makeshift bandage from a cut on her leg. There were people everywhere, all talking at once, and doctors and nurses moving at breakneck speed, trying to accommodate the victims of the storm.

Shocked, Frances grabbed Tommy's arm. "Oh, Tommy! Just look. Bless their hearts."

Tommy knew he had a few cuts and scratches on his back from shielding his family with his body, but he'd gotten worse building fence. Frances had a few bloody scratches on her face and arms, and one cut at the edge of her hairline. It had left a dingy brown stain in her short blond hair, but that only reminded him of how fortunate they were.

"I know, Frannie. This is awful."

Frances momentarily leaned her head against Tommy's shoulder, taking strength in the fact that they were all in one piece.

But Holly wasn't as appreciative. Her hand hurt, and all the noise and the bloody people scared her. She took one look at the chaos and started to wail.

A doctor walked by, saw the expressions on the couple's faces and bypassed the hospital's usual routine. Instead of finding a nurse and having them spend what was going to amount to hours filling out paperwork, then waiting, he stopped.

"Hey there, honey . . . what's making you cry?"

Holly hid her face as Tommy started talking.

"We were at church when the storm hit, and the kids were outside playing," he said. "When the siren sounded, they ran for the church, and Holly fell and got stepped on in the stampede. We didn't think she was hurt, but now she cries every time anything or anyone touches her hand."

"Then I think we'd better take a look at it," the doctor said softly, and laid a hand on Holly's arm. "Hi, honey. My name is Dr. Luke, and I'm going to be examining your hand, okay?"

"No," she said.

He grinned at Frances and Tommy. "She isn't the first one who's told me that today. Follow me."

It took what seemed like forever, but after his examination, then X-rays, then filling out paperwork while waiting for the X-rays to be read, they finally got a diagnosis.

Dr. Luke parted the curtains surrounding the area where they were waiting, and entered with a nurse and a Tootsie Pop.

"This is Jeanie. She's going to help me put a bandage on your hand," he said, then handed Holly the sucker. "And this is for you. Do you like grape?"

Holly nodded.

The doctor peeled off the paper and handed it to her. She put it in her mouth. Then he turned to her parents. "One of the small bones in her hand is broken. I'm going to set it and splint it."

Frances glanced at Holly, then lowered her voice. "Won't that hurt?"

"I'll give her a shot to deaden the pain," he said, and pointed to the lollipop. "Preventative medicine."

A pain shot, a meltdown and a lollipop later, Holly Maxwell's hand had a splint in place.

"There now," Luke said, as the nurse handed him the last piece of tape, which he wrapped around the splint. "You're going to need to wear this for a while, and keep it dry. I gave some written instructions to

Mommy and Daddy, but I think you three are cleared to go home. How's that?"

Still sucking the grape lollipop and eyeing the contraption on her hand, Holly nodded.

Frances leaned down and whispered in Holly's ear.

"What do you say to Dr. Luke?"

Holly took the lollipop out of her mouth and sniffed.

"Thank you for the sucker, and thank you for fixing my hand."

Dr. Luke patted her blond curls, then wiped a smudge of sticky purple from the corner of her lip.

"You're very welcome. My little girl used to like grape lollipops, too." Then he grinned wryly at the Maxwells. "Unfortunately, she's not so little anymore. She'll be a senior at Loyola University this fall. Time flies."

"You're right about that," Tommy said, and scooped Holly up in his arms, ready to head for home.

Their relief at finding everything still intact faltered some when they realized the power was still out. But Tommy quickly took charge and began hooking up the genera-tors. Frances sat down in her favorite rocker, lifted Holly and her dolly onto her lap and began to rock.

Between the comfort of being at home and

in her mother's arms, and having her dolly tucked under her chin, Holly began to relax. Finally Frances felt it was safe to talk about the events of the day.

"Honey, I'm so sorry your hand is broken. You know it was an accident, right? No one meant to hurt you."

Holly nodded.

"Everyone was running, including you, after the siren went off. You fell down so fast, the children behind you couldn't stop in time to keep from hurting you, right?"

"Uh-huh," Holly said, and looked down at the splint.

"It was a good thing Mrs. Earle picked you up when she did, or you might have been hurt worse."

Holly's eyes widened as she nodded again. The mention of Katie made her mind shift to Bobby. She'd heard everyone talking. She knew the story. They said Bobby had blown away in the storm, which made her sad. Bobby was her friend.

"Mama . . . ?"

"What, baby girl?" Frances murmured, as she smoothed the hair away from her little girl's face and continued to rock.

"Why did that happen to Bobby? He was my goodest friend."

Frances sighed. How did you explain

death to a child and not leave them afraid it would happen to them next?

"We don't always know why bad things happen, honey. We just have to trust in God to take care of us and help us through when they do."

Tears rolled from Holly's eyes and down her cheeks. "But, Mama, if God is taking care of us, then why did He let Bobby get taken away?"

Frances sighed as she pulled her daughter closer. She couldn't help but feel guilty at the joy of knowing she still had her child when Katie did not.

"It's complicated, Holly. Just know that God doesn't make bad things happen, but when they do, He helps us get through them."

Holly's eyes were closed, and she was silent for so long that Frances thought she'd fallen asleep. Just when she thought about getting up and carrying her to her bed, Holly's voice shattered the silence.

"God was wrong, Mama. Pastor William says God can make miracles, so He should have made a miracle and saved my friend. He shouldn't have let that happen."

Frances couldn't help thinking Holly was right. It shouldn't have happened. But it had. And there was nothing to be said that would change the outcome.

"I know how you feel," she said. "And I'm sorry you're so sad."

Holly nodded, but the tears that rolled from the corners of her eyes and down her cheeks tore at Frances's heart, which prompted her to add yet another explanation.

"You know what my grandma Sutton used to say about things like this when I was a little girl?"

Knowing her Mama had once been a little girl never failed to intrigue Holly. "When you were little like me?"

Frances smiled. "Yes, when I was little like you."

Holly almost smiled. "What did she say, Mama?"

"She used to say that when someone died suddenly, someone so loved that no one could believe it had happened, that God must have had a really special job up in heaven, and that He had picked the very best person He knew to do it."

Holly's features stilled. Suddenly she sat up.

"Mama! You mean God took Bobby because He wanted him to work?"

Frances frowned. That wasn't exactly the thought she'd meant to impart. She shrugged.

"I'm saying . . . that's what my grandma Sutton used to say."

Holly's lower lip trembled. "I hope God doesn't have any jobs for me, because I don't want to leave you and Daddy."

If Frances could have taken back what she'd just said, she would have, but it was too late. Unintentionally, she'd added yet another level of stress to her daughter's life.

"You aren't going to go anywhere, so don't worry," Frances said, and started rocking harder.

Holly snuggled, but she still wasn't satisfied. "How do you know that, Mama?"

"I just know. . . . But to make sure, tonight when I say my prayers, I'll make certain to let God know you don't want to go. He'll be fine with that, I'm sure."

That seemed logical to Holly, and she finally relaxed. Within a few minutes the pain meds finally kicked in and she fell asleep.

Frances was putting her to bed when she heard the air-conditioning come on, sending the first waves of cool air into the room. She blew her daughter a kiss and went to see if her husband needed any help.

Hurricane-force waves were breaking above

the deck of the offshore rig as the men who'd been left behind rode out the storm below.

Stanton Blalock was coming down from his last fix and had crawled into a bunk and gone to sleep, leaving J.R. with nothing to do but dwell on his own demons.

He wasn't too worried about their safety, although he'd said a few prayers just in case. It was the inland storms that gave him pause. Four men were in the mess hall playing cards, and the rest sat watching the wall-mounted television. The signal was so bad that the broadcast kept going on and off. But the men who had family in the storm's path were worried as to what was happening back home and kept watching, anyway. J.R. was among them.

He'd tried to call Bordelaise several times but hadn't been able to get through. In this kind of weather, that wasn't unusual, and it was no reason to assume there was anything wrong.

But as he sat with the others, watching the National Weather Center tracking storms across the state, he couldn't stop worrying.

If he hadn't been such a jerk and tried to force a move to New Orleans, they would still be together. He'd been living in motels for years. It wouldn't have killed him to keep it up a while longer, giving Katie time to accept the fact that his job and lifestyle really had changed. He'd been so sure that if he bought the new house she would come, and he was still in a state of shock that their lives had come to this.

Right now Bobby was their only link to each other. But that wasn't enough. Without Katie, J.R. felt like he was dying. During this imposed isolation, he'd come to a conclusion. As soon as this storm passed, he was going back to Bordelaise to beg Katie to forgive him. He would put the new house up for sale and drive to hell and back every day if that was what it was took to keep his family intact.

After hours of watching intermittent broadcasts of weathermen repeating the same warnings over and over, J.R. gave up. He grabbed a cold drink and some cookies from the mess hall, and ate them on the way back to his room. He was so keyed up, he wasn't sure he could sleep, but he needed to rest.

Eventually the weather would change.

A chopper would arrive.

And he and Stanton Blalock would be off the rig and heading for home.

Bobby woke up needing to pee. At first he couldn't figure out where he was or why his arms were stuck above his head when his legs worked just fine. Then he heard a sound behind him and turned his head just as Newt choked on a snore.

The sound was as startling as the sight. Bobby took one look at the nude and blistered body and, once again, began kicking and screaming.

Newt didn't hear the thin, high-pitched squeal, but when the bed began to bounce and a little heel caught him in the side, he woke up with a start.

"What the hell?" He sat up in bed, realized the kid was awake and reacted in anger and pain to being kicked. "Shut up!" he yelled, and clapped his hand across Bobby's face, leaving only his wide, frantic eyes exposed.

Bobby froze as Newt leaned over him.

"If I move my hand, are you gonna kick me again?"

Bobby shook his head.

"Fine," Newt said, and moved his hand.

Bobby took a deep breath but didn't move.

"Good job," Newt said. "I'll take the tape

126

off your mouth if you promise not to scream."

Bobby nodded.

"Little bastard," Newt muttered. "Can't you see I'm hurt, here?"

He reached for the tape, then winced, took a deep breath and tried again. He picked at a corner, trying to get enough loose to get a grip, but soon learned it was harder to get it off than it had been to put it on. Finally he peeled loose a corner and yanked.

Bobby moaned, but quickly swallowed the pain. He'd promised to be quiet.

"Sorry," Newt said, patting Bobby's leg. "It was stuck."

Bobby nodded, gulping back tears, but now that his mouth was free, he had a serious request.

"I need to go to the bathroom."

It suddenly dawned on Newt how long the kid had been here, and he knew it was a miracle he hadn't already peed the bed.

"Yeah, sure, kid," Newt said, and rolled carefully out of bed.

The more time passed, the stiffer and more painful his injuries were becoming. The skin was pulling, and the blisters that hadn't already burst were getting larger.

His steps were slow and careful as he circled the bed, then took the dangling ends of the panty hose between his thumb and fingers and pulled. They came loose from the slip knots easily, a simple task compared to removing the tape.

Within seconds Bobby Earle was free, but his arms were almost numb from being over his head for so long, and he kept wiggling his fingers, hoping the feeling would return.

He felt threatened by the nudity even more than the angry words. He'd seen Daddy naked plenty of times, but it had never seemed scary. He wished Newt would put the sheet back around his body or at least move back.

"Bathroom's right down the hall," Newt said, and led the way. "Follow me."

They walked single file from the bedroom. Bobby kept his eyes averted, and when they stopped at the bathroom, Newt pointed.

"In there," he said, but when the kid tried to close the door, Newt stopped it with his hand. "Leave it open."

Bobby shivered but was afraid to disobey, so he relieved himself with his back to the door. Afterward, he tried to turn on the taps to wash his hands, but no water came out.

"The power is still off," Newt said. "Just wipe your hands on that blue washrag."

Bobby stared at the washcloth, trying to find the color blue beneath all the grime, and opted for wiping his hands on his pants instead. He stepped out of the bathroom, then hesitated, uncertain what he was allowed to do next.

Newt knew he had to do some fast-talking or the kid might make a run for it. With the shape he was in now, there wouldn't be a lot Newt could do to stop him.

"Are you hungry, kid?"

Bobby shrugged; then, in spite of his intention not to, he couldn't help but stare at the man's blistered flesh.

Newt caught the look and figured he would try for some sympathy and explain himself in the process. He wanted the kid to get used to his body — to seeing him naked — and to being naked with him. But the latter would have to come later, after the shock wore off. And it would. He knew kids. They were the most resilient creatures on the planet. Most of them were taught to mind and please grown-ups, and Newt knew how to enrich the process to his gratification.

He walked the kid into the kitchen, then pointed at a chair. Bobby quickly took a seat. Newt sat down in the chair nearest the front door, knowing that with the lower half of his body shielded by the table, the kid would relax.

Then held out his hands and arms.

"We know it's rude not to wear clothes in front of people, right? But as you can see, I got myself a really bad burn. While you were asleep, I had to go help with cleanup downtown."

Bobby wanted to interject that he hadn't been sleepy, he'd been tied to the bed, but he was too afraid to correct the story.

"Anyway, I fell in some stuff that was . . . was . . . like poison. It got all over my clothes, and it burned my skin before I could get them off. The doctor gave me some medicine. It will take a while for it to heal, but until I get better, it hurts too much for anything to touch my skin. Understand?"

Bobby nodded. He was still uncomfortable about all that naked skin, but he was relieved to learn he couldn't catch what was wrong with the man.

Newt took one of the lunch sacks he'd picked up from the Red Cross tent and pushed it toward Bobby.

"This is yours," he said, then cursed beneath his breath as a ripple of pain poured through him. "I got it special for you. Dig in. There's one for me, too, and some bottles of water."

He pushed a water bottle toward Bobby, then popped a couple of pain pills and

130

downed them with a swig of water.

He watched Bobby slide the sandwich out of the wrapper and begin to eat, then smiled encouragingly.

"Way to go, kid. You'll feel better in no time."

Satisfied they were making progress, Newt took out his own sandwich and wolfed it down, before starting on the banana and cookie that had come with it.

He was oblivious to the fact that Bobby Earle was having trouble swallowing past the lump in his throat, but it did occur to him as he sat watching the kid eat that, since he'd just downed some more pain pills, he was going to have trouble staying awake.

So how was this going to work?

He couldn't leave the kid on his own while he slept. And if he tried to tie him back up to the bed and the kid fought him, he was in no shape to hold him down.

When his gaze fell on the pain pills, he got an idea. If they made him sleepy, they would make the kid sleepy, too.

He took out a pill, broke it in half and shoved it across the table.

"Here, kid. I'm sorry about the sores on your wrists and ankles. I doctored them already, but this will help them get well faster, okay?"

131

Bobby eyed the pill, then the pill bottle. He knew that doctors gave out medicine, and he'd watched Newt take some, so he didn't think they would hurt him. And his wrists and ankles *did* hurt. A lot.

He took the pill from Newt's palm and put it in his mouth, but when he tried to swallow it, it wouldn't go down. He began to gag, then cough, then choke.

Afraid he would spit it back up and waste it before he got the thing down, Newt yelled before he thought.

"You have to take a drink of water with it! Damn it to hell, boy! Can't you even take a fucking pill?"

Bobby flinched. The man was angry, and he'd cursed. Still gagging, but too frightened to cough, he took a big swig of water and finally swallowed the pill.

"Did it go down?" Newt asked.

Bobby nodded.

Newt smiled. "Good. You'll feel better in no time. In fact, since we'll be getting well together, that'll make us buddies, right?"

Again Bobby was afraid to argue, so he took another bite of his sandwich. But there was no mayonnaise on the bread, and the cheese was getting dry. He managed to eat a few more bites, then abandoned it for the cookie. It wasn't a homemade cookie like

Mama made, but it was sweet, and Bobby liked sweets.

"That taste good?" Newt asked.

Bobby shrugged.

"What's the matter? Can't you talk?" Newt asked.

"It's not as good as Mama makes," Bobby whispered.

Newt frowned. Now was the time to put that devil to rest. "Yeah . . . about your mama . . ."

Bobby's heart thumped hard against his chest. "Is she coming to get me?"

Newt leaned back in the chair. "No, kid, she's not. I'm real sorry to have to tell you this, but when I was out helping with the cleanup after the storm, Chief Porter told me that your mama didn't make it."

This time the heartbeat in Bobby's chest was so hard he felt sick.

"What do you mean?" he whispered.

"You remember the tornado, right? The one I saved you from?"

Bobby was watching Newt's mouth, hearing the words and feeling like he was going to faint all over again.

Newt went in for the kill without a qualm of conscience. "Well, your mama wasn't as lucky. They told me that she died in the church with a whole bunch of others.

133

Yeah . . . you were really lucky I found you and brought you back here, or you'd be dead, too."

Bobby's breath stopped as the monster's face blurred before his eyes. Paulie Bronson's mama was dead. She died in a car wreck when they were in kindergarten, so he knew that kind of thing happened.

"My mama's dead?"

Newt stifled a grin. This was perfect. They thought the kid had blown away in the storm, and now the kid thought his mama was dead, too. There wouldn't be any running away now. Not when there was nowhere to go and no one to run to.

"That's what Chief Porter said, and he's the police. They don't tell lies, right?"

Bobby's body began to shiver. Wave after wave of panic washed through him. "But you're the monster," he whispered. "And monsters might tell lies."

Newt stifled his surprise. "Why did you call me the monster? Is it because of how I look with the burns and all?"

"No . . . no . . . you're the monster from the window. I saw you in the dark. I saw you, and I told my mama and daddy. My daddy went looking for you, and he'll look for you again."

A sudden chill ran up Newt's spine. The

words sounded too much like a prophecy. He didn't know the kid had recognized him and put two and two together like this. And even worse, the family had taken the boy's story seriously enough to investigate. This drastically changed their situation. He needed to put out a few fires before this got out of hand.

"Now look, kid . . . you must be mistaken. I'm just Uncle Newt, right? I saved you from the storm, and there's no one left to take care of you but me."

"There's my daddy. My daddy will take care of me. You have to tell the police to find my daddy," Bobby whispered, then shuddered, the last of his bravado gone.

"There, there, kid . . . don't cry. Uncle Newt will take care of you. He won't let anything happen to you."

The pain in Bobby's belly moved up to his chest, expanding to such an extent that it hurt to draw breath, and still no sound came out of his mouth.

"You gonna eat the rest of your sandwich?" Newt asked.

Bobby leaned onto the table, hid his face in the crook of his arm and began to sob — deep, gut-wrenching cries that should have pierced the hardest heart.

Newt's eyes narrowed thoughtfully. He

135

hesitated briefly, then reached toward the boy. But instead of patting him on the shoulder in a gesture of comfort, he grabbed the cheese sandwich and began eating it as casually as if they were at a picnic, instead of the wake it had become.

The way he figured it, by the time the kid had cried himself out, the pain pill should have kicked in. It would be an easy trip to walk him back to the bedroom and tie him up again.

Hell. Maybe by the time they woke up the power would be back on. Despite his damned burns, things were already looking up.

Six

The hurricane had long since passed. The drilling crew that had been evacuated was back. Unfortunately, the new crew chief had yet to arrive, which meant J.R. still wasn't going home.

He had just come off a long shift and for the umpteenth time tried to call home, only to get a busy signal. He knew any calls to his home phone would have been forwarded to his cell. The inland storms must have been worse than expected. Usually lines that went down were fixed before this. He couldn't imagine what the hell was happening, but he knew he didn't like it. Frustrated, he crawled into his bunk, but he had been there less than an hour when he was awakened by a thunderous noise. For a moment he thought he was hearing waves pounding against the rig; then he realized someone was pounding on his door and

137

shouting frantically.

What now? he thought, as he swung his legs off the bed and ran to the door.

It was Charlie Watts, the day crew chief, and he was bleeding from a cut on his forehead and holding an even bloodier towel to his nose.

J.R.'s pulse kicked. A dozen different scenarios were going through his mind as he grabbed Charlie and pulled him into his room.

"Charlie! What the hell?"

Charlie mopped at the cut on his forehead, then poked the towel back up under his nose.

"There's a damn riot in the mess hall. I tried to stop it and got this for my trouble. There are so many fighting now, it's out of control. I need help."

"You need to get down to the med station," J.R. said, as he grabbed his jeans and put them on, then began pulling on his boots.

"No, no, I'm all right," Charlie said.

J.R. reached for a T-shirt. "Who started it?"

"Blalock, of course. He has his backers. You know that. Someone said something about Blalock being canned. Someone else laughed. One thing led to another and —"

J.R. pulled the T-shirt over his head.

"Let's go," he said, and ran out the door, with Charlie right behind him.

Long before he reached the stairs leading to the lower level, he could hear the racket. His belly knotted as he took the stairs two at a time, then skipped the last four in a running leap. As they rounded the corner leading to the mess hall, a chair came flying out the door, followed by the man who'd been sitting in it. No sooner did the man hit the floor than he was on his feet and running back inside.

"Shit," J.R. muttered, then dashed into the room. Inside, chaos reigned. With only seconds to assess the situation, he got an idea.

"Charlie, do you have your cigarette lighter?"

Charlie slapped it in J.R.'s palm, then ducked as a plate came sailing past his ear.

"Whatever you're gonna do, do it fast or we'll be eating off the floor," Charlie yelled.

J.R. grabbed an overturned chair, shoved it beneath a sprinkler head and then leaped up onto the seat. Dodging flying crockery and airborne furniture, he flipped on the lighter and held the flame close to the sprinkler.

The ensuing fire alarm blasted in a

earsplitting shriek as the sprinkler heads in the ceiling began to spew. Between the piercing alarm and the cascades of water now pouring down on the men, the fight ended as abruptly as it had begun.

There were a few moments of confusion as the men began looking around.

"Charlie! Get on the horn and tell maintenance to shut down the alarm and the sprinklers!" J.R. shouted.

Charlie nodded and quickly disappeared.

Still amped from the brawl, someone cursed. Another chose to kick a chair, sending it scooting through the water toward an adversary.

"Listen up!" J.R. shouted. "The next son of a bitch who moves or talks is fired. Do I make myself clear?"

The men froze, their focus suddenly locked on the man standing beneath the sprinkler. They'd all seen him around — the troubleshooter who'd come to get Blalock. They knew he was tall, but standing on that chair, he loomed. And with the wet T-shirt plastered to his body, it was impossible not to notice the muscles beneath. At that point, no one wanted to challenge his authority and lose their job.

Suddenly the sprinklers went off, followed by the alarm. The silence that came afterward was startling. The only sound in the room was dripping water.

Seconds later Charlie reappeared, still carrying the bloody towel. That was when J.R. lit into them.

"Which one of you is responsible for Charlie's injuries?" he asked.

Silence.

"You may as well own up to it, because I'm going to find out."

Someone muttered deep in the crowd.

"You have something to say . . . speak up or shut up!" J.R. said.

Stanton Blalock stepped forward with a swagger in his step. Before he could open his mouth, J.R. snapped.

"Your input isn't needed. Your ass is already fired. Get the hell out of here, and don't leave your room until I come to get you, or I swear to God, you'll forfeit whatever salary you have coming to pay for this mess."

Stanton's face flushed a dark, angry red, but he knew better than to argue with J. R. Earle. The man was bigger than he was, and had the balls and the authority to do what he'd just said.

Without comment, he stomped out of the room.

J.R.'s attention shifted back to the men.

141

"Charlie, who hit you?"

Before Charlie could answer, a thirty-something man with a bald head and a thin black mustache shoved through the crowd.

"I did. So what?"

J.R.'s muscles tensed. A challenge. Fine. The way he felt, he was more than up to the task.

"*So what?* This man is your boss, and you don't hit the boss."

"Then he shouldn't have gotten in my way," the man drawled.

"What's your name?"

"Quentin James."

"Now that we've been introduced, your ass is fired, too. Go pack your gear. You'll be leaving the rig with your buddy."

Shock spread across James's face. "You can't do that!"

"Actually, I not only can, I just did."

James's hands curled into fists. "Easy for you to say, standing up there like you owned the fuckin' place."

J.R. jumped off the chair. Water splattered waist-high. The effect was startling.

Before James could react, J.R. was in his face.

"Is this close enough?"

James's face flushed angrily as he doubled up a fist and swung.

J.R. blocked the blow with his left hand, then took the other man out with his right. James dropped like a rock, flat on his back into the water, his arms outspread, his eyes rolling back in his head as he lost consciousness.

J.R. paused, then looked up. "Who else in here has the hots for Blalock?"

There was a brief moment of silence, and then the crowd parted, revealing two men standing apart from the crowd at the back of the room.

Both men appeared nervous. One had an eye that had already swollen shut, the other a gaping cut on his cheek.

"Paulson and Henton, right?"

They nodded.

"Since you guys are such good buddies, I'm thinking you won't want Blalock and James to leave you behind when they go. Go pack your shit. You're fired, too."

Neither one of them wanted to repeat Quentin James's mistake. They hunched their shoulders, shoved their hands in their pockets and had started to walk out when J.R. stopped them.

"Hey!" he yelled.

They stopped.

"Don't forget your girlfriend," he said, pointing to James, who was regaining consciousness.

The trio left, much quieter than they'd been only minutes earlier.

"Is that it?" J.R. asked.

Charlie nodded. "That should do it."

J.R. needed to make sure. "Anyone else got a beef about Blalock?"

No one moved or spoke.

"Good. Then the rest of you can grab some mops and supplies, and clean up the mess you just made."

Thankful to have survived the purge, the remaining men scurried through the water to do as they'd been told.

J.R. shoved a hand through his hair, sending water droplets flying in every direction, then shook his head in disgust.

"Charlie, if you need me, I'll be in the office. I have to call headquarters and get an ETA on our ride home. They also need to know to cut final checks for four men, not just one."

"I'll stay here and help out," Charlie said. "We made a hell of a mess. If we don't fix this place up, the cooks are liable to put us on cold rations for a week."

J.R. headed for the office to make the call. The way things were going, there weren't going to be enough men left on the rig to keep it running.

Thursday morning

When Katie Earle woke up, the first thing she saw was a framed painting of Jesus Christ hanging on the wall, which didn't make sense. There was a mirror opposite their bed. What had happened to the mirror?

And then, like a wave crashing against the shore, everything hit her at once.

The fight with J.R.

The long, empty months sleeping alone in their bed.

The scream of the storm siren.

The tornado.

And living through it all when Bobby had not.

A tide of anger washed over her, flooding every facet of her being. Her body began to tremble as she stared at the painting. All her rage, all her pain, all her grief, was channeled toward the iconic image.

"How dare You?" she cried, her voice breaking with every word. "How dare You do this to me and then leave me behind?"

She started to get up, then realized she was bound to the bed by needles, tubes and monitors, which angered her even more.

145

"Why didn't You let me die?"

But He didn't answer.

The room blurred before her eyes. In frustration, she began yanking at the clips and needles and tubes. As she pulled off the heart monitor, a warning sounded, indicating that her heart had stopped.

Someone shouted out in the hallway. A sudden flurry of footsteps sounded as staffers came running toward her room. They thought Katie Earle had died, when, in fact, she'd just taken her first step back into the world of the living.

Penny Bates had spent an hour outside watering flowers, trying to put a bit of her own world back in order. As usual, her cat, Milford, had chosen to watch from a seat in an old wicker chair nearby. She'd been fighting a growing depression in the only way she knew how: by giving her attention to living things and trying to come to terms with what had happened to Bobby Earle.

Later, when she'd gone inside, she saw that the light was blinking on her answering machine. A message, telling her to come to the hospital.

In a panic, she'd grabbed her purse and made a run for her car. She didn't know if Katie was coming back to herself or if her condition had worsened, but her obligation to the young woman ran deep.

At the hospital, she'd parked close to the front and hurried through the lobby. Once she came out of the elevator onto the second floor, she hurried toward Katie's room. The door was ajar. She pushed it open as she entered the room, then came to an abrupt halt.

The room was empty.

The bed was made.

Penny gasped. What did this mean?

Had Katie died?

She ran out of the room and headed for the nurses' station, praying with every step.

"Where's Katie Earle?" she cried, as she came to a stop at the counter.

The nurse looked up. "Oh, hello, Mrs. Bates. Katie has been released to go home."

Penny stared at the woman as if she'd just lost her mind. Even after she came out of sedation, Katie had been basically comatose since Sunday.

"Is she awake and talking?"

"Oh, she's awake, all right. Doctor checked her over and signed her release. We called you because you were the only person listed on her chart, and she needs a ride home."

Penny leaned over the counter and spoke

slowly, as if trying to explain herself to a child.

"She doesn't have a home. It blew away the same day her child did."

The nurse frowned. "We understand that, but arrangements will have to be made elsewhere. This isn't a motel."

"Oh, for the love of God," Penny muttered. "Have you been able to contact her husband, J.R.?"

The nurse scanned the chart. "I don't see any mention of it."

Penny glared at the nurse, but the woman was otherwise occupied and didn't notice.

"Mrs. Earle just left a few minutes ago with an aide," the nurse said without looking up. "She'll be waiting in the lobby."

Penny gasped. She must have been coming up in the elevator as Katie was going down.

"Is she okay? Was she talking?"

"She had herself a fit and unhooked herself from everything, which gave us quite a start. We thought her heart had stopped. She demanded to go home, and we had no medical reason to keep her."

Penny bit back the angry retort on her lips and headed for the elevator. Her heart was pounding by the time she reached the lobby, nervous as to what shape Katie would be in, and what she was going to do with her.

Then she saw the younger woman across the room, wearing green hospital scrubs and a pair of flip-flops. Her face was devoid of makeup, and her long brown hair was loose around her face. From where Penny was standing, she could have passed for a teenager.

God help me, Penny thought, then lifted her chin and hurried across the lobby.

When Katie saw her coming, she stood and dismissed the aide.

"Thank you for coming to get me," Katie said.

Penny sighed. Katie's eyes were red and swollen, which meant she'd been crying again, but she couldn't blame her. She still cried herself, at least once or twice a day.

"Sweetheart! It's so good to see you up and talking again. I'm just glad you've come back to us. Are you ready to go?"

Reminded that she had nowhere to go to, Katie's bravado suddenly slipped. "Penny?"

"Yes, darling?"

Katie's body started to tremble. "I lost my little boy."

Penny wanted to weep. "I know. I'm so sorry."

"Have they . . . Did they ever . . . ?" She stopped, took a deep breath, and then made herself look into Penny Bates's eyes. "Have they found him?"

"No, darling, not yet."

It was as if all the bones suddenly melted in Katie's body. She went limp, then dropped backward onto the chair behind her.

Penny sat down, then reached for Katie's hand and held it. There wasn't anything else to say.

Tears pooled, then spilled down Katie's cheeks unchecked.

"It's all my fault, you know. If I'd moved with J.R., like he wanted, this wouldn't have happened."

Penny's eyes narrowed thoughtfully. So that was the reason for the separation! Everyone in town had wondered.

"J.R. was already mad at me," Katie said. "Now he's going to hate me."

The poignancy in Katie voice was nearly Penny's undoing.

"Honey . . . J.R. isn't going to hate you. He loves you."

"Not anymore," Katie said, then leaned forward, her voice just above a whisper. "Penny, do you think I'm a bad person?"

Penny tightened her grip. "Lord, no, honey! You're not a bad person. Why would you ever think such a thing?"

"I think God is punishing me."

"Why would you say that?"

"Because He keeps taking away the people I love."

Penny's heart felt as if it were breaking. How did one argue with such an overwhelming grief? Still, she had to say something.

"You know what Pastor William would say to that. He'd remind you that God didn't cause any of this, but He's there to lean on when the bad stuff happens."

Katie shook her head. "I leaned on Him for weeks after Hurricane Katrina. I prayed and prayed for Momma and Daddy to be all right, and you know what happened to them. I leaned on Him when J.R. left me, thinking we would find a way to work it all out, but it didn't happen. Then Bobby disappeared, and I prayed to God to help me find him. It seems to me that leaning on God is a huge waste of time."

Penny frowned. Katie's argument was far stronger than hers, which meant it was time to change the subject.

"God knows you're entitled to your feelings, but we've got the here and now to deal with. So until we can get hold of J.R., you're coming home with me. My house wasn't damaged, and the power is back on."

151

"Oh, Penny, I —"

"Don't argue," Penny said, and then her own voice broke. "If I could, I would have given my own life for your little boy, but it didn't happen that way. Now all any of us can do is take life one day at a time. Besides . . . I've got the teddy bear."

"Oliver? You found Oliver?"

Penny sighed. "No, honey, you did. They gave him to me in the E.R. He was pretty dirty, but I ran him through the washer and dryer, fixed his ear and his eye, and he looks almost as good as new."

Katie was confused and weary, but too numb to argue. When Penny took her by the hand and led her out of the hospital, she didn't resist.

Later, as they drove through Bordelaise toward Penny's house, Katie realized a major cleanup was in progress. So this was what had been happening while she'd temporarily checked out.

She felt almost abandoned, knowing life had a way of going on whether one chose to participate in it or not.

People were everywhere, some removing downed trees, others cleaning up debris, or replacing windows and doors in an effort to put their homes and their lives back together.

She watched for a while and then looked away. If only she could rebuild her own world as easily.

Frances was putting the breakfast dishes in the dishwasher while Holly sat at the kitchen table with a pad of drawing paper and a box of crayons.

Frances had noticed that Holly wasn't going through her normal routines — playing outside with her cat, Tigger, or riding in the swing Tommy had built for her under the big oak — and chalked it up to the splint she was wearing on her broken finger. Instead, Holly had chosen quiet games and indoor pastimes in order to stay close.

Frances understood Holly's fears. They'd all endured an almost unimaginable trauma. It was going to take lots of time and patience to get past what had happened, and she was willing to give Holly all the time she needed.

She glanced over at her little girl's bowed head, caught the intent expression on her face as she colored on the paper and decided now was a good time to start up a conversation.

"Hey, honey . . . what are you drawing?" Frances asked.

Holly laid down a green crayon and then reached for a blue one.

"Pictures of God," she said.

A bit taken aback, Frances wiped her hands on a towel and then sat down at the table with her daughter.

"Why are you drawing pictures of God?" Frances asked.

Holly frowned. "I don't know. I just am."

"May I see?" Frances asked.

Holly pulled a finished one out from beneath her tablet and shoved it across the table.

"Thank you," Frances said, as she smiled at her daughter, then looked down at the drawing.

It wasn't what she'd expected. There were no heavenly beings. No angelic figures with wings and halos, or puffy clouds and shiny auras. Just the playground at the church and cars on the street.

"Honey, this is a nice picture, but I thought you were drawing pictures of God?"

Holly looked up and frowned. "I am."

Frances pushed the picture toward Holly. "I don't understand. Where is God in this picture?"

Holly pointed. "He's right there."

Frances frowned. "But that's just a man in a blue pickup."

"No. That's God . . . when He came for Bobby," Holly said.

Frances's heart skipped a beat. "What do you mean . . . when He came for Bobby?"

Holly sighed. "Mama. You and Daddy both told me God took Bobby to heaven because He needed him to work, remember?"

Frances resisted the urge to argue. Instead, she took a deep, calming breath and then started over.

"No, baby. That's not exactly what we said, but never mind. What I want to know is . . . why do you think God came for Bobby in a blue pickup truck? Is that how you think God takes people to heaven?"

Holly shrugged. "I don't know. It's just what I saw, that's all."

Frances's breath caught. "What do you mean . . . that's what you saw?"

Holly shrugged. "Because that *is* what I saw," she said with the pure logic of a child, then reached for a yellow crayon to color the slide in her current picture.

Frances was getting scared. This didn't make sense.

"Tell me, baby. Tell me exactly when it was that you saw the man in the blue pickup take Bobby."

Holly frowned. "God. You said it was God, remember?"

Frances's head was spinning. Had her

daughter been a witness to something more than a storm.

"I know, I know," Frances said. "But maybe I was mistaken. I want you to tell Mama exactly what it was you saw and when you saw it, okay?"

Holly looked up. "Okay."

Frances sat without moving, listening to a story that chilled her heart, and when Holly was done, she got up from the chair and walked into the other room. She called Tommy first; then, after a brief conversation, she hung up and made a second call to the police.

Hershel Porter was on his way to the office. He had a steaming cup of his favorite chicory coffee in the cup holder and was wolfing down the last of the three home-made ham biscuits his wife had sent with him.

Bordelaise had made lot of progress since the storm. The phones lines were working; the power was back on. After no clues had turned up, he'd called off the search parties looking for the prisoners a couple of days back. As for Bobby Earle, all he could do was hope that eventually they would find the kid's body during the cleanup of the town. He was sick about it, but until more

156

debris was removed, there wasn't much else they could do.

On the plus side, he was finally spending nights at home. He couldn't remember his wife ever looking any prettier or her cooking ever tasting as good. Last night he'd crawled in bed and passed out before she'd gotten out of the shower. When the alarm went off this morning at 5:00 a.m., he couldn't believe it. He was still lying in the same position as he'd been when he'd closed his eyes.

He swallowed the last bite of his ham biscuit, then licked his thumb before chasing the biscuit with a careful sip of the hot coffee.

It pained him to think about the devastation Bordelaise had suffered, but it was heartening to know that all of Bordelaise's electrical power had been restored before he'd gone home last night. Today, the last of the telephone landlines had been repaired and his cell phone was working.

And when he suddenly heard day dispatcher Vera Samuels's voice come over the radio, he realized the communication system at the police department must be back up and running, too.

"Testing . . . testing . . . testing . . ." Vera said.

Hershel keyed up his mic. "This is Porter, reading you loud and clear."

"Ten-four," Vera said. "Chief, are you inbound?"

"Affirmative."

"Good. You have visitors."

"Be there in five. Porter out."

SEVEN

Hershel entered the station with a spring in his step. He'd long since given up being surprised by what hairstyle Vera Samuels was wearing in any given week, although he had to admit that the red curly style she had going today was far better than the one that had preceded it, which had looked, to him, like a pissed-off porcupine with pink-tipped quills.

"Morning, Vera."

"Good morning, Chief," she answered. "Katie Earle woke up this morning and went home with Penny Bates."

"That's good news, right?"

Vera's expression never wavered, although part of that had to do with the high arch she put in her eyebrows and the pout of color on her lips.

"Katie isn't exactly on the good-news list, Chief. We haven't found her son's body, and we still haven't been able to contact J.R."

Hershel's good mood shifted, then disappeared.

"Yeah, I didn't mean —"

Vera pointed toward his office. "Visitors waiting."

Hershel frowned. "Can't it wait until I top off my coffee?"

"I don't think so. They were acting very upset."

"Fine," he muttered, and headed down the hall toward his office, his steps dragging now.

He'd become accustomed to the constant sound of hammering and machinery as the back of the jail and roof were being rebuilt, but he didn't like the smell of dust and diesel that kept drifting into this part of the building.

However, when he turned the corner in the hall, he was pleasantly surprised to see Frances Maxwell and her little girl, Holly, waiting in the corridor.

"Good morning, Frances . . . Holly. Come in. Come in," he said, and stepped aside so they could enter his office. As soon as they were all seated, he smiled. "What can I do for you two this fine morning?"

Frances glanced at her daughter, who was suddenly focused on the toes of her own shoes, then handed Hershel a stack of child-

160

ish drawings.

Hershel gave them a quick look, but he was puzzled. "Well, these are real fine, but what am I to do with them?"

Frances's voice began to shake. "I'm not sure, but considering the gravity of the situation, I felt it important to let you know what Holly told me this morning."

"And what would that be?" Hershel asked.

"It all started with a misunderstanding," Frances said. "You see, Holly and Bobby Earle are . . . were . . . are really good friends, and when the storm hit and we all thought Bobby died in the storm, Holly was very sad."

Hershel's interest in their visit had changed immediately when he caught her switch from present to past and back to present tense. "What do you mean, 'thought' Bobby died in the storm?"

Frances pointed to the pictures. "See the man in the blue truck? If you'll notice, he's in all the pictures . . . in the same blue truck."

Hershel nodded. "Yeah, but what does that have to do with —"

"Please . . . just bear with me, Chief," Frances asked, then started over. "We were still at the Methodist Church Sunday when the tornado hit. We'd had a dinner for the

161

congregation after services, and Penny Bates had taken her Sunday school class outside on the playground. That's where all the smaller children were, Bobby and Holly included, when the siren started to blow. They came inside, but as you know, we all believed Bobby didn't make it in and that the storm caught him. Anyway, afterward, when Holly was so sad, we tried to explain what had happened by telling her God had taken Bobby to heaven and that he was okay . . . you know?"

Hershel glanced at the little girl with the sad face and nodded. There had been a lot of sadness and readjustments after the storm.

He nodded, indicating Frances should continue.

"So today we were in the kitchen, and Holly was drawing. I asked her what she was drawing, and she told me she was drawing pictures of God. But when I looked, there was just this man in a blue truck, and he was in all the pictures. When I asked her who the man in the blue truck was, she told me he was God."

Hershel looked down at the pictures, then back at Holly.

"So you think God looks like this and drives a blue truck?" he asked Holly.

She was a little intimidated by the sudden importance of her drawings, but when her mama patted her hand, Holly answered.

"Yep," she said simply.

Hershel stifled a smile. "Why would you think that?" he asked.

"Because I saw him."

Hershel's smile slipped.

"What do you mean . . . you saw him?"

"I saw God stop on the street in his blue truck and carry Bobby away."

Sweet Jesus. Hershel's heart thudded once very heavily as he suddenly grasped the significance of what she'd said.

He glanced at Frances, then back at Holly. "Let me get this straight. You saw a man you thought was God . . . get Bobby Earle from the playground and take him away in a blue truck?"

"Yep."

The hair on the back of Hershel's neck was standing up, and he could feel the ham biscuits he'd just eaten turning into a knot inside his belly.

"When did you see this, honey?"

"At church, right after the siren started making all that noise."

"Tell him, Holly. Tell him what you told me at home," Frances urged.

"Bobby and I were in the red tunnel on

163

the playground. The siren was really loud, and I got scared. I climbed out and ran toward the church with Miss Penny and the others, and I didn't wait for Bobby." Her lip quivered, and her eyes welled with tears. "I didn't mean to run off from him. I just got scared by the noise."

"That's okay, sweetie," Hershel said. "Then what?"

"We were almost at the church when I remembered. I stopped and started to go back when I saw Bobby coming out of the red tunnel. Only he fell, but he didn't get up. Then I saw God get out of a blue truck, put Bobby over his shoulders and drive away."

Hershel's heart was pounding. He knew his voice was shaking, but he was too stunned to subdue his emotions.

"You saw a man in a blue truck pick Bobby Earle up from the playground and drive away with him . . . before the tornado? Before you went inside? You're sure?"

She nodded.

"Why didn't you say something sooner?" he asked.

Holly frowned. "About what?"

"About the man taking Bobby?"

"It wasn't a man. It was God."

Suddenly, Hershel began to realize the

endless circle of confusion that had led to this mess.

"And you thought it was God because . . . ?"

Holly rolled her eyes, a little weary of having to explain herself over and over to adults who were supposed to know these things.

"Because everybody at the church said Bobby died, and Mama and Daddy said God took him. And Pastor William says that someday everybody will go home with God, that's why. And then my hand was hurt, and Mama and Daddy took me to the hospital, and they put a thing on my hand. See?"

"Yes, I see," Hershel said, looking at the little hand she held up to him, all the while thinking of the wasted days they could have been looking for the boy. Sweet Mother of God . . . The boy had been snatched, and they'd thought they were looking for a body. Jesus. After this many days, they might still wind up looking for a body, only for a different reason.

He glanced at the pictures. "Honey, can I keep these for a while?"

Holly nodded.

Hershel reached for a pen and notebook. "Can you tell me what the man . . . what God was wearing when you saw him take Bobby?"

Holly's eyes narrowed thoughtfully, then she counted off the garments on her fingers. "Jeans like Daddy . . . and a blue shirt with stripes . . . Oh, and a black cap, just like I drew in the pictures."

Hershel was taking notes as fast as Holly spoke.

"What about his hair? Did you see what color his hair was?"

"I think it was brown, but he was wearing that cap, so I don't know for sure."

"Right," Hershel muttered, then took another angle. "How tall was he? Did you see his face?"

Holly shrugged. "He was bigger than Daddy, with a big chest."

"Tommy is just under six feet," Frances offered.

"What color was his skin?" Hershel asked.

Holly pointed. "Like yours."

"Did he have a beard or whiskers?" Hershel asked.

"I don't know," Holly said, then turned to her mother. "Mama, can we go now?"

He realized he'd pushed about as far as he could go. A child's memory was often vague, and already four and a half days had passed, diluting it even more.

"I'm sorry," Frances said. "We had no idea."

"No, no, it's all right," Hershel said. "And thank you for bringing these in. We'll get on this right away."

Frances stood, then stopped. "Um, Chief . . ."

"Yes?"

"Has anybody been able to contact J. R. Earle since the storm?"

"Not to my knowledge. Why?"

"Well, when I called Tommy to tell him about what Holly told me, he reminded me that J.R. drives a blue truck. I just thought you'd want to know."

Hershel frowned. "Holly, do you know what Bobby Earle's daddy looks like?"

She shrugged. "I don't think so."

Frances explained. "J.R.'s job has kept him away from home a lot. The kids all know Katie, but not everyone is familiar with J.R."

"Right," Hershel said, while his mind shifted to the possibility of a parental abduction. "We'll look into this, and thank you again." Then he added, "If Holly remembers anything else, don't hesitate to call."

"We will," Frances said. "Come on, Holly. Let's go home."

Holly took her mother's hand, but her

focus was still on the pictures on Hershel's desk.

"I'll take good care of these," he said.

Satisfied with that promise, Holly nodded and smiled bashfully. Moments later they were gone.

Hershel grabbed the phone and hit Intercom. "Vera! Call the main office at Macklan Brothers Oil Company in New Orleans again, and as soon as you're connected, put them through."

"Will do," Vera said.

Hershel leaned back in his chair and picked up the pictures. There were variables in every one of them, except for the truck and driver. Then he thought of Katie Earle. He had to talk to her, but not before he checked in with the oil company. The fact that J. R. Earle was ignoring all their calls regarding the health and welfare of his wife and child had suddenly taken on new meaning.

Hurricane Bonnie had missed New Orleans, but the days after had been a hectic mess. On the Monday morning they'd been inundated by one terrific thunderstorm after another. Angela, the regular receptionist at Macklan Brothers Oil, had just gotten to her desk when she went into premature labor. Brent Macklan and a UPS delivery man walked in moments behind her and called 9-1-1, but they were told that all ambulances had already been dispatched to other emergencies. So, with the UPS man taking instructions over the phone and Brent following orders, they had delivered Angela's baby — a little girl she named Bonnie.

As soon as weather permitted, they had been transported to a hospital and arrangements were made for a temp to fill in, starting the next morning.

On Tuesday, a temp named Charlotte Perkins arrived to find an office filled with chaos. The mail had piled up. There were so many messages on the machine that she started to cry. The roof of her house had been leaking for days. She'd left bowls and buckets scattered around the rooms in an effort to save her furniture and flooring, but it was dicey. And coming in to a mess of these proportions had sent her over the edge.

Rattled by the demands of the job and the complicated phone system, she'd accidentally hung up on so many people that when the boss, Brent Macklan, stopped by the front desk to introduce himself, she thought she was in trouble and burst into tears all over again.

Still, she did her best, and when she'd taken two messages for an absent employee named J. R. Earle, one from a hospital and one from a small-town police department, she'd tried to relay them to a forwarding number, but the calls wouldn't go through. Overwhelmed by everything else on her plate and with no idea what to do next, she'd put the message slips on his desk next to a growing stack of mail and forgot all about them.

Then, on Thursday, as she was in the middle of putting through an overseas call for Brent Macklan, another phone call came through for J. R. Earle.

"Macklan Brothers Oil, how may I direct your call?"

"Hold for Police Chief Porter, please."

"Oh . . . wait," Charlotte said, and then frowned in confusion.

Brent Macklan was still on hold, waiting for his call to go through. But before Charlotte had time to panic about messing up the calls, there was a rough, urgent voice in her ear.

"This is Chief Porter. I need to speak to J. R. Earle."

"I'm sorry," Charlotte said. "Mr. Earle is

170

out of the office. May I take a message?"

"I already left a message that he didn't return. When do you expect him in?"

"I don't know, sir. I'm a temp, and I've only been here a few days."

Hershel frowned. "So Earle hasn't been in all week?"

"Not since I've been here, sir."

"Do you know where he is?"

"No, sir."

"I need to speak to Earle's boss."

"I'm sorry, sir, but Mr. Macklan is on an overseas call. I can have him contact you later."

"Tell him it's an emergency," Hershel said, then gave her the number and disconnected.

Charlotte was in the middle of writing the last three digits onto an official message slip when she realized Macklan's overseas call was on the line. In her haste to connect, she didn't even notice that she transposed the last two digits.

Hershel waited for nearly an hour without a return call.

Frustrated by the lack of communication, he decided he couldn't wait any longer to talk to Katie. After what Frances had told him, it wouldn't be long before word began to spread, and Katie deserved to hear the truth from him.

What bothered him was how to break the news. It wasn't exactly a case of "I have news — some good, some bad; which do you want to hear first?"

How did you tell a mother they had good reason to believe her child hadn't died but had most likely been abducted?

If the abductor was Bobby's father, then the chances of his life being in danger were probably nil. But if J. R. Earle was *not* the man who'd taken him, then not only did a total stranger have her little boy, he might already be dead, and no matter what, the man who'd taken him had a four-day head start.

Penny Bates was trying to figure out how best to help Katie Earle cope, along with wondering why J. R. Earle hadn't checked on his family, as she pulled up into her driveway, then parked beneath the portico.

"We're here," she said unnecessarily. When Katie didn't respond, Penny led the way into the house and down the hall. "This will be your bedroom. There's a private bath beyond that door. We'll make a list later, and go get you some clothes and toiletries."

Katie stared around the room, taking in the neat blue curtains and white spread, but

Penny kept talking, and she knew she was supposed to respond. Then she saw Oliver propped up against the pillows, and her heart twisted. She walked over to the bed and sat down, then pulled the bear up beneath her chin, the same way Bobby slept with him every night.

"Thank you," Katie said, then added, "I have money to pay for the stuff I need to buy."

"I know you do," Penny said, and then hugged her. "I'm going to go make us some lunch. Are you hungry?"

Katie slumped. How did you explain to someone that the pain in your heart is too sharp for the food to go down?

"Not much," she said, then saw the phone. "Do you mind if I use your phone? I want to call J.R."

Penny frowned. "Of course you can use the phone. Use anything you need, although you should know that neither the hospital nor the police have been able to contact him since . . . when you . . ." She sighed. "You know."

Shocked by the news, the knot in Katie's belly twisted tighter. "He never called back . . . ever?"

"According to the hospital, no. I can't speak for the police department," Penny

173

said, then pointed at the phone. "You make all the calls you need. Come to the kitchen when you've finished, and we'll have lunch."

Katie waited until Penny was gone, then picked up the receiver. She punched in J.R.'s cell phone number, then closed her eyes and willed herself to be calm as she waited for him to answer. She didn't know how she was going to tell him what had happened, because so far she had been unable to say the words aloud — even to herself.

When she heard the first ring, her palms began to sweat.

He's going to hate me.

When it rang the second time, her throat began to tighten.

Why wasn't I the one who died?

When the call rang a third time, then a fourth, before going to voice mail, she almost hung up. She didn't want to hear his voice and remember how it sounded when he whispered in her ear, or when he laughed, or the tenderness that used to be there when he just said her name.

"Hi. This is J.R. I'm away from the phone, but if you'll leave a message, I'll call you right back."

Her fingers curled around the receiver as she waited for the beep. Even so, when it came, she was caught off guard.

174

"Um, uh, it's me. I need you to call me as soon as you get this message."

She hung up, then rolled over onto the bed, curled up into a ball and closed her eyes. She kept remembering how she'd felt when she'd gotten the news that her parents' bodies had been found. Her pain then was nothing to what she was feeling now. She'd messed up her marriage and lost J.R. That she had accepted. But the pain of knowing she would never see her baby again was enough to make her want to die.

The stuffed bear's softness reminded her of Bobby, and she hugged it to her, aching for the feel of Bobby's warm little body squirming against her, aching for the sound of his voice and the peal of his laughter — aching, aching, in every facet of her being.

"Oh, God . . . why my baby?"

Her voice broke. She was still crying when Penny knocked on the door, then came hurrying in.

"Katie! Chief Porter is here to see you."

Katie's heart nearly stopped. She tossed the little bear aside and quickly rolled off the bed, tears still drying on her cheeks. All she could think was that the only reason he would be looking for her was to tell her that they'd found Bobby's body.

When Penny saw her face, she opened her

arms, her own voice trembling as Katie let herself be comforted. Finally it was the opportunity Penny had been waiting for.

"Katie . . . if it would bring him back, I would take my own life this minute."

Katie wrapped her arms around Penny's ample frame and hugged her as fiercely as she was being hugged.

"It's not your fault. Whatever happened, it happened because of the storm," she said.

Penny took a tissue out of her pocket and handed it to Katie.

"Here. Wipe and blow. Hershel seems anxious, so let's go see what he has to say, okay?"

Katie nodded, wiped her face and blew her nose, then followed Penny to the living room.

Hershel stood as they entered, then offered his hand.

"Katie . . . I'm sorry I didn't get by to see you in the hospital. Bordelaise has been in a bit of a mess. However, I need to get to the reason for the visit. I have news."

Katie's body went limp. "You found my . . . You found his . . ." She couldn't say the words.

"No, no, nothing like that," Hershel said. "I'm sorry. I should have said that the minute you came in."

Katie staggered backward to the nearest chair, then covered her face.

Penny frowned. "Chief, if you could get to the point . . ."

Hershel nodded. "We got news this morning that leads us to believe your son was not caught in the tornado, after all."

Katie's head came up as a bolt of joy shot through her.

"Oh, my God, oh, my God! What do you mean? Are you saying that he's alive? My little boy is alive?"

"I'm saying we don't think the tornado got him. But we still don't know where he is."

Joy turned to panic as Katie's voice rose. "I can't handle riddles! What are you trying to tell me?" she cried.

Hershel sat down in a chair across from her, then leaned forward with his elbows on his knees.

"Frances Maxwell brought her little girl, Holly, to the station this morning with a story that gave us a whole new take on your son's disappearance. According to Holly, she saw a man — who she thought was God — pick Bobby up from the playground, put him in his truck and drive away."

Penny gasped.

Katie's heart skipped a beat, then she

moaned.

"Abducted? You're saying Bobby was abducted?"

"If we believe Holly, I'd say yes."

The room started to spin. Katie held on to the arms of her chair to keep from falling out.

"Oh, my God . . . why didn't she say something sooner?" she wailed.

"It's a long story," Hershel said. "But suffice it to say, she heard too many people say Bobby was dead, heard too many people talking about God taking people to heaven, so she thought she'd seen God as he came for Bobby."

Katie's mind was reeling as fast as her hopes were being dashed.

"But maybe she was just confused and really didn't see —".

Hershel picked up a stack of papers from the table beside him and handed them to Katie.

"That's what I might have thought, too, only Frances showed me these."

Katie frowned as she leafed through the drawings, then laid them aside. "What do these have to do with Bobby's disappearance?"

"See the man in the blue truck . . . in all those pictures Holly drew?"

178

"Yes, I saw him, but what does he have to do with any of this?"

"According to Holly, that's what God was driving when he came for your son."

Foreboding. It was the first thing Katie felt as she looked back at the pictures and began grasping the implications.

"She saw a man in a blue truck snatch my son and thought he was God?"

Hershel nodded. "That's what we think. Now I have a question to ask you. I've been told that your husband, J.R., drives a blue truck. Is that true?"

Katie's heart skidded to a stop. Oh, my God. He wouldn't. He *couldn't.* "Yes, he does, but —"

"When's the last time you talked to him?" Hershel interrupted.

Katie thought back. "Friday, because he called to tell me he couldn't come get Bobby because of work. The last thing he said was that he'd come see him as soon as he could."

"He hasn't returned my call. Have you heard from him since the storm?"

Katie's body was beginning to shake. Surely to God J.R. wouldn't snatch Bobby? Surely. She didn't trust herself to speak and just shook her head.

"When's the last time you tried to call him?"

Katie swallowed around the lump in her throat. "About ten minutes ago."

"And no answer?"

Her voice was barely above a whisper. "No."

"Well, then," Hershel said, "is there anything else you can tell me that might lead me to believe someone other than J.R. could have taken your son?"

"No," Katie said, then remembered. "Oh. There *was* one time when Bobby had a bad dream and swore there was a monster at his window."

Hershel sighed. "That's pretty much every kid's nightmare, isn't it? Either at the window, in the closet or under the bed. Was anyone there?"

Katie frowned. "No. And it was before J.R. left, so he went outside and looked around, but he didn't see anything suspicious."

Hershel nodded. "Did it happen again?"

"No," Katie said, then remembered her last conversation with Bobby. "But when we were walking to church last Sunday, Bobby said he liked staying in New Orleans with J.R. because the monster didn't live there."

Hershel frowned. "Did you ever consider this might be something J.R. was feeding him to get him to persuade you to move?"

Katie shivered. "I never thought of it like that," she whispered. "Once I would have said J.R. would never do something like that, but now . . . I don't know what to say, because I never thought that we'd ever be living apart, either."

"Okay," Hershel said. "That's about all I can tell you for now."

"Chief, do you believe Bobby Earle is still alive?" Penny asked.

Hershel didn't hesitate. "Yes, I do."

Penny's eyes welled. "Thank the Lord. Thank the Lord."

"What are you going to do? How will you know where to look? Do you think it was J.R.? What if it's not? What if there really was a monster and he has my son?" Katie's thoughts were examining a dozen different scenarios at once, and with every question she asked, her voice rose in panic, and her hands curled into fists as she suddenly clutched them against her belly. Then she gave voice to what Hershel had been thinking from the moment he'd heard Holly's story. "What if it's too late? What if the monster who took my son has already done what he wanted to do?" Her voice sank to a whisper. "What if he's the kind of monster who doesn't leave witnesses?"

Hershel's gut knotted. "I can't read the future, Katie. But we won't leave a stone unturned in looking for him. And I need to talk to J.R. Since he's the obvious suspect, we need to rule him out. I don't have to tell you that if you hear from him, you need to tell him to call me — immediately."

"Yes, I will," Katie said.

Hershel nodded. "Well, I guess that's all for now. I'm sorry I don't have better news."

Katie stood as well, then impulsively threw her arms around him and gave him a hug.

"You don't understand," she said. "The news you gave me was nothing short of a miracle. This morning my son was dead. Now he's alive. It's the kind of miracle a parent prays for."

Hershel blushed as she took a quick step back. "Yes, ma'am. That I understand. I'm relieved beyond words myself, but I won't feel good about any of this until we find your boy. Say your prayers, and I'll stay in touch."

Penny saw him to the door. When she turned around, Katie was nowhere in sight. She went looking for her and found her in the kitchen, digging through drawers.

"Honey, what are you looking for? Let me help," Penny said.

"Pen and paper. I need to make a list. I

need to get some clothes and shoes. I need a phone — mine went with the house. I need to talk to Holly Maxwell. I'm going to make so many calls to J.R. that he'll *have* to call back." Then her face lit up. "Oh, Penny! My little boy is alive!"

Penny nodded but chose not to remind her that if J.R. didn't have their child, given that he'd been abducted days ago, there was a very good chance that no matter what Chief Porter said, Bobby was, in fact, still dead — just not from the storm.

EIGHT

The sea was rough today, but the sun was shining. White foam hung on the edges of the waves like lace on a skirt as the massive waves pounded against the base of the rig, while gulls circled above it in ever-widening orbits.

Even though J.R. was standing stories above the belly of the rig, the loud and steady thump of the massive pumps rang incessantly in his head.

Sick and tired of his forced stint on the rig, he'd chosen to go topside and had been at the helipad for nearly an hour, waiting for the arrival of the inbound chopper and, with it, the new crew chief. Stanton Blalock and his cronies were standing nearby, talking among themselves and casting angry glances when they thought he wasn't looking. He knew they were pissed, but he didn't give a damn. They'd all four broken hard and fast rules. All he'd done was enforce them.

He kept watching the sky as he paced, anxious to leave. He hadn't spoken to Katie in days, and it was driving him crazy. At first he'd laid blame on the storm for his being unable to get through, but now, while all his calls went through, he kept getting busy signals, or messages that the number was no longer in service, and that made no sense. What he did know was that she wasn't answering the phone. He knew she was mad at him, but he hadn't expected her to isolate him like this from Bobby.

Frustrated by the fact that the chopper still wasn't here, he glanced at his watch. It was a little after one in the afternoon. He couldn't help wondering where Bobby and Katie were, and what they were doing. Katie always loved summer, when Bobby was out of school. He could imagine them at the park or at the city pool, having a picnic or swimming, just as they'd always done — and always without him.

He glanced at Blalock, making sure the troublemaker stayed within his sight, then took out his cell and walked a short distance away, determined to call one more time in hopes of getting through. When he flipped open the phone, he realized he'd missed a good half dozen calls.

He scanned the numbers quickly. One was a message from his phone carrier, which he deleted, four were from the accounting firm that did payroll for Macklan Brothers Oil and related to the men who'd been fired and one was from a number he didn't recognize.

Anxious to call Katie, instead of listening to the message he opted out of the list and made his call.

When the call began to ring, his hopes rose, and then the recorded voice came on again, stating that the number was no longer in service. At that point the hair rose on the back of his neck. He didn't know what was going on, but he didn't like the odds that it would be good. Just as he was about to go back to the menu to check that last call, Blalock yelled.

"Chopper! Inbound!"

J.R. turned. It was barely a spot on the horizon, but it was definitely the chopper, and it was coming fast.

Finally, he thought, and walked back to where he'd left his bag.

It took a good half hour to welcome the new crew chief and the four replacements, and give them a tour of the rig. Once he'd introduced the new crew chief to Charlie

Watts, his duties were over. Leaving the two men to their business, he went back up top to check on Blalock and his cronies.

They were right where he'd left them, seemingly as anxious to get off the rig as he was. When he saw the pilot coming across the deck, he turned to Blalock.

"Load up and buckle in," he said shortly, as he picked up his bag and tossed it into the belly of the chopper, then slid into the seat beside the pilot.

The rotors were turning, making it difficult to be heard inside the cockpit, so he gave the pilot a thumbs-up.

"Everyone turn off your cell phones," the pilot yelled.

The men reached into their pockets.

Moments later, they lifted off.

J.R. never looked back.

Newt woke up needing to pee. He glanced down at the blisters on his belly and winced. One of them looked infected, so maybe he would finally go back to see the doctor and get the dressings changed, and they could figure it out there.

He glanced over at the small dark-haired boy beside him and grunted. Thanks to the constant round of sleeping pills he kept putting down the kid, the boy's presence had posed no further problems.

But there was a downside to keeping him doped that Newt didn't like. It critically limited the time they had together, which would also make bonding with him that much harder.

With a regretful glance for what he was missing, he eased himself up from the bed and exited the bedroom. A few minutes later he emerged from the bathroom and headed to the kitchen. As he was in the middle of making a pot of coffee, there was a knock on the door.

"What the hell?" he muttered, and peered through the venetian blinds.

It was Sam. That was when it dawned on him that it was rent day.

Newt cursed. "Hell's fire, doesn't he know I got more problems than worrying about my rent being a day or so late?"

It occurred to Newt that if he stayed quiet, Sam might leave. Then the knock came again. Fearing the noise would wake the kid, he called out, "Just a minute!"

He shuffled to the bedroom, retrieved the sheet he'd been using as a robe and wrapped it around him toga-style, then closed the door behind him as he left — just in case.

He was careful not to open the front door too wide and give Sam the mistaken belief it was an invitation to come in.

"Hey, Sam. What's up?" he asked.

Sam frowned as his gaze slid across what he could see of Newt's blistered body.

"Damn, man, you look awful."

Newt frowned. "If that's the only reason you came, you might be interested to know that isn't news."

Sam sighed. "Sorry. I didn't mean to be rude. It's just shocking to —" Then he shook his head. "Never mind. Today is rent day, but I thought I'd see if you need some groceries or maybe a ride down to the doctor's office. Shouldn't you go back and see him sometime?"

"Yeah, I probably should," Newt said.

"So how do you think you're doing?" Sam asked.

"I think I'm getting an infection."

Sam craned his neck, peering over Newt's shoulder into the darkened room. Even though he could smell coffee brewing, he saw nothing but clutter.

"I think Mrs. Waller at trailer ten cleans house for people. If you want, I could see about getting her here to help you out. Might keep down infection and the like if the place was a little cleaner."

Newt frowned. "I don't need you telling me how to live my life. I appreciate the ride, but I don't like visitors, understood?"

"Yeah, sure, Newt. I was just trying to help."

Newt's frown deepened as he pointed to his truck, all but invisible among the downed trees.

"If you want to help, you could get those trees cut away so's I could get my truck out."

Sam nodded. "Yeah, I know, I know. But it's not like you can drive yet, and there's not a spare chain saw to be had in the whole of Bordelaise. Everyone has their own debris to clear or is already hired out by others."

"Well, hell, Sam. You can't just leave the damn trees there," Newt snapped.

Sam's chin jutted angrily. "Like I don't already know that? My boy lives up north of Baton Rouge. He promised to come down this coming weekend and help me clear all this out."

This was Thursday, Newt thought. A couple more days couldn't matter. Not when everyone thought Bobby Earle was dead.

"Well, yeah, that would be okay, I guess."

"Great. So . . . when do you want your ride?"

"What time is it?" Newt asked.

"Almost eleven."

"Give me thirty minutes to get myself together."

"Right," Sam said. "I'll be back here at eleven-thirty to pick you up."

"Thanks," Newt said. "I'll bring the rent check." Then he stepped back, and closed and locked the door.

No sooner had the door swung shut than he heard a thump from the back of the trailer. The kid must be awake. Good. That left him just enough time to get the kid up, let him pee, then feed him and dope him back up. He thought again that he hated to keep drugging him, but at this point he didn't really have a choice.

There was another thump, and then a high-pitched squeal.

"I'm coming," he muttered. "I'm coming."

Bobby Earle was dreaming.

He was sitting at the kitchen table, watching Mama making pancakes. A big tub of butter was on the table in front of him, and his favorite brown sugar syrup was in that little blue pitcher with the tulips on it.

Mama was talking to him, but he couldn't hear what she was saying, and every time he asked her to repeat herself, she got smaller and smaller, until finally, the last time he called her name, she completely disappeared.

In the dream, he was crying.

Then all of a sudden he was awake. That was when he remembered. Mama was dead. She'd died in the tornado. That was why she'd disappeared in his dream. She wasn't real anymore.

A huge ache welled up and gushed through his body, and then he was crying in real life, too. God had taken his mama away and let the monster catch him. He couldn't understand why this had happened. He didn't tell lies, and he wasn't mean to people, so why was God punishing him like this?

He could pray to God again and ask, but he was mad at God and didn't want to talk to Him anymore.

He would have to ask Daddy. Daddy knew the answers to almost everything. Only Daddy didn't know about Mama yet. Daddy was in New Orleans. Bobby knew he needed to get free. Then he could find someone else to help him — someone who wasn't smelly and scary, someone who didn't yell at him and tie him to the bed.

In frustration, Bobby kicked and yanked against his restraints, then began screaming and rolling his head from side to side, trying to dislodge the gag.

192

A cockroach ran across his shirt. At the sight of the bug, he flopped and kicked until it ran scurrying from the bed.

He hated those bugs. They crawled on everything, making this house even scarier — almost as scary as the monster who lived in it.

He thought of his house, of his bedroom and his clothes, and how good they always smelled, and how good it felt to put on clean clothes. For the first time in his life he actually wanted to take a bath, but that would mean taking off all his clothes, and while he wasn't sure why, that didn't seem like a good idea.

The monster already watched him eat. He watched him go to the bathroom. He watched him do everything, just like their neighbor's cat watched for gophers to pop up out of their holes — lying in wait for hours and hours, not moving so much as a whisker, until a gopher stuck his head up out of the ground. Then the cat would pounce. That was how the monster made him feel: like he was waiting for him to make a mistake, so he could pounce and eat him up.

Bobby kicked the mattress again, yanking hard on the ties that bound him to the bed and then stopping when the room started spinning. Frightened that he would get sick and throw up beneath the gag, he closed his eyes, willing the bed to settle. Then he kicked again, taking comfort in the angry thump as the headboard bucked against the wall.

Suddenly the door flew open.

Bobby flinched.

"Hey, hey, now!" Newt cried, as he scooted onto the side of the bed beside Bobby and began removing the gag. Once it was gone, he smoothed the hair back from the kid's sweaty little face. "Glad you're awake, little guy. I'll bet you need to piss, don't you?"

"That's a bad word," Bobby muttered, then held his breath, afraid he would be chastised for talking back.

But Newt was on a deadline and couldn't afford to cause a ruckus. He needed the kid to do his business, eat some food and down another sleeping pill.

Choosing not to confront the sass, he quickly untied Bobby's wrists and then urged him to the bathroom.

"Go do your business, and then come into the kitchen. I've got some real good bologna and cheese. I'll make sandwiches. You like mayonnaise, right? See, Uncle Newt knows what you like. He's taking real good care of you."

Bobby slipped into the bathroom and, before Newt could stop him, closed the door in his face.

"You little bastard," Newt muttered, then added louder, "Just so you know, the lock don't work, so as soon as you're done, get yourself to the kitchen before I get mad — and you already know, you don't want to make Uncle Newt mad."

Bobby shivered as he relieved himself. His act of defiance was over. He looked longingly at the small window above the tub. It was too high for him to reach, and there was nothing inside the bathroom for him to stand on.

When he washed up afterward, he scrubbed hard at his face, wanting to make sure that the tears were all gone. He'd already learned that showing weakness to this man could be dangerous. As for accepting the status quo, Bobby Earle was nothing if not his father's son. Instinct told him that even if Mama was in heaven, Daddy would come find him.

It wasn't much comfort, but it was enough to get him out of the bathroom and into the kitchen without further tears.

He did, however, come out with far less

bravado than when he'd gone in. He scooted a chair up to the table and grabbed the sandwich without looking up.

When he took a big bite and began to chew, Newt joined in, wolfing down his own food in short shrift. He glanced at the clock, then reached for an Oreo, stuffing the whole thing in his mouth.

Eat up, kid. Your day is coming, he thought, and was reaching for another Oreo when a sharp burning sensation suddenly ran up his arm. He looked down, eyeing two blisters that had suddenly broken open in the palm of his hand.

Bobby saw the sores oozing fluid and pus, and shivered, afraid that the monster would put those hands on him.

"Finish your Pepsi," Newt said.

Bobby grabbed the drink and downed it, then started on his own stack of Oreos. He was in the middle of his third cookie when the floor started to look wavy. He grabbed his stomach, afraid he was going to be sick.

Newt had been watching him, waiting for a sign that the pill had kicked in. When he saw a sheen of cold sweat break out across the kid's upper lip, he relaxed.

Bingo.

"What's wrong, kid? Don't you feel good?"

196

"My tummy feels funny," Bobby muttered.

"Maybe you better go lay back down," Newt said.

But that meant being tied back up, and Bobby didn't want to give in.

"No," he said. "I don't want to lie down."

Newt stood, purposefully letting the sheet fall to the floor. Even if he couldn't do anything about it, he liked being naked in front of the boy.

"Come on, I can't have you throwing up on my floor."

Confronted by the horror of all that burned and peeling flesh right under his nose, Bobby stood and then started backing away.

Before he knew it, he'd backed himself all the way down the hall and into the bedroom. Once again, he was trapped.

"Lie down," Newt ordered.

Quiet tears welled and ran down Bobby's face, but he did as he was told.

When the man began retying his wrists to the bed, the stench of the unwashed body and running sores was frightening. And when Newt reached for the gag, Bobby begged.

"No, no," he pleaded. "Not that. I'll be quiet."

"Sorry," Newt said. "You were naughty shutting the door in my face earlier. Now you have to accept your punishment."

Bobby's nostrils flared as he watched the gag coming closer.

In a last ditch attempt to defy his captor, he blurted out, "My daddy is going to be mad at you."

Newt slapped the gag over Bobby's mouth, then tied it tighter than usual just to prove that he was the one in charge.

In mute panic, Bobby felt the knot growing tighter and tighter, and feared what was going to happen next.

To his relief, the man just got up and moved across the room to the closet.

That was when Bobby closed his eyes and started to pray.

Please God, please help Daddy find me.

Indifferent to the kid on the bed for once, Newt was digging through the closet for the loosest shirt and pants that he owned. It would be hell having to wear clothes, but he couldn't show up at the doc's office wrapped up in a sheet or they would start talking hospitalization. He couldn't let that happen.

Just before he left to go meet Sam, he glanced back at the bed. The kid was out like a light.

"I'll be back," he said softly, as he pocketed his checkbook, blew Bobby Earle a kiss and left to catch his ride.

Katie was on a mission. She didn't know how to feel about the news she'd been given. Part of the time her heart soared from the unfettered joy of knowing Bobby had not died in the tornado, and part of the time she felt sick to her stomach, knowing that he had been kidnapped. Her only hope lay in believing that J.R. had been the one who took him, because that meant he would be safe. Even if J.R. wanted to hurt Katie, he would never hurt his son. She was betting her life, and the life of their son, on that. But she couldn't just do nothing. Not when she'd been given a new reason to live.

Within an hour of hearing Chief Porter's news, she'd talked Penny into driving her to the bank to get cash from her account. From there they'd gone straight to Target, where she'd purchased three changes of clothes, along with shoes and underwear, toilet articles and a prepaid phone.

It was kind of Penny to give her a place to stay, but she couldn't start running up Penny's phone bill trying to find her missing husband. Even though Chief Porter had assured her that he was trying to find J.R., she wasn't willing to wait.

She was going to start making calls on her own until she got some answers. In her heart, she couldn't believe he was the one who'd taken Bobby.

Unless . . .

And this was where doubt crept in.

Unless he had truly grown to hate her.

Unless he no longer wanted to be married to her and had no intention of sharing custody, so he had abducted their son with the intent of disappearing and living somewhere new under a false identity.

She knew things like that happened when families broke up. She didn't want to believe it of J.R., but the fact that he had not cared enough to come to Bordelaise and check on them, and had not returned calls from the hospital or the police, made him seem guilty as hell. She knew Angela, the secretary at Macklan Brothers, would know what was going on. Angela knew everything, and she was going to call her as soon as they got home.

She tossed the sacks with her purchases in the back of Penny's car and then got inside. Penny was right behind her with bags of her own.

Penny winced as she slid behind the wheel. The leather seats were scorching.

"It's so hot! Thank goodness the power has all been restored so people can run their air conditioners again."

Then she realized how unimportant that was in the grand scheme of Katie's life. "I'm sorry, Katie. That was a thoughtless comment. I'm sure the weather is the least of your concerns."

Katie frowned. "My troubles don't supersede everything else. It *is* hot, and it *is* a blessing power has been restored."

Penny frowned. "What are you going to do about your house? Are you going to rebuild? Do you need help contacting your insurance company . . . or anything like that?"

Katie shrugged. "I don't know what I'm going to do. My whole future hinges on finding my son."

"Do you think J.R. really took him?"

Katie frowned, then looked away. "I don't know what to think." Then she added, "But I do want to thank you for all your help."

Penny reached across the seat and took her hand. "Honey, it's my pleasure. I wish I could do more. I wish I had *done* more. I still can't believe I let —"

"Stop! Stop right there!" Katie said, and held up her hand. "You didn't let anything happen. You didn't cause the storm. You didn't order up a man in a blue pickup to swing by the playground and snatch my son when no one was looking. If there is blame to be laid, it belongs at my feet." Katie's eyes welled. "Oh, God . . . none of this would have happened to Bobby if I'd only agreed to move like J.R. wanted."

Penny shook her head vigorously, making her salt-and-pepper curls bounce. "I think we both need to stop talking about blame and look at things from a different angle. We were given a miracle today. In a manner of speaking, your little boy came back from the dead. He might be missing, but I won't let myself believe that he's dead. Not now. Not again. All we have to do is start praying for the police to find him."

Katie's eyes narrowed angrily. "I'll pray, all right, but I'm not waiting. I'm going to start looking on my own, and the first person we need to find is J. R. Earle. I pray to God he has Bobby, and then *he* better pray to God I don't kill him."

"Is there anyplace else you need to go?" Penny asked.

"No."

Penny started the car. "If you don't mind, I need to pick up an order at the garden center before we go home."

"You do what you need to do, but I'll wait

in the car. I'm not in the right frame of mind to start talking to people about anything . . . you know?"

"Absolutely," Penny said, as she drove out of the parking lot. "It won't take long, and I'll leave the car running so you'll be cool."

"I bought a prepaid phone. I'm going to start making calls while you're inside. If I ever get J.R. to answer his phone, it will take more than an air conditioner to cool me down."

NINE

Charlotte Perkins was finally getting the hang of her temporary job at Macklan Brothers. It was often hectic, but there were the down times, as well. And the best part was that she hadn't disconnected anyone since yesterday, and she had also lost the urge to cry every time Brent Macklan walked past her desk.

She glanced at the clock, gauging the length of time she had left on her lunch break, then took another bite of her sandwich. She'd made an executive decision to put the switchboard on voice mail and was in the break room, scanning through her new issue of *People* magazine as she ate, relieved that, for the moment, the office was peacefully quiet.

Brent Macklan had gone to lunch with a client, and except for a geologist who was at the next table studying maps, she was alone.

A couple of calls came in, but she ignored

them, knowing voice mail would pick up. She reached for her drink as she turned a page, took a quick sip, then kept on reading.

Katie couldn't believe it! The world had gone completely to hell. The phones at Macklan Brothers never went to voice mail. Frustrated, she disconnected without leaving a message. She didn't want to talk to a machine. Her hands were shaking as she dropped the phone into her lap. This didn't make sense.

"Damn it, J.R. . . . where are you? Why don't you call?"

Struggling with a growing panic, she didn't know what to think. She'd always been able to contact him — anywhere in the world, any time of day or night. And if for some reason she'd been unable to get to him directly, she'd always gone through the home office. It was beginning to seem like a conspiracy, and she was the only one who didn't know the game or the rules.

She just couldn't believe J.R. would take Bobby and scare her like this. But what else explained his lack of concern when the police and hospital had tried to contact him? Why else wouldn't he call back?

The only reason she could think of was that he just didn't care what happened to

Katie, and he knew Bobby was fine.

But the minute she thought it, her heart rejected it.

She picked up the phone. "One more time, John Robert. I'm going to call you one more time — and if you know what's good for you, you'll answer."

Her hands were shaking as she called his cell again.

"Please, God . . . please, God . . . please," Katie whispered, as she began to count the rings.

Once.

Twice.

Three times it rang.

And on the fourth, it went straight to voice mail. She couldn't listen to his voice again, telling her he was away from the phone and to leave a message and he'd call them right back — because that was a lie. She ended the call with a lump in her throat, then leaned back against the seat and closed her eyes.

A car pulled into the parking space beside her, but she chose to ignore it. She didn't want to see someone she knew and have to talk. She couldn't bear the pity on their faces.

But when she heard the high-pitched voice of a child, the longing in her was so intense that she had to look.

The result was to be expected. The pain of seeing someone else's child happy and healthy increased her guilt. If she'd been a competent parent, none of this would have happened.

But like someone witnessing a wreck, even though it was painful, she couldn't look away. She was mesmerized by the animation on the little boy's face, by hearing the rapid-fire cadence of his questions as he held his daddy's hand.

And in that moment time turned backward and she was walking down the street with Bobby, listening to their last conversation together as they were on their way to church.

He'd been so happy and carefree, and she'd been so wrapped up in her own misery that she'd failed to savor the joy of the moment. When the child's face began to blur, she turned away.

The knot in her stomach was growing. Despite everything Chief Porter had told her this morning, one thing still hadn't changed. Her child was lost to her, and she didn't know where to find him. Awash in despair, she finally gave in to her sorrow.

And that was how Penny found her — doubled over in the seat with her head on her knees, sobbing uncontrollably.

"Oh, honey . . . oh, Katie . . . bless your heart."

By the time Penny got them both home, she was crying, too.

Talking to Katie Earle had been difficult for Hershel. On the one hand, he'd given her hope, but then, on the other, he'd taken it right back. He was close to convinced that J. R. Earle was the one who'd taken Bobby.

Couples separated. Kids got caught in the middle. Every so often one of the parents flipped out and went on the run with the kid. It happened all the time. Just because he knew these people, that didn't automatically preclude them from acting irrationally. Still, he knew he had to cover all the bases.

By the time he got back to headquarters, he had a running list of avenues to investigate regarding Bobby Earle's abduction, and they needed to be followed up ASAP.

He needed an up-to-date listing of all the registered sex offenders in the parish, as well as a listing of everyone who owned a blue and, from Holly's description of it as "shiny," late-model pickup.

He strode into the office with his hat jammed on his head and a frown on his face. It was a look that Vera, the dispatcher, had seen before, and she knew it meant trouble.

"Call Tullius. Get him back here on the double," Hershel snapped.

"Is everything okay?" she asked.

"Hell, no, everything's not okay, and you know it. I've got four missing prisoners. We buried three of Bordelaise's finest citizens today, and I have a child whose status has gone from dead to just plain snatched."

Vera's mouth dropped. "Bobby Earle? Are you talking about Bobby Earle?"

Hershel yanked the hat off his head and slapped it against his thigh in frustration.

"Yes, I'm talking about Bobby Earle. According to Frances Maxwell, her daughter witnessed a man in a blue truck snatch the boy while the siren was blowing last Sunday."

Vera gasped. "Lord have mercy! Why is she just now telling?"

Hershel sighed. "It's complicated, but it only works if you're thinking like a seven-year-old with very specific ideas about God and how you get to heaven."

"What in the world?"

Hershel nodded. "That's what I first thought. But it seems that Holly Maxwell heard all the adults around her talking about Bobby being in heaven and safe with

God — you know the drill — and what she saw got tangled up with what she heard, until she decided that what she'd seen was God coming after Bobby in a blue pickup truck."

Before Vera could comment, Lee Tullius burst into the room.

"Chief! Is it true what I just heard? About Bobby Earle being alive?"

Hershel's shoulders slumped. "How fast news does fly," he said. "And yes, it seems to be true, only we don't know where he is. However, I'm glad you're here. Whoever took him has more than four days' head start on us. There's something I want you to do."

The phone rang, and Vera answered.

Hershel moved away from the desk so that their voices wouldn't interfere with the call.

Lee followed, anxious to hear more. "I don't understand, Chief. If we know he's alive, why don't we know where —"

Before Hershel could answer, Vera called for his attention. "Chief, phone call for you."

"Is it an emergency?" he asked.

She shrugged. "DEA?"

He sighed. "I'll take it in my office. Wait here," he told Lee, then headed down the hall. Once inside his office, he took a seat and then picked up the receiver.

"Chief Porter here."

"Chief. Stewart Babcock, Captain, DEA. I understand you have some prisoners in your jail. By any chance, is one of them a man named Nick Aroyo?"

Hershel frowned. "He was here, but he's not anymore," he said. "Not him and not the drug ring he was running with."

"You turned them loose?"

"No, sir. Last Sunday our town was hit by a tornado. Among other things, it took out the back of the jail, and as far as we can tell, the prisoners went with it. We don't know if they were taken by the tornado or if they're on the run. I had search parties scouring the area for days, and they found nothing to lead me to believe they were still alive. We called off the search a couple of days ago."

"Damn it," Babcock said. "Look, I want to send a team down to help you search."

"You can send whoever you want, but they'll be on their own. I can't afford the manpower to go back out again, because we're working the case of a kidnapped child."

"Tough," Babcock said. "What's the ransom?"

"There never was a request for ransom. We're leaning toward the theory that it's either the father or a child molester."

There was a long moment of silence, and then Babcock cleared his throat.

"That's a tough one," he said. "As for the missing prisoners, if you do find them, you need to let me know immediately. Nick Aroyo is one of us. He's been undercover with that drug ring for months."

"The hell you say!" Hershel said, thinking back to the dark-eyed man who'd been so quiet during booking.

"Yes," Babcock said. "So be on the lookout for my men. I'll have them check in with you to get them started."

"Glad to help out," Hershel said, and they disconnected.

He was scratching his head as he headed back up the hall, surprised by the news. Still, he had bigger fish to fry.

When he walked into dispatch, Vera was on another call. Before he could give Lee directions, Vera hung up the phone and sent everything spinning.

"Chief! There's a four-car pileup on the Abalone Road west of town. The road is blocked. There are multiple injuries, with one man pinned in his car. I'm dispatching emergency services now."

"Crap," Hershel said. "Where's Carter?"

"Outside putting oil in the cruiser," Lee said.

"Go tell him what's happening, then both of you proceed to the scene ASAP. You know what to do."

"Where are you going, Chief?"

"I'll already be there," Hershel said, and headed out the front door as Lee took off through the back, his plan to start a search for Bobby Earle sidelined by a blowout.

Dr. Luke peeled off his surgical gloves and tossed them in the trash as the lab tech left with the specimen he'd just collected from the festering sore on Newt Collins's belly.

"You can get dressed now," the doctor said.

Newt swung his legs off the side of the examining table and sat up.

"So, am I gonna live?" he asked.

"I'm still reserving judgment," Luke said, as he sat down to write a prescription. "Get this filled and use it as directed. I want to see you back in here on Monday. If this infection isn't beginning to clear up by then, I *will* admit you to the hospital. And if you go against my orders again, I will be forced to withdraw as your physician."

Newt panicked. "But I —"

Luke held up his hand.

"No buts. What the hell is the matter with you, anyway? Don't you understand the seriousness of your situation? You're a walking invitation to MRSA infection, staph infection . . . any number of infections, all of which could kill you! For all I know, you already have one of them, although we won't know until I get the lab results back."

Newt frowned. He didn't want to hear this.

"What's MRSA?"

"Ever hear of flesh-eating bacteria?"

Newt's lips went slack. Shit. "Yeah, I heard of that." He looked down at the festering sores on his belly. "Is that what that is? Is it going to eat all the flesh off my belly?"

"MRSA will eat more than your belly. If you get it, or staph, or any invasive infection in these burns, you can lose limbs, internal organs —"

"What about my dick?" Newt asked.

Luke stared in disbelief. "You lose limbs and internal organs, you won't be needing that dick," he snapped.

Newt shuddered involuntarily. Maybe he had been too casual about all this.

"So what's your best guess? *Is* . . . this staph? Or . . . that MRSA?"

The doctor sighed. "I don't know what it

214

is. But look at yourself, man! This isn't good. You're beginning to heal in places, but some of these blisters are a festering mess. Wounds like those need to be cleaned and dressed daily. This is just as serious an injury as if you'd been burned by fire . . . maybe more so, because the chemicals not only burned your skin, you absorbed some of them through the open wounds, as well."

Newt's eyes widened in shock. "What's that mean?"

"Basically, it means you poisoned yourself and are acting like you don't give a damn. Aren't you in pain?"

"Hell, yeah . . . but at home I don't wear any clothes and it's not so bad. Besides, when it gets too bad I just take a pill and —"

"You can't depend on pain pills to heal you. All they're doing is masking the pain. Are you taking the antibiotics like I instructed?"

"Took one yesterday morning, but the rest spilled down the sink and —"

Luke's voice rose in anger. "Those are more important than the pain pills. They're meant to keep down infection. Get this prescription filled today, and don't miss a dose. If things get worse, you come back to the hospital immediately or I won't be

215

responsible for the outcome. Look . . . let's be honest here. What's so important that you refuse to be admitted? Is it about money, a lack of insurance? Because if it is, we can always work out a payment plan."

Truth wasn't an option, so Newt blurted out the first thing he could think of.

"I'm afraid of hospitals. Sorry. Can I go now?"

Dr. Luke shrugged. "If you're asking if I'm finished with your treatment and exam, then the answer is yes, but don't expect me to condone your choices."

"I'll be better. You'll see," Newt said, and started dressing.

By the time he finished, he was in misery. His hands were still tender and raw, and the waistband of his pants was rubbing against his skin. It was all he could do to walk to the lobby.

Sam saw him coming and stood. "That didn't take so long," he said. "Are you ready to go?"

Newt handed him the prescription. "Gotta get this filled before you take me back, but these clothes are killing me. I don't think I'm gonna be able to walk in the pharmacy and wait."

"I'll do it," Sam said, and held the door open for him as they went out.

About a half hour later they were pulling into the trailer park. Sam stopped in front of Newt's trailer, eyeing the jumble of uprooted trees around Newt's pickup, and sighed.

"Real sorry about those trees. We'll be getting to them come Saturday, for sure."

Newt was in so much pain that, at that moment, he couldn't care.

"Yeah, right. Thanks for the ride," he said, and headed for the front door with the bag holding his new prescription and a softball he just bought as a bribe for the kids, desperate to get out of his clothes.

The moment he turned the lock, he began stripping and didn't stop until he was naked again. Relief was instantaneous. He groaned softly, then popped both an antibiotic and a pain pill into his mouth at the same time, and chased them with water straight from the tap.

It was just after two. The kid should still sleep for a couple hours — maybe more. That would give the pain pill he'd just taken time to kick in and let him get some rest.

He kicked at an empty pizza box as he walked past his favorite chair, sending cockroaches scrambling in a dozen directions at once.

"Dirty bastards," he muttered, but kept

on walking, without realizing the irony of his remark.

He paused in the doorway to his bedroom, eyeing the sleeping child and thinking about what they were going to do when he got well. He looked at his dick, willing it to an erection, if for no other reason than to assure himself it still worked.

Nothing.

He sighed. If he had this to do over again, he wouldn't have snatched the kid, but it was too late to rectify the error.

The doctor had made a believer of him. He didn't want to lose a limb, and he damn sure didn't want his dick to rot off.

He lay down on the bed, scooting the kid's leg over to his own side of the bed, and then closed his eyes. The last thing he remembered thinking before he drifted off to sleep was that he needed to wash these sheets.

J.R. glanced down as the chopper entered New Orleans airspace. Even though several years had passed since Hurricane Katrina's devastation, it was still easy to spot the hardest-hit areas. Very little had been done toward reclamation, which made that part of the city look like a war zone. As for the mighty Mississippi, it might look like a lazy snake from up high, but he knew all too well

218

how fast that could change.

When they flew over the area where Katie's parents had been found floating in their own attic, he said a silent prayer, then looked away. After all the overtime he'd put in, he was due for some downtime. Whatever was waiting for him at the office could go on waiting. He was going to Bordelaise.

As the pilot began descending, J.R. looked down at the helipad behind the home office and saw Brent Macklan waiting near the back door.

J.R. was the first to get out. He retrieved his bag, and then ducked as he ran out from under the spinning rotors and headed toward his boss. Blalock and his three buddies followed more slowly, and while none of them were happy about having to face Macklan, they wanted their severance checks.

Brent grinned wryly as he shook J.R.'s hand.

"That little trip I sent you on sure backfired, didn't it?"

J.R. smiled. "Yes, sir, that it did."

Brent nodded. "Anyway, it was much appreciated, and we're glad to have you back. I think I can promise it won't happen again. The new troubleshooter is already on the job."

"That's good news," J.R. said, then glanced back toward the chopper. "There are your bad boys. I'll leave you to put the fear of God into them in private."

Brent frowned. "No need. They blackballed themselves, especially Blalock. The word is already out that he's a user. No oil company is going to touch him with a ten-foot pole. His days on the rigs are over. He just doesn't know it yet."

"That's good. He was an accident just waiting to happen."

As J.R. started to walk off, Brent called him back.

"Hey! I almost forgot to tell you — you missed a lot of excitement on Monday."

"I don't know," J.R. said. "There was a lot of excitement out on the rig Monday. Hurricane Bonnie gave us hell for hours."

"Yeah, well, I'll bet no one gave birth out there," Brent said.

J.R.'s eyes widened. "Angela? She had her baby?"

Brent grinned. "In the office. In the middle of the storm. They transported mother and baby girl Bonnie to the hospital after the worst of the storm had passed."

"Oh, man," J.R. said. "Who delivered?"

"Me and the UPS guy," Brent said.

J.R. laughed out loud. "Poor Angela."

"Hey. We did all right."

"I'm sure you did," J.R. said. "And speaking of mothers and babies, I haven't been able to get through to Katie and Bobby, although I've tried several times since the storm. I don't suppose you've heard anything about how things are going down there? All their power out or something?"

Brent's smile slipped. "To my knowledge there aren't any more power outages in the state, but I could be wrong."

J.R. frowned. "So it was out down there? For how long?"

"At least a couple of days." Then Brent added. "You *have* talked to her since Sunday, right?"

"No, why?"

Brent hesitated, then pointed at the four men who were heading their way.

"Wait there!" he ordered.

The quartet stopped. They weren't about to argue with the man holding their money.

"What?" J.R. asked. "What about Sunday?"

"Man . . . I thought you knew."

J.R.'s heart hit a beat so hard it hurt his chest.

"Knew what? Damn it, Brent! What happened to my family?"

Brent held up his hand. "Whoa, whoa . . .

221

I'm not saying anything did, but they are still down in Bordelaise, right?"

"Yes, damn it. Talk!"

"It was hit by a tornado. Went right down the middle of town — even took out part of the jail. I remember hearing something about some missing prisoners and three or four deaths, but no names."

J.R. staggered, then turned his back to the men and covered his face.

God, no, please no.

Brent put a hand on J.R.'s back. "Are you all right? Is there anything I can do?"

J.R. spun, his face twisted with pain. "Why didn't someone say something to me? Has anyone from Bordelaise called the office wanting to talk to me?"

Brent frowned. "I couldn't say. We have a temp working the office while Angela is on maternity leave. Her name is Charlotte. You could go check with her. She probably forwarded any messages to your cell." Then he sighed. "Although I will admit she's not the brightest bulb in the lamp."

J.R. was already heading for the back door. He strode through the hallways, past the offices and conference room, then past his own office to the front desk.

The young woman sitting in Angela's chair was on the phone.

He strode up to her desk, yanked her headset off and then leaned down until they were eye to eye.

She screamed.

It was actually more like a squeak, but on the spur of the moment, it was all she could muster.

"I need to ask you a question," he said quietly.

Charlotte bit her lip and nodded rapidly.

"I'm J. R. Earle. Have there been any messages for me from Bordelaise?"

Her eyes widened, then she nodded.

"Who from?" he asked.

"Um, one from a hospital and, uh, two from a Chief Porter . . . I think."

J.R. groaned as his legs went weak. "Woman . . . what have you done?"

Charlotte started to cry. "I don't understand. What was I supposed to do?"

He pulled a handful of tissues from a box on her desk and handed them to her.

"Why didn't you forward the calls to my cell?"

She took the tissues but continued to bawl. "I tried, but they wouldn't go through. I thought it was because of the weather."

J.R. straightened, then shoved a hand through his hair in disbelief. This was a

223

nightmare. Damn this job and damn the storm.

"Why didn't you try later, after the weather had cleared?"

"Because I forgot," she said, and then let out a wail. "They're on your desk. I put everything on your desk."

J.R. ran down the hall toward his office. As she'd said, there was a stack of mail on one side and a handful of messages in the middle.

His hands were shaking as he leafed through the messages. Finding the one from Bordelaise General Hospital was like a fist to the gut. When he found the two from Hershel Porter, the room started to spin. He dropped into his chair and took out his cell, then stopped, uncertain of who to call first.

That was when he remembered he hadn't turned his phone back on after they'd landed, or checked that last message. His hands were shaking so hard he could barely hold the phone. He didn't recognize the number, but when he went to voice mail and heard Katie's voice and the desperation in every word, he felt sick.

"Call me," she'd begged.

"God . . . oh, God . . . what isn't she saying?"

Now that he knew the call was from Katie, he was even more concerned. Where was she? What had happened? Why wasn't she calling from home?

He started to call her, then stopped, staring down at the number pad until the numbers all ran together. Suddenly he took a deep breath and flipped the phone shut.

Every instinct he had told him the news was going to be bad, and he knew that whatever it was, he needed to hear it from her — face-to-face, not over a phone.

Then he picked up the message from the police department. The least he could do was check in. Let them know he was coming.

He punched in the numbers, then waited as the phone on the other end started to ring.

"Bordelaise Police."

He recognized Vera's voice. "Vera. It's J. R. Earle. I just got the chief's message. Tell him I'm on my way home."

"Wait! Wait!" Vera cried, but he'd already disconnected.

He took the car keys from his desk, found his bag just inside the back door and headed for the company parking lot on the run.

Soon he was driving east out of New Orleans. During the drive, he kept reliving the fight that had split them apart. It was like a nightmare that had been hardwired into a loop in his brain. He could see the tears on Katie's face and the confusion in his little boy's eyes. He remembered the pain and emptiness of the past few months, and wondered if this was God's punishment for what he'd done.

Panic finally got to him, and as he was passing a semi, he accelerated. The engine roared as he gunned it, but once he'd passed the truck, he didn't let up on the gas. Instead, the scenery soon turned into a blur. He drove faster and faster, until the sound of the tires on the pavement was a high-pitched hum. By the time he reached the Bordelaise city limits it was fully dark and a storm was brewing. There were distant flashes of lightning in the east, and if the storm continued in this direction, they would most likely get rain before morning.

It took a while for him to figure out what was wrong. There were blocks and blocks of missing streetlights. He could see signs of wind damage, but in the darkness, it was difficult to see how bad it was. It wasn't until he started up Main Street that he saw the first major signs of the devastation. Panic resurfaced.

Get home. Get home. It was all he could

think of to do. He needed to see Katie's face. He needed to be holding her in his arms when she said what she had to say.

But when he drove past Pinky's Get and Go and saw the boarded-up windows, he suffered his first huge moment of doubt. And the farther he drove toward the street on which they lived, the more certain he was that he was driving through the direct path that the tornado had taken.

When he got to the intersection where he needed to turn, he lost his sense of direction. There were no street signs, no landmarks, no houses of any kind left, only piles and piles of debris.

He knew where their house should have been, but like everything else on both sides of the block, it was missing. Stunned, he hit the brakes and shoved the transmission into Park. As he got out, hot, muggy air hit him in the face like a slap. Not so much as a blade of grass was stirring. It was as if God was holding His breath, waiting to see if there was anything down here worth saving.

"Sweet Mother of God."

The words came out like a prayer as his knees went weak. Had they been inside when the tornado hit?

"Katie . . . Katie . . . where are you, baby?"

Even though he knew she couldn't answer,

just her name on his lips brought tears to his eyes. This was his worst fear come to life: that he would be gone when his family needed him most. And now, with the house destroyed, he didn't even know where to start looking for them.

His hands were shaking, and he kept blinking back tears as he scanned his cell for her earlier call. Still frowning at the unfamiliar number, he hit Redial, then held his breath, waiting for someone to answer.

TEN

It was just after eight. Supper was over, and the lingering scent of the cornbread Penny had baked to go with their brown beans and ham still hung in the air. She was sitting in her favorite recliner with a lap full of knitting, but her hands were idle. She couldn't focus on the television show for looking at Katie. It was a sad thing to witness a woman coming undone. Even though she sat quietly, Katie's face was streaked with tears.

The news that Bobby Earle hadn't been swept away by the storm had been superseded by the growing belief that J.R. had taken him and was on the run. She could only imagine Katie's despair, fearing she might never see him again.

When the phone rang, the sudden look of hope on Katie's face was wrenching. Penny picked up the receiver.

"Hello?"

"This is J. R. Earle. Is Katie there?"

Penny gasped, then nodded quickly at Katie to indicate it was him. Thank you, Lord, she said silently. "Yes . . . oh, yes!"

"Who is this?" J.R. asked.

"Oh. It's Penny Bates. Katie is —"

"Tell her I'm coming."

"Wait. You can tell her —"

The line went dead in her ear.

Katie had scooted to the edge of the couch. Her heart was pounding.

"Was that J.R.? Why wouldn't he talk to me?"

Penny's knitting hit the floor as she jumped to her feet.

"All he said was, 'Tell her I'm coming.' "

Katie started to shake. She didn't know what that meant or how long it would take him to get here, but her prayers had been answered. If he walked into this house with their son, she would never ask God for another thing as long as she lived.

"Honey, sit down. There's no telling where he was calling from. It could be tomorrow before —"

"No," Katie said, and ran to the window. "He's here . . . somewhere. He's looking for me."

Penny looked over Katie's shoulder and out into the empty street, then gave her a quick pat on the back.

"I hope you're right or we'll never get a minute of sleep tonight," she said, then picked up her knitting, leaving Katie standing watch at the window.

The streetlights on Penny's street were still standing, but only one of them was lit. Within seconds, a car drove past, while another approached from the opposite direction. Katie was so focused on watching those two vehicles that she missed seeing a third one turn the corner.

Then she heard a roaring engine and saw the third vehicle coming down the street — coming fast. When it passed beneath the streetlight, her heart leaped. It was him!

"They're here!" Katie cried, and ran for the door.

J.R. took the turn up Penny Bates's driveway so fast that the tires squealed. He slammed the pickup into Park and killed the engine just as the front door opened. When he recognized the familiar silhouette of his wife in the doorway, he went weak with relief.

Katie! Thank God!

Seconds later he was running toward the house as Katie flew down the steps, and then she leaped into his arms.

"You didn't come and —"

"I didn't know you —"

"They called and called —"

"Trapped on the rig —"

"I thought —"

J.R. groaned, then smothered her lips with his, stifling the words. She was warm and alive, and he couldn't stop touching her. He kissed her over . . . and over . . . and over, running his hands up and down her body, through her hair, tilting her face to his in the moonlight, making sure she was truly okay.

For Katie, the emotion was just the same. She had been dying, and now she was alive again. Resurrected from despair by a simple touch and a kiss. For a few frantic moments she forgot — and then Bobby's face slid through her mind, and she roughly pushed him away.

What was the matter with her? How could she feel this joy? She needed to know if he had Bobby.

J.R.'s heart sank. Was she angry? Would she ever forgive him?

Katie looked over his shoulder toward the truck just as J.R. looked over her shoulder toward the house. At the same moment, they both asked the same question.

"Where's Bobby?"

Katie heard the words, spoken in perfect synchronicity to hers, and felt the ground tilt beneath her feet.

"Noooo!" she screamed, and began beating on his chest with her fists. "I thought . . . I prayed . . . Oh, God, oh, God!"

J.R. grabbed her wrists and pulled her close. He knew before he asked that it was going to be bad.

"Katie . . . baby . . . where's Bobby? Where's our son?"

Her cheeks were wet with tears. The words were acid on her lips.

"He's gone! He's *gone!*"

J.R. staggered. "What do you mean, he's gone?"

"Up until this morning, we all thought he'd died in the tornado. There were search parties and . . . Chief Porter said . . ." She stopped, then took a deep breath. "They just couldn't find . . . couldn't find him anywhere."

J.R. was listening, but the words didn't make sense. This wasn't happening. It couldn't happen.

Katie shuddered, then took a deep breath. "This morning the Maxwells showed up at the police department and told Chief Porter that while the tornado siren was blowing, their little girl, Holly, saw a man in a blue pickup snatch Bobby from the churchyard. Chief Porter suspected you. Even while I couldn't believe you would do that, I kept praying it was you. At least then I would know he was alive. And then, when they called to notify you I was in the hospital, you didn't call back, and when I left you that message and you still didn't answer, we didn't know what to think."

J.R.'s heart was pounding so hard that he couldn't hear. He kept seeing his little boy's laughing face; then suddenly he turned away and vomited.

Katie moaned, then grabbed the back of his shirt and held on. They were together again, bound by misery, and on their way to hell.

Penny was watching their reunion from the window, and when she saw Katie suddenly start hitting J.R.'s chest, and then saw J.R.'s reaction to what he'd been told, she knew the news was bad.

This reunion had become a horrible demonstration of irony. While they'd found each other, they had also confirmed everyone's worst fears. J.R. did not have his son.

"Lord, can this get any worse?"

Then she clapped her hand over her mouth, sorry that she'd given life to the words and ran for the phone. Hershel Porter needed this information.

■ ■ ■ ■

Hershel Porter had been home less than an hour when he decided to make himself some supper. Tonight was his wife's book-club meeting, which meant he cooked. By choice, his cooking usually consisted of a pastrami on rye with a thick coat of cracked mustard and a tall glass of sweet iced tea. He was spreading mustard on the bread when the phone began to ring.

"Dang it all," he muttered, licking the mustard off his thumb as he answered. "Porter residence."

It was the night dispatcher from the police department.

"Chief, Penny Bates just called and said J. R. Earle is at her house, and that you'd want to know."

Hershel waited, remembering that J.R. had called but had never mentioned his son. "Does he have the boy?"

"She said no."

"Sweet God Almighty, this isn't good news." He looked longingly at the makings of his sandwich, but the decision was already made. "If you need me, call my cell. I'll be at the Bates home."

"Yes, sir," the dispatcher said, and disconnected.

Within minutes, Hershel was on his way to Penny's.

J.R. couldn't stop shaking. Even when he walked into Penny's house, his legs felt like rubber.

"Come in . . . sit here," Penny said, urging them both inside.

Katie sat down on the sofa, then pulled J.R. down beside her. He couldn't bear to look at her and see the blame in her eyes.

"It's my fault. If I'd been here, none of this would have happened," he said.

Katie gasped, then reached for his hand. "No! No! That's not true! I'm the one to blame. I should have moved when you wanted me to."

J.R. shuddered, then looked up. He had his Katie back, but at what cost?

At that point, Penny intervened.

"Neither one of you is to blame for this! Someone abducted your child . . . in broad daylight!"

J.R.'s eyes suddenly narrowed as memory surfaced. "The monster!"

Katie shivered. "Monster? Did he talk about the monster to you again, too? He only mentioned it to me one other time, and that was last Sunday on the way to church."

"He's talked about a monster off and on for months . . . ever since we . . . since I bought the new house."

Katie paled. "What did we miss? Why didn't we know this was real?"

Before J.R. could answer, there was a knock at the door.

"That will be Chief Porter. I called to let him know you were here," Penny said, as she went to answer.

J.R. stood as the police chief walked in.

"I'm going to make some coffee," Penny said, and quietly disappeared.

Hershel gave J.R. a steady look.

"You've been a hard man to find," he said.

Awash with guilt, all J.R. could do was explain.

"I've been on an offshore drilling rig for the past week. The chopper that was supposed to evacuate us went down in the gulf, then it was too late to send another, because of the storm. We were stranded. At first, when I couldn't reach Katie, I just assumed the power lines were down or something. Then I began to worry, but I had no way off the rig until my replacement showed up. I just got back into New Orleans this afternoon and found all the messages that had been left for me, although they were supposed to have been forwarded to my cell."

Katie shuddered. "I still don't understand. Angela is always so —"

"Angela isn't there. She had her baby early," J.R. said. "There's just a temp who was unaware of the protocol."

Hershel shook his head sympathetically. "It's not often that I wish a parent had snatched his own child, but I have to say, given the alternative, we were sure hoping you had him."

J.R. reached for Katie's hand. "We've had our ups and downs the past few months, but I would never have scared Katie like that. Ever."

"Okay," Hershel said. "So that's that." He took out a notebook and pen. "Had either of you noticed someone paying too much attention to Bobby?"

Another wave of guilt washed over them as they looked at each other. Because of the fight, their son had been living two separate lives.

"We never saw anyone, but I just found out that he's been talking to J.R. about a monster living in Bordelaise. The only time he ever mentioned it to me was on the way to church last Sunday. He said something about the monster not living in New Orleans."

"Can you pinpoint an incident that started his fears?" Hershel asked.

Katie nodded. "It started a few months ago, right after J.R. had come home for the weekend. Bobby woke up screaming. Nearly scared us to death. By the time we got to his room, he was crying hysterically and claiming there had been a monster looking in his window."

J.R. nodded. "We wound up sleeping with him the rest of the night. He talked about the monster at my house, too, but I never put it together like that. I thought the monster had to do with him being upset that Katie and I weren't living together. I thought he was acting out because of the stress."

Hershel started making notes. "How can you be sure he wasn't referring to a fictional monster, like the one under the bed . . . or in the closet, like other kids?"

"He never had imaginary friends," Katie said. "And he never had bad dreams, unless he was sick. When he ran a fever, he sometimes had nightmares. When he mentioned the monster Sunday, I was shocked."

"Why?" Hershel asked.

Katie glanced up at J.R., then back at her

hands. "He was talking about Daddy's new house, and how he was going to get a puppy because of the big backyard, and that he liked going to New Orleans because the monster didn't live there. It was the first time he'd ever said anything to me about a monster being in Bordelaise. When he mentioned it, I immediately thought of that night."

Hershel turned to J.R. "Tell me exactly what he said about this monster when he was with you."

"There were several times it came up, but each time I always thought he was trying to find a reason for me to move back or for Katie to come with him . . . you know? He's seven. He didn't always have the words to express the way he might be feeling."

"For instance?" Hershel asked.

J.R. thought for a moment. "One day we were shopping for groceries. Without thinking, I put a jar of orange marmalade in the grocery basket."

"I don't get it," Hershel said.

"I'm the only one in the family who likes it," Katie said.

Hershel nodded. "Okay . . . you forgot Katie wasn't with you for the moment. How does that —"

"Let me finish," J.R. said. "When Bobby

240

saw me do it, he called me on it, reminding me that was Mama's jelly, but that Mama wouldn't get to eat it unless he took it back to Bordelaise."

Katie had never let herself think of what Bobby's time had been like with J.R. Knowing that her little boy had been trying to compartmentalize his allegiance set off a new wave of guilt.

"Oh, Lord," she said, and covered her face.

J.R. put his arm around her and pulled her close as he continued with his story.

"Anyway, I asked him if he missed his mother when he was in New Orleans with me. He hesitated, then said yes. Then I asked him if, when he was in Bordelaise, was he sad because I wasn't there? He shrugged and said that he was used to me being away sometimes, but he wasn't used to being away from Mama."

"Why didn't you tell me?" Katie cried.

"We weren't talking, remember?"

Katie's shoulders slumped.

"Back to the subject of the monster," Hershel said.

J.R. nodded. "It was what he said next that made me think he was just trying to gain some leverage and get us back together. He said that we should try and get Mama to move to New Orleans because the monster lived in Bordelaise."

"Oh, my poor baby," Katie said. "He was telling us over and over that there was a monster, and we didn't believe him."

"This isn't definitive by any means," Hershel said. "But it does give us a place to start. It's obvious he wasn't taken for ransom, or we would have heard something by now. We'll be cross-checking the DMV listing in this parish against owners of a newer model blue truck to see if any names pop out. And I'm also requesting a list of registered sex offenders for this area."

J.R.'s stomach rolled again. He couldn't let himself think about what Bobby might be going through. He wouldn't think about the emotional damage that could result. All he wanted was his son back — alive.

"What can we do?" Katie asked.

Hershel sighed. "Let me do my job."

"I can't just sit here and wait," she insisted.

"You can pray," Hershel said. "God knows we're going to need all the prayers we can get to make this right."

At that point Penny came back with four coffee-filled mugs and a plate of cookies on a tray. She stopped in front of Katie first.

Katie's stomach rebeled. "I don't —"

"Shush," Penny said. "You didn't eat enough at supper to even dirty your plate."

Katie didn't argue. She just took her coffee and cookies, and watched as Penny served the two men.

"Thank you," Hershel said, and promptly downed a cookie in three quick bites.

"So do we have a plan?" Penny asked.

Hershel frowned. "There's always a plan. Problem is, they don't always pan out. I can't make promises about anything except that I won't stop looking until we bring Bobby home."

Suddenly, J.R. remembered Brent mentioning that several people had died.

"My boss told me there were casualties. Needless to say, my heart nearly stopped until I found that message from Katie on my phone."

Hershel nodded. "Yes, four, actually. Old man Warren died during the evacuation of the nursing home after the storm was over. Heart attack. His funeral was Wednesday. Then today we buried the Norths."

"All of them?" J.R. asked.

"Yes."

"Good Lord," he said.

The last time he'd seen Frank and Maggie North, they'd been beaming proudly at one of Carolina's book signings. It was a source of pride for everyone in Bordelaise that one of their own had become a famous author.

J.R. pulled Katie a little closer, quietly thanking God that she was still alive.

"I'm sorry," Hershel said then, as he set his coffee aside. "I'd better be going now. If either of you remembers anything else, call me."

"We will," J.R. promised.

Penny showed the police chief to the door. Once he was gone, she turned with her hands on her hips, a don't-argue-with-me expression on her face.

"You'll both be staying here with me until this is over."

"We accept, with much gratitude," J.R. said. "Are you sure it won't be too much trouble?"

Penny glanced at Katie, then sighed. "Obviously she hasn't told you, but I feel as guilty about Bobby as the both of you want to feel. I was the one who was watching the children when the sirens went off. I'm the one who let this happen."

Katie immediately spoke up. "No. That's not true," she insisted. "Holly and Bobby were playing in one of the tunnels. When the siren went off, Holly got scared and ran for the church. She forgot about Bobby being in the tunnel, and Penny didn't know. She looked behind her to check, and the playground was clear. . . . It was crazy. Of course she assumed he was on his way inside with the other children."

"Then how did Holly know?" J.R. asked.

"She finally remembered him and started to go back. Just as she turned around, she saw him climbing out of the tunnel, and then he stumbled and fell. And then Holly said she saw a man get out of a blue truck, throw Bobby over his shoulder and get back in the truck, then drive away. Before she could say anything, she was knocked down in the rush to get inside and hurt her hand. I'm sure that injury made her forget. Later she heard everyone talking about the tornado taking him and her parents said he'd gone with God, so she put her own spin on it and decided she'd seen God taking Bobby to heaven in his truck."

"My God," J.R. muttered. "So how did they find out what she'd seen?"

"Pictures," Katie said.

"Pictures?"

"Frances said she kept drawing pictures of the storm and the church and the playground, and in every one, there was a man in a blue pickup. Holly said he was God, and everything snowballed from there."

"Katie's right," J.R. said to Penny. "It's not your fault. We're the parents. We misunderstood the warning signs. The horrible truth is that the monster he's been so afraid of is real, and he finally saw his chance and took it."

Penny blew her nose, then stuffed the tissue back into her pocket.

Unable to talk about what had happened without crying, she said, "Katie can show you where you'll be sleeping. There are clean towels in the bathroom. Help yourself. I'm going to wash up the dishes and go to bed."

"Good night, Penny, and thank you again," Katie said.

"Thank you for taking care of Katie for me," J.R. added.

"You're both welcome — now stop thanking me," Penny muttered, then grabbed the tray and hustled out of the room.

"I'm going to get my bag from the truck. I'll be right back," J.R. said, then hesitated when Katie grabbed his hand.

"I'm sorry," she said softly.

"Like we just told Penny, you have nothing to apologize for."

"If I had moved when you wanted, this wouldn't be happening, and you know it. The monster lived in Bordelaise, not New

Orleans. Remember?"

"I'll say it one more time, then this subject is forever closed between us, understand?"

Katie nodded.

"The only person at fault in this nightmare is the sick son of a bitch who took our son. And I promise you, Katie, when they catch him, if the law doesn't kill him, I will."

Katie shivered as she watched J.R. walk out the front door. She knew her husband well enough to know that was not an idle threat.

As soon as he came back inside, he stopped long enough to lock the door behind him, then held out his hand.

Katie threaded her fingers through his.

"The bedroom is this way," she said.

J.R. followed, emotionally torn. On the one hand, he was relieved to learn Katie had escaped injury, even though the house was destroyed. But it was impossible to rejoice. This was a nightmare from which he needed to wake. All he could think about was how small Bobby was, and how innocent, and what he might be going through.

Katie closed the door to the bedroom as J.R. dropped his bag at the foot of the bed. When she hesitated, he took her in his arms. Twice he started to speak, and both times failed. Finally his voice grew husky; then it started to shake as he said, "I have to say this. I have to say it aloud or the words are going to explode inside me."

"Say what?" Katie asked.

"What if we never see him again? What if we never know what happened . . . if he suffered . . . if he died thinking we —"

Katie put her hand across his mouth. "Don't! I will not believe that. I will not believe that God would do that to me twice," she said fiercely.

J.R. groaned as he pulled her close, then buried his face against the curve of her neck.

Katie held him, needing his comfort as much as he needed hers. They were as wounded as two people could be and still be breathing.

Finally it was J.R. who pulled back. He cupped her face, then lowered his head and kissed her. Once. Gently. "Forgive me?"

"For what? I'm the one who —"

He pressed a finger to her lips and then shook his head. "For leaving you alone. I should have waited. I shouldn't have tried to force you."

Katie took his hand and placed it over her heart. "You shouldn't have had to try. It was a fabulous opportunity for you to finally be home with us, and all I could think about was myself. I should have gone with you." Then her voice broke. "Now I have something I need to ask you, and you have to swear you'll tell me the truth."

"Always."

"What if I'm wrong?"

"Wrong how, baby?" he asked.

The words spilled out, one on top of the other, as if she was afraid they would get caught and choke her to death before she got them said.

"What if we never see him again? You say it's not my fault, but how will you feel as time passes? When months pass and his birthday rolls around. Will you look at me and think, If she'd just come with me, we'd still have our son? Will you, J.R.?" She dug her fingers into his arms. "Will you? You have to tell me now, because I won't be able to bear losing him — and you — all over again."

J.R. groaned. "No, baby, no. I don't have the words to explain what you mean to me. All I can say is that you and Bobby are the reason I draw breath. If something happens to one of you, that won't make me turn on the survivor. I'm not made that way."

Katie shuddered. "I'm so scared."

"So am I, Katie, so am I."

"Will you hold me? I've been alone for so —"

"Hold you? God forgive me, but I need more than a hug."

Katie sobbed, then threw her arms around his neck and pulled him to her. Making love to him now had nothing to do with lust. Emotionally, it was what they needed to seal their promises to each other — vows as honest as the ones they'd spoken the day they were married.

J.R. pulled Katie's shirt off over her head, unzipped her pants and slid them down around her ankles, then picked her up and laid her down on the bed.

Katie was trembling as she watched him undress. He'd always been fit, but now she could see he was thinner — evidence of his own stress and suffering.

Please, God . . . you gave me back my husband. Please give us back our son. Please, God, please . . . give me a second chance.

Then J.R. was on the bed beside her, kissing every inch of her body, loving her with words as well as touch. She didn't know that she was crying. The universe was centering on the building need deep in her belly and the man who slid between her legs.

J.R. groaned. She felt so good. But guilt

was battering his thoughts. It seemed obscene, taking this pleasure when his son was lost and suffering. Then Katie slid her arms around his neck and nothing else mattered. He needed to be healed as badly as she did. They needed to forgive each other before they could go forward, and making love to Katie was his way of setting things right. It was an affirmation of their faith and trust in each other, and a combining of their strengths to face the uncertainty of the days ahead.

He looked down at her face, saw the tears on her cheeks and began kissing them away.

Katie trembled. He was deep inside her, yet motionless. For the first time in months she felt complete. She pulled him close, then whispered in his ear, "Make love to me, Johnny."

J.R.'s vision blurred. For a second, her words transported him back to another place and time — to their senior year in high school, just after Halloween, the night they first made love.

Make love to me, Johnny.

He could no more refuse her now than he could then. Bracing his hands on either side of her body, he started to rock. When she shuddered, then moaned, his pulse leaped.

"I love you, baby," he said softly, then

251

began moving a little faster, a little deeper.

One minute turned into two, and then three, and still he rocked inside her. Heat built between them until they were slick with sweat and lost in the motion. Over and over, harder and harder, deeper and deeper — while the coil tightened in their bellies.

Suddenly Katie lost it. The climax was like an explosion, sending shock waves throughout her body.

When J.R. felt her tremors, he didn't hold back. He came hard and fast, then collapsed on top of her.

Katie was still trembling when he wrapped her in his arms and shifted her until they were lying back to front, spooned against each other. Their embrace was desperate, fueled by a subconscious fear that if they parted again, neither would survive.

Slowly their labored breathing eased and the room grew quiet. It took forever before he felt her body relax. She'd finally gone to sleep.

But tonight, sleep evaded him. He couldn't quit thinking of Bobby. The ache in his chest continued to swell until tears were running down his face.

"I will find you, son," he said softly. "Just have faith. Daddy's coming."

Katie flinched in her sleep, as if echoing his promise.

ELEVEN

Friday

A half dozen men were waiting in the outer office of the police department when Hershel got to work. Despite their matching haircuts and casual clothes, he would have recognized them by their serious expressions alone. When he noticed they were carrying, he knew he was right.

DEA.

Babcock's search team had arrived.

The tall, sandy-haired man nearest the door stood first, as the others followed.

"Chief Porter?"

"That's me," Hershel said. "Gentlemen, would you join me in my office?"

Vera's eyes were big as saucers, but she knew enough to refrain from comment. Still, he could only imagine what she was thinking. Six armed men waiting for him to walk in. She'd probably been freaking out until he got in to work. As he walked past her desk, it occurred to him to wonder what the agents had thought about her. Sometime between last night and this morning she'd gone from red and curly to long and blonde. He sighed. Vera sure was fond of her wigs.

"Hold my calls," he said shortly.

She nodded, watching curiously as the men followed her boss down the hall.

Hershel entered the office, stepped aside for the men to enter, then closed the door and offered his hand.

"I'm Hershel Porter, police chief of Bordelaise. Sorry, I don't have enough chairs for all of you."

"Chief Porter, pleasure to meet you, sir," the sandy-haired man said. "Agent Edwards, DEA." Then he went down the line, introducing the other men. "As you've probably guessed, Captain Babcock sent us. We'll be helping you search for the missing prisoners. What exactly is the status of the search?"

"It was called off a couple of days ago. I ended up with four search teams going in four different directions. We were looking for the prisoners, and also the body of a little boy who'd gone missing. However, we just learned last night that the child was not a victim of the storm but, we believe, of a child molester."

The men were visibly concerned about

255

the news.

"That's a rough one. I take it you had no luck with the search for the prisoners, either?" Edwards asked.

"Not so much as a footprint or a shred of clothing. You understand that this is bayou country. That means swamps and gators in abundance. If those prisoners had the misfortune to go airborne, then land in the swamps, their bodies are long gone."

Edwards blanched. He was friends with Nick Aroyo, the missing undercover agent, and the thought of his friend meeting such a fate was daunting.

"If you don't mind, we'd like to see the jail, then we'll begin our own search from there."

"Yeah, sure. They're about finished with repairs. Still have to shingle the roof, but the concrete-block walls have been replaced. Follow me."

Although it was close to 8:00 a.m., Katie was still asleep. A short while earlier J.R. had awakened with tears on his face, but it hadn't taken long for his despair to turn to anger. He wasn't going to sit back and wait for the police to find Bobby. Too many days had passed, and they were going to need all the help they could get.

As he looked down at the woman in his arms, his heart twisted. She seemed so frail. All that dark hair and pale skin, all the scratches and fading bruises from the injuries she'd suffered during the storm, just reminded him of what she'd gone through alone. He brushed a kiss across her forehead.

"I'm sorry, Katie girl. But you're not alone anymore," he whispered.

Katie stirred, but didn't wake.

Carefully, he scooted out of bed, grabbed some clean clothes from his bag and headed for the bathroom.

It was the smell of freshly brewed coffee and the sound of the shower in the adjoining bathroom that woke Katie up.

J.R. was home!

The moment she thought his name, she opened her eyes and the memories came flooding back. There was no home anymore. She was at Penny Bates's house, and Bobby was missing. Her stomach knotted as a familiar pall settled back over her soul.

Then she reminded herself that there was a positive to this. She'd thought he was dead, but now there was hope. That was something she'd thought she'd lost.

She threw back the covers and got out of

bed just as she heard the shower go off. A couple of minutes later J.R. came out wearing Levi's but minus his shirt. His body was so beautiful to her — washboard abs and that olive complexion. Then she thought of last night and how much it meant that they were no longer at odds. The distance that had stretched between them was gone. If they could only find Bobby, their life would be perfect.

"Good, you're up," J.R. said, then reached for a T-shirt and pulled it over his head. "I've been thinking about something off and on all night, and I want to run it by Chief Porter. As soon as we eat breakfast, let's go down to the office."

"Give me five minutes and I'll meet you in the kitchen," Katie said.

He cupped her cheek as he bent down and kissed her, then whispered in her ear, "Good morning, my love."

"Thank you," Katie said.

"For what?" he asked.

She shrugged. "Oh . . . just for you being you."

He nodded. "Want some toast?"

"I don't think . . ."

"I was just being polite by asking. You *will* eat some breakfast before we go."

She sighed. He was right. She needed to

keep up her strength for the days ahead.

"Then yes to the toast."

He nodded. "See you in a few."

Katie hurried into the bathroom. There was no time to dawdle. They had places to go and people to see. And if they were blessed, they were also one day closer to finding Bobby.

J.R. pulled up in front of the police department and got out.

Despite the questions Katie had asked during breakfast, he'd been evasive about what he was going to suggest to the chief. She had finally given up, but he could tell her curiosity was as sharp as ever.

She joined him on the sidewalk; then they walked in together. Vera was already on duty. Katie tried not to stare at the very fake blonde wig, then gave it up as a lost cause. "Nice color," she said.

Vera beamed. "I think it goes good with my skin tone, don't you?"

"Oh, absolutely," Katie said, and tried not to smile.

"Is the chief in?" J.R. asked.

"Yes. Go on back. I'll let him know you're coming."

They started down the hallway, only to have the chief step out of his office and motion them in.

"Good morning," he said, as they settled in chairs in front of his desk. "Can I get you some coffee?"

Katie shook her head.

"No thanks," J.R. added. "I'm going to get right to the subject. I have a question regarding Bobby's disappearance."

Hershel leaned forward, resting his elbows on the desk.

"Not sure I'll have an answer, but ask away."

"Something has been bothering me about the timeline of the abduction."

"Like what?" Hershel asked.

"What I want to know is, how long did the sirens blow before the tornado actually hit town?"

Hershel looked at Katie, then shrugged. "I'd say no more than five minutes, probably less. What do you think, Katie?"

"That sounds about right."

"Then that means whoever took Bobby had to seek shelter immediately, which means he most likely lives here, and if he does . . ."

Hershel's eyes widened. "I never thought about it that way. Unfortunately, until you showed up last night, we were all pretty certain it was you who'd taken him."

"I know," J.R. said. "And I understand. It would be a logical assumption when I didn't return any of the emergency calls. This whole thing has been one big screwup, and I'm sorrier than I have the words to say."

Katie reached for his hand.

He glanced at her, then had to look away. He didn't know what was going to happen to her if they couldn't find Bobby. She'd nearly come apart when her parents died. This would be the end of her. He knew it.

"The point I was trying to make is . . . if the abduction was happening at the same time the tornado was hitting the other side of Bordelaise, then there's no way he could have outrun the storm by driving out of town."

"But he's had nearly a week to make a getaway," Hershel pointed out.

"Well, what if he couldn't? What if he never intended to leave? Everyone thought Bobby had been taken by the tornado, so he had a free pass. No one would be looking for Bobby, only his body."

"Oh, my God," Katie whispered, then scooted to the edge of her chair. "You're right! Dear Lord, J.R., you're right! Up until Thursday, everyone thought he was dead, including me."

J.R. nodded.

"That's a damn good theory," Hershel said. "And like I told you, I've already got one of my deputies contacting the DMV for a list of people who own blue pickups, and another working on a list of registered sex offenders. If he's on those lists, we'll find him."

"What if he isn't registered?" Katie asked. "What if it's someone living among us and nobody knows?"

Hershel shrugged. "It's possible, I'll admit. But checking those lists is a start."

"We're going to start looking in town for men with blue trucks," J.R. said.

Hershel frowned. "You'll just be wasting your time. Half the people in here drive out of town every day to work, most of them in Baton Rouge, the others on the fishing boats. You can drive all over town and still miss half the owners."

"I can't just sit and wait," J.R. said.

"Then look, if it will make you happy," Hershel offered. "But don't approach anyone on your own. Just write down tag numbers and addresses, and we'll go from there."

J.R. nodded, then stood, but Katie still had a question.

"Chief, when do you think you'll get those lists?"

"It's going to take a little time. Surely by this afternoon, though. I'll definitely keep you updated on our progress. I thought about putting out an Amber Alert, but once that hits the media, it will also alert the perp that we're on to him. Plus we'd be inundated with calls, and we'd have to follow up. That would take time and manpower — manpower I don't have — and it will be a better use of the men I do have to investigate those lists."

"When you get them, let us know," J.R. said. "Katie and I can come here and help you cross-check names to see if any show up on both lists."

Reluctant to get civilians involved in matters of the law, Hershel played it safe. "We'll see how it goes," he said, then walked them to the door. "Remember what I said about not confronting anyone on your own. That's my department."

"Yes, sir," Katie said, J.R. nodded at Vera, who was just coming up the hall, as he closed the door behind them.

"Lord, Lord," Vera said to Hershel as she entered the office, then wiped her eyes and blew her nose on a tissue. "If this isn't just the saddest thing."

Hershel frowned. "Sad doesn't even come close. Where's Tullius? He's supposed to be

263

working on getting me that list from the DMV."

"I'll put out a call," she said.

"When you find him, put him through to my office," Hershel said, then stomped out of the room.

Newt had been awake for almost an hour, and had just finished taking a shower so he could apply fresh dressings to his burns. Dr. Luke had scared the shit out of him. He didn't want to catch that flesh-eating disease. He didn't want his dick to fall off. And more important, he didn't want to die. He and the kid hadn't even had a chance to play.

He turned off the shower and stepped out, leaving the wet washcloth in the bottom of the tub. After two failed attempts to dry off, he gave it up as too painful and reached for the medicated salve.

Bobby was awake. He'd awakened just as the bad man was getting out of bed but had pretended to still be asleep. As soon as he heard him turn on the water in the bathroom, he began to tug on his bindings — pulling harder and harder, until the old panty hose began to stretch.

The man had quit tying his ankles days

ago, but back then he'd been afraid to try anything. Now, as the days continued to pass, he'd begun to get angry. His clothes smelled bad, and his head itched. Even though the sores around his wrists were nearly healed, he wanted a bath, and he was tired of bologna and cheese sandwiches. And most of all, he didn't like the drinks the monster kept giving him. They made him dizzy and left a bitter taste in his mouth.

With a glance toward the open doorway to make sure the bathroom door was still closed, he began digging his heels into the mattress and pushing himself toward the headboard. Even though his wrists were still tied, he managed to push himself to a sitting position.

Frantic that he would get caught before he could get away, he began pulling on the nylon around his wrists even more, using the added leverage of his body weight and his teeth to stretch them.

All of a sudden one hand slipped free! The feeling of freedom was so heady that he almost yelled in triumph. Desperate to get his other hand free before the monster came out of the shower, he continued to pull and tug. When the second hand slipped out of the bindings, he vaulted from the bed and started running.

■ ■ ■ ■

Newt was still in the bathroom when he heard a loud thud. Frowning, he paused to listen. All of a sudden he was hearing footsteps moving fast past his door.

"Holy shit!" he yelled, and grabbed the doorknob.

His fingers were still slick from the ointment he'd been applying, and they slipped futilely off the knob. When he finally got the door open, Bobby Earle was all the way into the living room and heading for the door. Panic surged.

"Hey!" he yelled. "Hey, you little bastard!"

Bobby stumbled, then caught himself before he fell. He didn't know he was crying as he reached the front door, but when he tried to open it, it wouldn't give.

Locked. It must be locked.

With only seconds to spare, he finally got it to work. When the knob turned, he sobbed with relief. The door opened, and the wet heat of a Louisiana summer hit him square in the face. It was the best feeling he'd ever had. He took off without looking back.

Newt was too far away to stop him, and he knew it.

"You take one step out of this house and you're gonna be sorry!" Newt yelled, but the kid kept going.

All of a sudden he saw the softball, grabbed it and threw it as hard as he could.

In his mind, Bobby was already running out of the trailer park and down the street. Then, all of a sudden, there was a sharp pain at the back of his head and everything went black. He hit the ground with a thud, face-first.

Newt was panting and cursing as he waddled toward the door. Frantically, aware of his nakedness and grateful for the shield provided by the fallen trees, he hurried down the steps and pulled the kid back inside, then looked around to make certain they hadn't been seen. Satisfied that no one had been watching, he stepped back in and locked the door. When Newt turned around, he was shaking so hard he could barely stand.

"What the fuck? Damn you, you little bastard."

The kid's nose was bleeding, and it occurred to Newt that if the boy bled into his throat, he could choke to death, so he picked him up and carried him back to the bed.

Bobby was already coming to as Newt

dropped him on the mattress. He opened his eyes, and when he saw the monster retying his hands to the headboard, then his ankles, as well, he started to cry.

"It's your own damn fault," Newt said. "You shouldn't have tried to run away from me."

"You hurt my head. You made me bleed. I want my daddy!" Bobby cried, and then started to scream. "Help! Help! Help!"

"Son of a bitch!" Newt said, and grabbed a sock off the floor and stuffed it into the kid's mouth.

Bobby tried to spit it out. It tasted bad, and he felt as if he was going to be sick. Tied once again like the fatted calf ready for slaughter he'd read about in the Bible, he felt his rebellion die. He'd tried his best to get away, and it hadn't been enough.

Daddy, Daddy, please come find me.

There was blood in his mouth. He choked and gagged, then closed his eyes and turned his head, defeated in spirit and in body.

"Hey! You're bleeding all over the pillow!" Newt yelled, and pulled the sock out of his mouth, then used it like a rag to stop the flow from the kid's nose.

Bobby wouldn't look. He couldn't.

Newt got the wet washcloth from the bottom of the tub, squeezed out the excess

268

water, then came back and started cleaning up the blood while he talked.

"Look, kid, Uncle Newt doesn't like to be mean. But you broke a rule, and you know what happens when kids break rules. You have to be punished. One of these days, when I get well, we'll load up the truck and head for Texas. Would you like to visit Texas? Cowboys and Indians and all?"

Bobby didn't answer and wouldn't look.

Newt cursed, then tossed the bloody washcloth aside.

"You're not bleeding so much anymore. It'll quit soon. I'm sorry this happened."

A shudder rocked Bobby's little body as tears tracked through the blood on his cheeks.

"I was just going to fix us some supper. Are you hungry, buddy? I've got some ice cream. Would you like some ice cream? Just tell Uncle Newt what you want."

Daddy. I want my daddy.

But Bobby didn't say it aloud. He didn't say anything.

Newt sighed. This was a major setback. He had never been in such a mess. Always before, he'd created an immediate bond with the little guys by giving them candy and toys, and anything else they wanted to put them at ease. Now, because of that

269

tornado and his burns, everything had gotten turned upside down. He'd never had to tie anyone up before. He'd never had to drug them. And he'd never gone this long without playing with them in the most intimate of ways.

He didn't want to think it, but it was beginning to seem as if this wasn't meant to be. If things got worse before he got well, he might be forced to overdose the kid and then get rid of him. A dead witness was almost as good as no witness at all.

He stood, then looked down at the bed. He'd never killed anyone before and wasn't sure he could, even if he had to. Distressed by the turn of events, he walked out of the bedroom, then closed the door behind him. He would fix them some supper. Everything looked better on a full belly.

Tomorrow was Saturday. Sam's son was supposed to come saw up the fallen trees that were blocking in his truck. Newt began to think about leaving Bordelaise. Even though he had no place more specific than all of Texas in mind, he was leaning toward the notion that packing up and leaving would be the safest thing. This near-escape had unnerved him. It had been close — too close. If Bobby Earle had gotten away, it would have been the end for him.

Still rattled, he grabbed a dirty pan from the sink, turned on the water and stuck it under the tap to rinse it out. Satisfied that it was clean enough to reuse, he opened a couple of cans of soup. It was too bad that he'd had to deck the kid like that. He'd had no idea Bobby would go down face-first. Now the kid's mouth would be too sore to eat solid food for a while. Soup would be easier to get down. And he could slip the sleeping pill in the soup, rather than a Pepsi. Every day it had been harder and harder to get the soda down him. It was as if he knew what was in it. But that was impossible. The kid was just seven.

A few minutes later he went back to the bedroom, carrying the bowl of soup. He didn't dare let the kid up again to feed himself, but he couldn't let him starve.

"Hey, kiddo, look what we've got here," he said, then sat down on the side of the bed, careful not to let the hot bowl get too close to his bare belly.

Bobby smelled the soup. His stomach growled. He was hungry, so hungry. But he hurt, and all because the bad man had hurt him.

"Open wide," Newt said, as he moved the spoonful of soup toward Bobby's mouth.

Bobby wanted to say no, but his survival

instincts wouldn't let him. His mouth opened almost of its own accord. It was noodle soup. One of his favorites. The last time he'd had noodle soup had been at Daddy's house, along with a grilled cheese sandwich.

The spoon clicked against his teeth as the soup went in. He choked a little, then swallowed.

"Hey," Newt said. "I think we need to sit you up a little, okay?"

He untied Bobby's ankles, then pulled the boy up until his back was against the headboard.

"Now then. That's better, right?"

Bobby shrugged. He didn't want to talk, but he wanted the food. He hoped it wouldn't take one to get the other.

Newt started to argue, then eyed the kid's swollen nose and puffy lip, and decided he'd had enough for one day. From the way it looked, he would probably have two black eyes in the morning, but so what? No one ever died from a bloody nose or black eyes.

"Here's another bite. Open wide for Uncle Newt."

Bobby shuddered, but the soup was still too enticing, and he did as he was told.

The meal continued until the bowl was almost empty. But something was wrong.

Bobby could feel that heaviness coming over him again. The one that always made him sleepy. Suddenly he realized that the bitterness taste he'd been tasting in his Pepsi was now an aftertaste in his mouth.

"Just a few more bites," Newt said, "and then I've got a cookie waiting for you for dessert."

Bobby wanted the cookie, but he was angry. The monster was tricking him again.

"Open up," Newt said, and tapped the spoon against the edge of Bobby's lips.

Bobby opened his mouth, but as soon as the soup hit his mouth, he spat.

Noodles and salty broth hit Newt's belly. The soup wasn't that hot, but it was unexpected, and when he flinched, he dumped what was left in the bowl in his lap.

"Son of a bitch!" he yelled, as the salty broth soaked into his open wounds. He jumped up from the bed. "What the hell did you do that for?" he yelled.

"You're making me sleepy!" Bobby cried. "You're a bad man! *A bad man!* You put bad stuff in my Pepsi, and you put bad stuff in my soup!"

Newt was stunned. The kid was smarter than he'd thought.

"No! I never," Newt said, and looked

down at the noodles stuck in the hair on his belly.

"You did. You lie! You hurt me, and you tell lies, and you give me bad stuff in my food! I hate you! *I hate you!*" Bobby screamed. "I want my daddy!"

Newt was stunned. Where had all this come from? He'd never met any kids this defiant.

"You better shut up or you'll be sorry," he yelled back.

"Daddy!" Bobby screamed. "I want my daddy!"

"Shit," Newt muttered, and headed for the dresser, grabbed the roll of duct tape and tore off a strip, then headed back on the run.

All he needed was for someone to be walking by the trailer in the middle of this. He slapped the tape across Bobby's mouth, then yanked the boy's legs out from under him and retied his ankles, even though the kid fought him every step of the way.

By the time he was finished, his belly was bleeding and he was cursing at the top of his voice. When he finally stepped back, he was so pissed he was shaking.

"You little bastard! You fucking little bastard!" he screamed. "I'll make you sorry.

274

You'll see! When I get well, I'll make you sorry!"

Then he staggered out of the bedroom and back into the bathroom, where he spent the next half hour under the shower, picking bits of noodles out of the hair on his belly and washing the salt out of his sores. When he came out, Bobby Earle was asleep.

Newt wiped the soup off the bed as best he could, and then cleaned up what was left on the floor.

He was tired and aching, and wanted to sleep, too. But he was so mad at the kid, he didn't trust himself to lie down beside him without silencing him for good.

Pissed that he only had the one bed, he grabbed a pillow and a sheet, and headed for the living room. He'd slept on the sofa before. It wouldn't kill him to do it again.

He popped a couple of pain pills as well as his antibiotics, then swiped some more ointment on his sores. Tomorrow, after the trees were cleared away, he was done with this place. He might take the kid with him, and he might not. The way he felt right now, he would be happy to choke the ever-living life right out of him and never look back.

TWELVE

It was getting dark. J.R. and Katie had been driving all over the north side of Bordelaise, taking photos of license tag numbers on all the blue trucks they saw. They had yet to cover a third of the city and already had more than twenty-five tag numbers.

But the more time that passed, the quieter Katie became. Just after she'd taken the last shot, she'd recognized the driver, then sighed and dropped the camera into her lap. Frustrated, she'd leaned back against the headrest and shut her eyes. She'd just realized it was the third time she'd taken a picture of the same man in the same blue truck, but in three different locations.

"What's wrong?" J.R. asked now.

"I can't remember the numbers anymore, but I'm beginning to recognize the drivers, and that's the third time I've taken a picture of this one."

J.R. sighed. "I'm sorry. Do you want to quit?"

"I can't. It would be like quitting on Bobby."

"No. It's not the same, and you know it. You're tired. It's getting dark, and I say we give Penny a call, let her know we're on the way home and see if we can bring her some supper along with our own."

Katie couldn't bring herself to care one way or the other.

J.R. felt her disconnect and gave her hand a squeeze. "I'm feeling lonesome, honey. Scoot over here by me," he said gently.

Katie undid her seat belt and scooted across the seat.

"That's better," he said. "Just like old times."

Katie's face crumpled. "Oh, J.R. I want that back. I want all of it back. What if we don't find Bobby? I don't think I can bear it."

The words were like a vise around J.R.'s heart. She'd said the same thing when her parents had gone missing, and he honestly thought if it hadn't been for the presence of their son, she might never have survived. This was the moment he'd been dreading ever since he'd learned of their son's fate. She was warning him now that she wasn't going to be strong enough to survive another emotional trauma. He was scared. He needed to shift her focus. He wasn't sure what he was going to say, but he knew where he wanted to be when he said it. When he turned down the street where their house used to be, Katie flinched.

"No, J.R. Not here. I don't want to see this," she said, and looked away.

J.R. pulled to the curb where their house had once stood, then took her in his arms.

"I don't like to look at this either, baby," he said softly. "But there's something you need to understand. Life isn't about what we want, Katie. It's about what we make of what we're given. We can get through this, but only if we lean on each other. If one of us checks out, that will take the other one down, too. I'm willing to fight for you. Will you fight for me?"

The poignancy in his voice tore through Katie's conscience as she threw her arms around his neck.

"Oh, J.R.! Oh, sweetheart . . . I'm sorry. I'm so sorry. I didn't mean to make this all about me. I didn't mean to come across as the only one who's suffering. It's the guilt . . . the guilt. It's eating me alive. I *will* fight for you. Always."

She pulled back just enough that she

could see his face. The tears on his cheeks were like stakes in her heart. Why was it that all she seemed to do was hurt the ones she loved? With a sigh, she put her hands on his cheeks and leaned forward.

Breath caught in the back of J.R.'s throat as her lips centered on his. Soft, trembling, yet firmly sealing the promise she'd just made.

He groaned beneath his breath as her mouth shifted to his cheek, then his chin, then the hollow spot at the bottom of his throat.

"Katie . . . Katie . . . I love you, girl. We *will* get through this. I promise," he whispered.

Katie hid her face against his chest, taking solace from this brief moment of found peace at the end of a sad and brutal day.

Suddenly a car horn honked from behind.

They turned to watch as a car pulled up to the curb behind them, then dimmed its lights.

"Who's that?" J.R. asked.

"I can't tell for sure," Katie said, "but the car looks like the one the Maxwells drive," Katie said.

"You mean Frances and Tommy?"

Katie nodded.

J.R. opened the door and got out. Katie

scooted out past the steering wheel and joined him just as he and Tommy Maxwell met beside their cars.

Tommy held out a hand. J.R. ignored it and engulfed the man in a huge, back-thumping embrace. It lasted all of a couple of seconds, but it was telling of how deeply J.R. appreciated the other family's part in helping to find their son.

Tommy was a little embarrassed but quickly shook it off as he nodded to Katie. "We heard you finally made it back," he said.

J.R. nodded, as he pulled Katie under the shelter of his arm.

"You won't believe the screwup that led to all this," he said. "I didn't know a thing about any of this until yesterday afternoon. You can imagine the panic I was in driving home."

Tommy's eyes widened. "Man! What's the deal? Were you out of the country?"

J.R. shook his head. "No, but I might as well have been. I was on an offshore rig when Hurricane Bonnie took a turn toward Houston. We had already initiated evacuation procedures and removed half the men. I was with the second half, waiting for the other chopper's arrival when it went down in the gulf. We rode out the hurricane on board. Then, between downed power lines and an office temp who should have been dipping ice cream instead of answering phones, every message that should have been sent on to me was either mislaid or forgotten."

"How awful," Frances said, walking up beside her husband, and then looked at Katie. "Uh, Katie . . . I hope you don't think we were interfering, but a bunch of us from church got together Monday afternoon and went through the debris here at your place. We were looking for keepsakes that had made it through the storm. You were so . . . so . . . sick, and we didn't want to take a chance on things getting rained on again before you were well enough to do it your-self."

Katie's eyes welled up again. Just when she thought she didn't have a tear left in her body, something would happen to prove her wrong.

"Frances! That is such a loving, thought-ful thing to do," she said. "Please tell everyone how much we appreciate it."

"Absolutely," J.R. added.

"Mama! Can I get out?"

It was the child's voice that shifted the conversation and sent everyone's thoughts toward a little boy lost.

The knot in Katie's stomach tightened. "I didn't know Holly was with you," she said. "Will you let her get out? I want to thank her."

"So do I," J.R. said.

Tommy grinned, then turned. "Yes, Holly. You can get out. Come on over here by Daddy, okay?"

The little girl emerged from the car, then ran toward her daddy. When Katie knelt down to her level, she ducked her head and grabbed his hand.

"Hi, Holly," Katie said.

Holly smiled bashfully. "Hi, Mrs. Earle."

"I want to thank you for telling everyone about Bobby. You did a very good thing."

Holly's smile died. "I ran off. The siren blew loud, and I got scared."

J.R. squatted down beside Katie. "Hi, Holly. I'm Bobby's daddy. Do you remember me?"

"I think so," she said.

J.R. knew she didn't. Yet another chink in what had been the apparent order of their life. He'd grown up here. Knew practically everyone in town. But for the seven years this child had been on earth, he'd spent most of his time somewhere else.

"It's okay," he said. "And don't worry about being scared. You were supposed to be scared. You did everything exactly right. What happened to Bobby is not your fault. In fact, Katie and I think you're a very brave little girl for stopping to look back and then paying attention to what you saw."

Holly's eyes grew wide. "Really?"

"Absolutely," J.R. said, then patted Holly's head as he stood. "Tommy, Katie and I can't thank you enough for getting the information to the police like you did."

"Don't thank me. Thank Frances. She's the one who caught on to what was happening."

Unwilling to be the center of attention, Frances quickly changed the subject.

"Katie, when we heard you were out of the hospital and that J.R. was back, we thought we'd bring your things. Tommy helped me load up what we salvaged, and we were on our way to Penny's when we saw you here. There isn't a lot, and you may still want to go through the debris yourself. All we could do was look for things that were still in one piece, and also try and find as many pictures as possible. That's what I would hate losing. The pictures."

"Again, I am so very grateful," Katie said. "You can put everything in the back of our truck."

J.R. opened the tailgate as Frances and

Tommy came over carrying a box apiece.

"We have a couple more," Tommy said.

"I'll help," J.R. said, and walked back to their car.

Katie had climbed up into the truck bed and was poking through the boxes as Frances got back in the car with Holly. Although it was getting too dark to see details, she was still elated at what they'd found. In the midst of her joy, she spied the back of a picture frame. Even before she took it out, she knew what it was. She rocked back on her heels, then sat down in the truck bed and clutched it close to her chest, running her fingers along the edges of the ornate metal frame, grateful beyond words that this, of all things, had once again been spared.

She would never forget finding this picture once before, in her parents' house, after the floodwaters had receded and her parents' bodies had been found.

It had been months before Katie had been able to go to the house. Even though they'd worn face masks, the jumble of rotting furniture and the black mold on the walls and floors had been a horrific reminder of what her mother and father had endured before they'd finally succumbed in the attic.

Katie had insisted on seeing the entire house. She'd wanted to get a sense of what they'd endured. She'd needed to be where they'd last drawn breath. Despite J.R.'s urging against it, they'd gone up the narrow staircase into the attic.

He was the first to notice that something had been wrapped in a black plastic bag and tied to the highest rafters: the photograph she now held in her hand. The discovery had gone a long way toward helping Katie heal. It was like finding the last gift her parents would ever give her, and she'd cherished it beyond words. Now, to have it back again was like a miracle.

When J.R. came back with the last box, he could just make out Katie sitting against the cab of the truck.

Frances and Tommy had Holly in the car and were driving away as he slid the last box in beside the others. Moonlight glinted off of something metal in her lap, as well as what appeared to be tears rolling down her cheeks.

He frowned. The reality of their situation had obviously returned. He got up into the back of the truck, then sat down beside her.

"Katie . . . honey . . . what do you have?" he asked.

She couldn't speak, and when he tried to

take the frame out of her arms, she wouldn't let go.

J.R. sighed, then leaned back and closed his eyes. He was at his wits' end as to how to help her. All he could think to do was pray.

Help me, Lord.

In the grand scheme of things, it was a small request, but only God knew how desperate J.R.'s life had become.

Suddenly he felt Katie's hand on his arm. When he opened his eyes, she was holding the picture toward him.

Thank you, Jesus.

It was completely dark now. He couldn't tell what was in the frame, but it was enough that she was opening herself up enough to share the pain.

"What is it, honey?" he asked softly.

"It's Mama and Daddy's wedding photo. The only thing they owned that Hurricane Katrina didn't destroy."

He sighed, then put his arm around her. "And now it's gone through a second storm and still come out whole. That's a pretty powerful sign, if you ask me," he said.

He felt her body relaxing against him and tried not to weep.

"Why?" she asked.

"I think this is a sign . . . sort of a mes-

286

sage from your mama and daddy telling you that you can get through your sadness a second time and still be okay. That's what I think."

Katie shuddered, but she didn't pull back.

"I hope you're right," she whispered.

J.R. glanced up, wondering how the sky could be so beautiful while their world was coming apart.

"Lord, Katie . . . so do I."

Saturday morning

It was the sunlight coming through the broken blinds that woke Bobby up. As soon as he tried to move, he remembered why he couldn't. He needed to go to the bathroom. As much as he hated it, that meant he needed for the man to come back. And it hurt to move. Bobby's nose ached, his lip felt swollen and everything in the room kept going around and around.

He began kicking and yanking at the ties on his wrists and ankles, and making all the noise he could. In less than a minute, he'd gotten results.

Newt came stomping through the door with a frown on his face. Since he was expecting the men to remove the debris today, he'd dressed for the occasion in a pair of loose gym shorts and an old T-shirt, soft from hundreds of washes.

"So, you're awake," he said. "I'm guessing you need to take a piss, right?"

Bobby nodded vigorously.

Newt smiled slyly as he yanked the masking tape off of Bobby's face, uncaring if it caused him pain.

"One of these days you're gonna have to give Uncle Newt something special to make up for all the problems you've caused."

Wisely, Bobby didn't answer. He was too afraid of getting hurt again to argue. When he was finally untied, Newt grabbed him by the arm and practically dragged him to the bathroom door.

"Make it snappy," Newt said. "I've got breakfast ready."

Bobby flew into the bathroom and relieved himself, but when he turned to the sink to wash up, he caught a glimpse of himself in the mirror and gasped.

His mouth was all puffy. His eyes were turning black, and his nose was twice its size. He touched it with the tip of his finger and then winced from the pain.

"Hurry up in there!" Newt yelled. "We got things to do today."

Bobby quickly washed, although there was no soap at the sink, and dried his hands on his pants. When he came out, he ducked his head and meekly followed Newt into the kitchen, grateful for the simple fact that the bad man was no longer naked.

Newt watched the kid slide into his chair and then stare down into the bowl of dry cereal, as if checking whether he could see anything there that didn't belong.

Newt snorted beneath his breath. The little brat was getting too smart for his own good.

"Want me to slice a banana on that cereal for you?" he asked, hiding his simmering anger at the whole situation.

Bobby shrugged. A banana sounded good, but he wasn't willing to admit it.

"Fine. Then I'll make the decision for you," Newt said, and sliced half a banana into Bobby's bowl, then sliced the other half of it into his own.

He picked up the carton of milk and started to pour when Bobby suddenly flattened his hands over the top of the bowl.

"No milk," Bobby said, then held his breath, afraid the monster would be mad.

"There's nothing in it," Newt said.

"I don't believe you," Bobby said, then ducked, expecting to be hit.

Newt was on to him now. "Look. I'm putting it on mine," he said. He poured the milk into his own bowl, then picked up his spoon and started shoveling the cereal into his mouth. "I think it needs a little sugar. You want some on yours?"

Bobby's certainty wavered. Maybe the milk was okay. He shoved his bowl across the table.

"Just a little milk," he said softly.

"No problem," Newt said. "You say when."

He poured slowly, watching Bobby Earle's face with a measure of lust and delight. Such pretty dark eyes. It was a damn shame they were turning black, but that would soon go away. Such a pretty little mouth, even if it was puffy. He was sorry about the kid's nose and wondered if it was broken. Not that it mattered. No way was he taking the kid to a doctor.

"When!" Bobby cried.

Immediately, Newt stopped pouring. "Need some sugar?"

Bobby nodded.

Newt shoved the sugar bowl toward him and then continued to eat, purposefully ignoring what Bobby was doing in the hopes of allaying his fears.

The meal passed in relative calm. When they were through with their cereal, Newt had a trick up his sleeve. He needed the kid out of the way while the cleanup was in progress. Which meant he had to find a new way to get the needed sleeping pills down him without a fight.

He got up from the table and took a small bowl of scrambled eggs out of the microwave, then got a couple of paper plates and divided them up. Half on his plate. Half on Bobby Earle's. He knew if the kid watched him dividing the eggs, he would assume they were also safe to eat. Thing was, Newt had stirred a crushed sleeping pill into half the eggs a while ago, before putting them back on the plate with the rest. All he had to do was be careful which half he ate.

He slid the eggs toward Bobby, handed him a fork, then proceeded to salt and pepper his own eggs before pushing the condiments toward the kid. He already knew Bobby would not only want the salt, but the pepper, as well. And he also knew that the pepper would hide whatever bitter aftertaste the pills might have left.

Bobby downed the eggs in a few bites, then sat back, watching to see what came next. To his surprise, Newt pulled a coloring book and a pack of crayons out of a drawer, and slid them across the table.

"When I was a kid, I liked to color," Newt said, as he moved about the kitchen, dumping paper plates and bowls in the trash, and rinsing off their forks and spoons. "Do you like to color?" he asked.

Bobby didn't answer, although he was leafing through the pages.

When Newt saw him pause, then reach for the box of crayons, he turned his back and smiled.

This is how it begins.

When he looked back a few minutes later, the kid had his head down, intently coloring the picture of a dinosaur.

"Do you know what kind of critter that is?" Newt asked.

Bobby paused, then shook his head.

"It's called a brontosaurus," Newt said. "Some people call them long-necks. Pretty cool, huh?"

Bobby shrugged, but he kept on coloring.

Newt didn't push it. He was feeling too good about what was happening to cause another scene.

As he cleaned up the kitchen, he kept looking out the window, keeping an eye on the front of his place. He needed to make sure the kid was well out of sight before they started sawing up the downed trees.

"I need to go to the bathroom," Bobby said.

Newt turned around. "Well, go on," he said. "Don't forget to flush."

Bobby got up from the chair, ruefully eyeing the front door as he passed. There would be no more attempts at freedom. He'd learned the hard way that there was no escape from the monster, and he'd been here so long, he was beginning to feel as if the whole world had deserted him.

THIRTEEN

Hershel walked into headquarters carrying a to-go cup of coffee and a sack of dough-nuts from the Bordelaise bakery. His wife was suffering a migraine attack, so he'd stopped there for breakfast rather than make noise in the kitchen back home. He set the sack beside the coffeepot, then topped off his coffee before pulling a chocolate glazed out of the sack.

"Brought breakfast," he said, as he took a bite and started to chew.

Vera tossed back a lock of her long blond wig and managed to look interested as she continued her phone conversation.

His deputies, Tullius and Carter, were at their desks with their heads down, going through paperwork, and didn't look up.

"What's all that?" he asked.

Tullius paused, then leaned back in his chair. "The lists you asked for, Chief. I have the DMV list of the owners of late-model blue pickups. Carter has the list of registered sex offenders."

"Keep me posted if you get any matches," Hershel said, and headed to his office. He had a proposition he needed to run by the Earles before he put it in motion.

The hunt for Bobby Earle was about to move into overdrive.

Penny was taking biscuits out of the oven when her telephone rang.

"J.R., honey, would you get that?" she asked.

"Yes, ma'am," he said.

Grateful that the emotional distance between him and Katie was over, he couldn't help but touch her shoulder reassuringly as he got up from the breakfast table and grabbed the phone.

"Bates residence," he answered.

"Oh, good, it's you," Hershel Porter said. "Just who I needed to talk to."

The chief's voice made J.R.'s heart skip nervously. "Do you have any news?"

Katie jumped up from the table and hurried to where J.R. was standing, anxious to hear what was being said. He pulled her close as the chief continued to talk.

"Not news in the sense you're referring to," Hershel said. "Just wanted you to know we're hard at work cross-checking current owners of late-model blue pickup trucks with registered sex offenders."

"Is there anything we can do to help?" J.R. asked.

"Actually, that's why I called. Remember earlier when I talked about putting out an Amber Alert and said I'd decided against it because everyone still thought Bobby had died in the tornado, and we didn't want to give the guy a reason to run?"

"Yes?"

"Well, the situation has changed," Hershel said. "That's all they wanted to talk about at the bakery this morning, and I got to thinking, since it's already common knowledge, it's bound to change the dynamics of whoever has him."

"What do you need us to do?" J.R. asked.

"I need a photo of Bobby. I know that's a hell of a thing to ask for considering everything you guys owned just blew away, but do you think you could find —"

"We have pictures," J.R. said. "When do you want them?"

"Anytime this morning. I'm going to work on the statement now. We don't have a lot to go on, but the eyewitness account of a blue truck and having your son's picture is better than nothing."

"We'll bring the photo down right after breakfast," J.R. said.

"Good. See you then," Hershel said, and hung up.

"What did he say?" Katie asked, as J.R. disconnected.

"They need a picture of Bobby. They're going to issue an Amber Alert."

Katie gasped. "But I thought —"

"Hershel said it's all over town now that Bobby wasn't a victim of the tornado, and since I showed up, no one can claim parental abduction. He's afraid that if the kidnapper is a local and still has him, the news could cause him to make a run for it, anyway, so we're better off if people are looking for him."

Penny had been listening without interruption, but when she saw Katie starting to panic, she quickly spoke up.

"Biscuits are ready. Sit. Sit! It won't take you long to eat breakfast, and whatever it is you need to do will sit better with a little food in your stomachs."

Katie was ready to bolt. "But the chief needs a picture of —"

"Penny's right," J.R. said. "And those biscuits do smell good. He's working on a statement. We'll eat, drop off the picture and go from there."

Katie sat, but her stomach was rolling all over again. Even as she was buttering a biscuit and adding some pepper to her eggs, she couldn't help but think of Bobby. She knew he was afraid. That was a given. But was her baby in pain? Was he hungry? How could she eat this wonderful food without knowing if he was being fed?

"Katie."

She blinked, then looked up. J.R. was watching her. She felt his concern and, at the same time, his strength. She reached across the table and took his hand.

"I'm fine."

"I know you are, baby," he said softly, then smiled.

That his smile made her think of Bobby only added to her pain. He hadn't said it, but she got the message, anyway. *I need to be strong for Bobby.*

"These biscuits look wonderful, Penny. Would you pass the jam?" she asked.

Penny beamed. "Absolutely. It's peach. I made it myself."

"That makes it even better," J.R. said, and took some, too.

But all the time he was eating, he kept thinking of his son. Remembering the last time they'd shared a meal, the sound of his laughter, the way his eyes crinkled when he smiled. His gut hurt all the way to his backbone, but he couldn't let it show. Katie was barely hanging on. He had to be strong for the both of them — and for their little boy.

Hershel had the info ready to release to the media and was waiting for the Earles to bring their photo when Vera buzzed his office and sent everything into a tailspin.

"Call for you on line one," Vera said.

"Thanks," Hershel said, and then switched extensions. "Chief Porter."

"Chief, Agent Edwards here. We have info regarding your missing prisoners."

Hershel stood abruptly. "I'm listening."

"We discovered a car in a creek several miles outside Bordelaise. It was reported missing by a Tom Dailey right after the tornado. There's blood on the seats, back and front. We've lifted prints and faxed them to Quantico. Just got verification that the driver was our missing agent, Aroyo."

Hershel was speechless.

"Prints and blood aside, you're sure it wasn't dumped in the creek by the tornado?"

"Not unless tornados are in the habit of going backward and forward at the same time."

299

"What?"

"According to our information, the storm that spawned your tornado was still moving inland after it hit Bordelaise. And the car went missing after the tornado hit your town. So it couldn't have been dumped where it is by the storm, because this is in the opposite direction. It got here because someone was driving it, and Nick Aroyo's prints are on the dash, the steering wheel and the door panel. Also, we found four bloody jail-issue jumpsuits among the storm-damaged clothing from the local department store that was waiting to be picked up by a salvage company. We're guessing they just crawled in through the broken windows, took fresh clothing off the racks, then dumped their prison clothes in with the damaged goods on the way out of town."

"Shit," Hershel muttered.

"It's not bad news from where we're standing," Agent Edwards said. "This means our man is probably still alive."

"I am glad to know it, but at the same time, this also means I have three very bad guys on the loose in my parish," Hershel snapped, then immediately shifted mental gears. "Sorry. Didn't mean to go off on you. Thank you for the information. Give me your location. I'll send my deputies out with a tow truck to bring in the car. You understand we'll have to collect our own evidence."

"No problem, Chief. Just wanted to keep you up-to-date. You'll find the car just off the bridge over Bonaventure Creek. And just so you know, we intend to continue our search until we locate our agent. If your missing prisoners are still with him, we would be happy to assist you in returning them to your custody."

Hershel sighed. "When we arrested them for possession of meth, there were already arrest warrants out on them from New Orleans. They were here on a holding basis only, awaiting transportation," he said. "If you find them, don't bring them back to me."

"Understood," Agent Edwards said.

Hershel disconnected, then headed up front. Both deputies were still going through the lists.

"Tullius. Call Marvin's Towing and tell him to follow you boys out to Bonaventure Creek. Tom Dailey's car just turned up."

Lee frowned. "But, Chief . . . we're never gonna get through these lists if we keep getting pulled off. I want to find Bobby Earle in the worst way. Why can't Vera just make the call?"

Hershel sighed. "Because our missing prisoners have just been resurrected. According to the DEA search team, they found four bloody jail-issue jumpsuits in the department store refuse, and when they found Dailey's car, their inside man's prints were all over it, along with blood evidence on both front and backseats, which means both seats had been occupied — most likely by those damned missing prisoners — and because we have to make sure the chain of evidence isn't broken after Marvin pulls the car out of the creek and hauls it in."

Lee Tullius's shoulders slumped. "Yes, sir. I understand."

He gave the printouts a regretful glance, then pushed them aside and reached for the phone.

"Carter, make sure you get blood samples, prints, all that stuff. I know the DEA already gathered their own evidence, but those were our prisoners. They escaped on our watch. We may be small-time, but we can still gather our own evidence."

"Yes, sir," Carter said, and pushed his own printouts aside.

A few minutes later, as the deputies were going out the back door, the Earles were coming in the front.

Hershel glanced at the abandoned print-outs, sighed in frustration, then turned to greet them, shaking J.R.'s hand and nodding to Katie.

"Morning, folks. Did you bring me that picture?"

"Actually, we have two that might work," J.R. said. "One is a full-length shot. The other is his latest school picture."

"Perfect," Hershel said. "I wasn't sure you'd have anything, considering what happened to your house."

"While I was in the hospital, the women from our church went through the debris at the house to salvage pictures and keepsakes," Katie said.

"That's good news," Hershel said. "I'll take good care of these and get them back to you as soon as possible."

"When are you releasing the Amber Alert?" J.R. asked.

"This is all I was waiting for. It will go out immediately."

Katie shuddered. "God . . . it just has to work."

"Yes, ma'am," Hershel said.

"What about those lists? Have you come up with any suspects?" J.R. asked.

Hershel glanced over at the deputies' desks and frowned. "Not yet. It's slow going, you understand. We're not set up like the big cities to cross-check by computer."

Before J.R. could respond, Tullius's voice came over the radio.

"We're on our way, Chief. Tow truck is following."

J.R. spun toward the windows as a patrol car sped past.

"Was that Lee and Carter?" he asked.

Hershel nodded. "Had a bit of an emergency."

"If they're gone, who's working the lists?"

"No one right now, but as soon as —"

J.R. grabbed Hershel by the arm. "Chief! Please! I know this is out of line, but this is our son's life. We've wasted so much time already. . . . Show us what to do. We can read. If it's just a matter of cross-checking names . . ."

Hershel's first reaction was immediate and stronger than it had been the first time the subject came up. "Police procedure dictates . . ."

Then he stopped. It was the look on Katie Earle's face that did him in. "What the hell," he muttered, then pointed at the desks. "To make things simple, this is the list from the DMV. It's got every late-model blue pickup in the parish. Check every owner's name against the sexual offenders list. You can see where Tullius left off. But there's always the possibility that someone was driving a stolen or borrowed a truck when he made the snatch, so even if there's no match, we can't rule out any owner with a local address, so put them on that list over there. We want to eliminate them, make sure they still have their vehicles."

J.R. sat in one chair, Katie in the other. Without saying a word, they put their heads down and got to work as Hershel headed back to his office. He had an Amber Alert to get out.

Bobby had gone to sleep at the kitchen table with a red crayon in one hand and a yellow one in the other, the picture he'd been coloring only half-finished.

It was what Newt had been waiting for. He took the crayons out of the boy's hands and picked him up. He lusted longingly after the small, fragile body as he carried him back to the bedroom, thinking of what it would be like when they could play.

He was still fantasizing as he tied Bobby up, but when he started to put duct tape over his mouth, he took a second look at the kid and changed his mind. His nose was so swollen, there was a danger his airway was already partially blocked. Shutting off the possibility of being able to breathe through his mouth could be a death sentence. Reluctantly, Newt put down the duct tape, smoothed the dark, ruffled hair on Bobby's head, then shut the door as he left.

After a quick glance out the front windows, he turned on the television, then grabbed a beer. It had been days since he'd felt like doing anything but eating and sleeping, and it felt good to be up and moving around. Even though it wasn't quite ten o'clock, he popped the top on the beer and began channel-surfing.

A few minutes later someone knocked on the door. He hit Mute, then got up to answer. It was Sam.

"Hey, Newt! Great to see you dressed and moving around a little better. I take it you're healing up okay?"

"Yeah, yeah, just fine," Newt said. "That your boy?"

Sam smiled and nodded at the heavyset man lifting a large chain saw from the bed of a green Dodge 4×4.

"Yep. That's my Freddy. He'll get this debris cleared up off your truck in no time," Sam said.

Newt nodded. "I appreciate it," he said. "I've got someplace to be tomorrow."

Sam glanced at the raw and peeling skin

on the palms of Newt's hands.

"Reckon your hands will be well enough for you to drive?"

"I'll manage," Newt said, then glanced over his shoulder toward the hall. "Look, I got something on the stove. I gotta go."

"Yeah, sure," Sam said. "Anyway, sorry for the delay."

"No harm," Newt said. "As long as those trees're gone today."

"Count on it," Sam said, then pulled a pair of gloves out of his pocket and went down the steps to help his son as Newt closed and locked his door.

"About time," Newt muttered, as he returned to his chair. He picked up his beer and took a sip, then kicked back in his recliner and upped the volume on the TV.

Within minutes the loud buzz of a chain saw split the air, indicating the work had begun. Newt smiled to himself and continued to skip through channels before finally settling on a John Wayne movie.

He was just downing the last of his beer when the show he was watching was suddenly interrupted. The loud, intermittent beeps were similar to those that preceded a severe weather warning, but he knew for a fact that there wasn't a cloud in the sky.

"What the hell?"

"We interrupt this programming for an important announcement. An Amber Alert has just been issued for a —"

Then they flashed a picture on the screen, and he didn't hear another word.

The kid! They were looking for the kid! The last Newt had known, they thought he'd died in the tornado. What the hell had changed their minds?

Then he focused back on the announcement and got an answer for which he wasn't prepared.

"— last seen being picked up by a white male wearing a T-shirt, blue jeans and a dark ball cap, and driving a blue, late-model pickup. If you see anyone answering this description accompanied by the child in this photo, call —"

Newt's heart was pounding as he catapulted himself out of the recliner. He ran to the front windows, then to the back, peering through blinds, pushing aside curtains, looking to see if the place was surrounded. All he could see was Sam Walker and his son, Freddy, sawing up the trees.

For a few frantic moments he couldn't think. His first instinct was to get in the truck and run. Leave the kid behind and get out while he could. But the longer he paced, the calmer he became.

The description of the abductor was vague. It could fit any number of men. And they didn't have a tag number or model for the truck. It could be anything, Ford, Dodge, Chevy . . . even a foreign model. There were thousands and thousands of late-model blue trucks. He was panicking for nothing.

Still, he couldn't stop pacing. He'd been living in Louisiana for all these years without registering as a sex offender. He'd managed to fly under the legal radar without calling attention to himself because he'd stayed out of trouble. If only he hadn't taken the kid. If only . . .

"Shit. It's too late for that," he muttered. "What's done is done. Now, what am I gonna do about it?"

He ran to the bedroom, just to reassure himself that the kid was still out, which he was. But as he stood and watched Bobby Earle sleeping, he realized he didn't want to give him up. And that was when he made the decision.

He was going to make a run for it.

With the kid.

As soon as his truck was free, he was leaving Bordelaise for good. He ran to the kitchen, grabbed the box of garbage bags he used for trash days, then headed for the bedroom. He emptied the drawers of his dresser onto the floor, stuffed in as many clothes as the bag would hold, then tied it off. He grabbed another bag, then another, filling them the same way until his closet was empty. And so he went, room by room, filling garbage bags with his belongings until he got to the kitchen.

His hands were shaking, and despite the steady hum of his window air conditioners, he was sweating profusely. That made his clothes stick to his body, which aggravated his healing burns, which meant he needed to shower, put new meds on the sores and get into some dry clothes.

"Son of a bitch," he muttered, and stripped in the kitchen, leaving his clothes on the floor where he'd been standing.

But his intent was immediately thwarted when he realized he'd already packed his clean clothes and towels, which meant he had to dig back through the trash bags until he found what he needed. By the time he finally got into the shower, he was shaking. He kept thinking he was hearing knocking on the door and people shouting. By the time he was finished, he was convinced the cops had found him.

It wasn't until he turned off the water and stepped out of the tub that he realized what he'd been hearing was the movie he'd been watching. It wasn't cops at the door. It was John Wayne in his living room.

"Lord, Lord," Newt muttered, as he carefully patted himself dry.

His hands were shaking as he spread new ointment on his sores and then pulled a fresh T-shirt over his head, followed by another pair of loose shorts. As soon as he was dressed, he ran to the windows again.

Sam and Freddy Walker were gone. The trees that had been blocking him from leaving had been cut away, sawed into firewood and stacked at the side of the trailer.

He grabbed the car keys from the cabinet and made a mad dash outside to check on his truck. One fender had a dent. There was another on the passenger side door, along with a multitude of scratches and the shattered back windshield. All he cared about was if it would start. He slid behind the wheel and, with shaking hands, jammed the key in the ignition.

"Please, please, please," he whispered, then turned the key.

The truck started without a hitch.

"Yes!" he shouted, and slapped the seat with the flat of his hand, then winced from the pain. "Shit," he moaned. "Reminder to self. Don't do that again."

He killed the engine, then headed back inside. Within moments he was loading the back of the truck. The microwave went in first. He wrapped the television in a blanket and shoved it against the cab, then did the same with his computer system. He wanted his table and chairs, and his recliner, but knew he would never be able to move them on his own.

All he had left were the garbage bags — and the kid.

He began loading the bags into the back of the truck as fast as he could carry them, until the truck was overflowing with black plastic bags filled to bursting. He opened the passenger side door, then stopped on his way back into the trailer and gave the trailer park a long, studied look. The only vehicles in the park belonged to Sam and a couple of guys who worked nights, which meant they were asleep. Sam's son was gone. Hopefully Sam had gone with him.

Satisfied that he was still unobserved, Newt ran back into the trailer and on to the bedroom. He untied the kid's wrists and ankles, then rolled him up in the bedspread and carried him over his shoulder like a rug. He went down the steps in record time and dumped the kid into the truck seat, then slammed the door shut.

He started to get in, then noticed he'd left the front door wide open. No need to advertise his absence, he thought, running back to close and lock it.

Seconds later he was behind the wheel. He put the truck in gear, backed away from the trailer, then slowly drove away. The truck had less than a quarter of a tank of gas. He could get gas on the west side of town on his way toward the interstate.

He drove through the backstreets, taking care not to call attention to himself. By the time he got to the city limits, he felt as if a weight had lifted off his shoulders.

"Dallas, Texas, here we come," he crowed, and stomped on the gas.

FOURTEEN

More than two hours had passed since J.R. and Katie had begun cross-checking the lists. At first it had been awkward, getting into a routine of checking one against the other, keeping track of local owners of blue trucks, along with a separate list of registered sex offenders in the parish, even though they didn't own or drive blue trucks.

The first time J.R. recognized a name on the sex offender list, he'd been shocked. It had taken further digging to realize how a teenage mistake could haunt a grown man. He remembered the incident that put the man on the list; it had happened during their senior year of high school. A friend of his who'd been on the high school football team had been dating a fifteen-year-old girl from a neighboring town. They'd gone out for several months before her parents suddenly decided he wasn't good enough and demanded they quit seeing each other.

When they were caught sneaking around together, the girl's father filed a rape charge against the boy because the girl was under-age. And it had stuck. J.R. hadn't realized how such a brand could linger through a grown man's life, but there it was.

It was yet another reminder of how a single act could change a life forever, which was what the fight between him and Katie had done. And he knew, without doubt, they would have continued to grow further and further apart had this tragedy not hap-pened. He needed to put his family back together — but to do that, they had to find Bobby. He shifted his focus back to the list and kept on working.

Katie's list was even more overwhelming. The number of late-model blue trucks in town just kept growing. She was beginning to realize this might be an impossible task. In frustration she suddenly stopped, then pushed herself up from the desk and stalked off to the bathroom without comment.

J.R. paused to watch as she walked out of the room and knew she was struggling. He felt her pain. This was beginning to feel like an exercise in futility, and yet they couldn't stop.

"There's coffee and doughnuts," Vera said, pointing to a table at the back of the room.

J.R. nodded, then proceeded to pour coffee for himself and Katie, adding just the right amount of sugar and creamer to hers, while keeping his black. He took a doughnut out of the sack, tore it in half, and when Katie walked back into the room, he handed a piece to her.

"Eat," he said.

"I'm not hungry," she muttered.

"Neither am I," he said, and downed his half in two bites.

Katie almost smiled. "Good thing you're not hungry," she said, then took a bite. Then another. And another. Before she knew it, the doughnut was gone and that horrible knot in the pit of her stomach seemed a little less painful.

When she took her first sip of the coffee, it added just enough heat in her belly to settle her nerves.

"Okay. That was a good idea," she admitted, then lifted her face for the kiss she saw coming.

It didn't matter to J.R. that Vera was only a few feet away. He needed to know Katie was hanging in there. When their lips met he tasted sugar, as well as a hint of her sweetened coffee. And when he suddenly cupped the back of her head and deepened their kiss to a hard, hungry raid on her

316

senses, Katie sighed. That was what he'd been waiting to hear. Their emotional connection was still there, and for now, that was enough.

When he pulled back, Vera giggled.

"Sorry," he said.

"I'm not," Vera said, and giggled again.

Katie leaned her forehead against J.R.'s. "Thank you for reminding me to breathe," she said softly.

"No problem," he countered. "Ready to get back to work?"

"Absolutely," she said, and back to work they went, fortified by coffee and a new attitude.

When twelve o'clock noon rolled around, the bells on the Catholic Church began chiming the hour.

Just as Katie looked up, she saw J.R. pause over a name.

"What?" she asked.

"The farther I go down this list, the more I realize how out of the loop I've been in your lives. I don't know half these names, even the ones who live right here in Bordelaise."

Katie frowned. "Really? Like who?"

He shoved the list toward her. "Be my guest."

Katie scanned the list, going name by name.

"Morgan Detweiller bought the old Freneau place on Bartlett Street. He's legally blind. A victim of some war. I forget which. I wonder why he still owns a truck?" She moved to the next name. "A. Pendelton. That's Abby Pendelton. She's the lady who has that big blackberry farm."

"Oh. Yeah. I remember that place. I just didn't know her name."

Katie nodded, and then continued to run down the names on the list, satisfying herself that she knew who the people were. It wasn't until she got closer to the bottom that she came to a name that gave her pause.

"Here's one I don't think I know," she said. "Newton Collins. Hmm. The name sounds familiar, but I can't place him." She turned in her chair and called out, "Hey, Vera! Do you know a man named Newton Collins? His address is Walker's Trailer Park here in Bordelaise."

"The name is familiar," Vera said. "But I can't place why."

Hershel caught the last part of Vera's comment as he walked into the office. "What name?" he asked.

"Oh. You're back," Vera said, and handed him a stack of messages. "None of these are

318

urgent, but . . ."

Hershel took them without looking, then asked again. "What name?"

"Newton Collins," Katie said. "He lives in Walker's Trailer Park, but I can't place him."

Hershel nodded. "Oh. Yeah. He goes by Newt. He's the bus mechanic for the public schools," he said. "In fact, he got himself hurt pretty bad during cleanup the day of the storm."

"Oh," Katie said, and shrugged it off, as she moved to the next name.

"What does he look like?" J.R. asked.

Hershel frowned. "Oh . . . middle-aged white guy with a big chest and no chin. I've never seen him in anything but baggy jeans and big T-shirts. Oh . . . and a cap. Always wears a cap."

Suddenly the skin crawled on the back of J.R.'s neck. That was what Holly Maxwell's pictures of God in the blue truck had been wearing. It could be a coincidence, of course, but it still made him think.

He took the sex offender list and quickly ran a check on the name, but nothing came up. Frowning, he shoved that list aside and started to go back to his own, and then a thought occurred to him.

"Chief. How long has this Collins fellow lived in Bordelaise?"

Katie turned. There was a look on J.R.'s face she knew all too well. When he got something in his mind, he was like a bulldog until he figured it out.

"Why?" she asked. "What are you thinking?"

J.R. shrugged. "Nothing. It's just that the chief's description of Newton Collins is exactly what the man in all of Holly's pictures was wearing. But it's a common outfit. Something we all wear. I'm sure it's no big deal."

Katie grabbed her list.

"I've already looked. His name's not on there," J.R. said.

Hershel frowned. "That list is only of sex offenders in this parish. They come and go without registering all the time, and we never know unless they reoffend."

Katie's heart skipped a beat. Something was beginning to click. She could feel it. "How can we check?" she asked.

"I can run his name through the national database," Vera said. "Our system is old, but it eventually does the job. Want me to check it, Chief?"

"Sure. Why not?" Hershel said, then nodded toward the list of local truck owners. "Who else popped up?"

J.R. handed him the list.

Hershel was still looking it over when his two deputies walked in.

When Lee Tullius saw Katie, he ducked his head. He hadn't seen her since the day he'd taken her to the hospital and wondered if she remembered. When she didn't react, he guessed that day was most likely a blur, for which he was glad. He still had nightmares about the sound of her cries and the depth of her despair. He'd even called his mom in Savannah and talked to her about it. She'd immediately gone quiet, and he realized she was remembering the day she learned his oldest brother wasn't coming home from Iraq. Then she made a comment he would never forget.

"That's the sound a mother's heart makes when it's broken, and nothing — not even time — can ever make the loss of a child okay."

He shook off the memory and headed f his desk. That was when he realized J.R. a Katie had been working the lists he Carter had had to abandon.

He glanced at Hershel, who shoo head and frowned. It wasn't protocol civilians into police business, but this week could qualify as an exceptional to break a lot of rules.

"Did you get the car taken care

shel asked.

"Yes, Chief," Carter said. "Want me to run the evidence up to the crime lab in Baton Rouge?"

Before Hershel could answer, Vera suddenly let out a squeal.

Everyone jumped, including the chief.

"Vera! Damn it! You nearly stopped my heart. What in hell is wrong with you?" he said.

"Chief! Come quick!"

Hershel moved toward the computer screen where Vera was pointing.

"I'm printing this out as we speak, but look. Look! Newton Collins is in the national database. But according to this, he's still in Los Angeles, California. I ran a quick check of his last known address and came up empty. According to this, he's been off the radar for at least nine years. Then I checked employment records, and he's been working for the Bordelaise School District for over eight years. Talk about prime hunting grounds . . ."

J.R.'s heart skipped a beat. "What are you saying?" he asked, as he raced toward her desk.

Katie was right behind him. She leaned over the counter, trying to see over Vera's shoulder.

"What else?" she cried. "What else does it say?"

Hershel cursed. Out loud. And for the first time in his life, he did not apologize to the women present for it.

Then, "Are we absolutely positive it's the same Newton Collins?"

Vera nodded. "Same Social Security number."

"God in heaven, how did this happen?" Hershel muttered, as he grabbed the printout.

"Chief! What the hell did he do?" J.R. asked.

"Newton Collins has a rap sheet. He has several convictions for sex offenses against minors. All boys."

Katie gasped. She kept thinking of her little boy, afraid of a monster at the window, and no one believing his claims. What had they done? What in God's name had they done?

"Where does he live?" Lee asked.

Katie grabbed her list. "Walker's Trailer Park — lot four."

"We're on it!" Lee said.

When Hershel started out the door with his deputies, J.R. called out, "I'm going, too!"

Katie grabbed J.R.'s hand.

"*We're* going," he amended.

Hershel frowned. "It's best if you —"

"Chief. We're going. Either with you, or on our own." Something in J.R.'s tone said there was no point in arguing with him.

Hershel sighed. He'd already broken protocol. Might as well go all the way.

"Just stay out of the way. I don't need civilians getting hurt."

J.R. didn't answer. He just grabbed Katie's hand and headed out the door.

Hershel pointed at Vera. "Stand by. And watch the radio traffic. I don't want everyone and their hound dog who has a scanner showing up for the fireworks."

"Do you think this is the man who took Bobby?" Vera asked.

Hershel frowned. "I think it's a pretty damned big coincidence that we've got an unregistered sex offender who matches the description of our perp, right down to the vehicle he drives," he said, and bolted out the door.

The sun was hot coming through the windshield of Newt's truck, even though he had the air conditioner blasting to keep himself cool. One thing he still couldn't tolerate on his healing flesh was heat.

He glanced down briefly, assuring himself

that the kid was still out. Which he was —
curled up in the floorboard of the truck with
the bedspread tucked around him like a
cocoon.

"Boy, oh, boy, we're gonna have ourselves
a high old time," Newt said, and then
returned to his driving, thinking of all the
places they would go and all the things they
could do in Texas. There was a great theme
park called Six Flags Over Texas. He'd never
been there, but knew it was somewhere
around Arlington. A theme park was a
guaranteed kid pleaser, and he needed to
please this kid. There had been too many
traumatic moments between them already.
As soon as they got resettled and he got
himself healed up completely, it was gonna
be party time.

It had been nearly an hour since he'd left
Bordelaise, and he was beginning to feel
easier. A few miles back a highway patrol
car had suddenly appeared in his rearview
mirror, and he'd had a few panicked seconds before it passed him without notice
and kept on going. After that, he began letting down his guard. According to the growl
in his belly, it was past time to eat. He
glanced at the clock on the dash.

Ten minutes to twelve. Almost noon. He
needed gas again. Damn, this truck was shit

on mileage. He would stop at the next fuel station, fill up and raid their deli at the same time. He made a mental note to pick up some cookies. The kid liked cookies.

He patted his shirt pocket, making sure that the sleeping pills he'd been using were at the ready. He didn't need to have the kid go all wonky on him again and try to make another run for it, calling attention to them. Plus there was the fact that the kid was sporting two black eyes and a swollen nose. It would be just his luck if some do-gooder went and reported him to the authorities for child abuse.

Satisfied that he had a workable plan for the next few hours, he turned on the radio, settled back into the seat and began watching the roadside for signs leading him to the next gas station.

Bobby was dreaming. He was in Mama's lap in the big rocking chair beside the window, with Oliver clutched beneath his chin. She was reading *Peter Pan,* and they were almost to his favorite part, where Captain Hook began hearing the ticktock-ticktock of the clock inside the alligator's belly. Even though he knew what was going to happen, he held Oliver just a little bit tighter and leaned into Mama's embrace.

He could feel her breath on the side of his face, and the steady back and forth motion of the rocker as she read. It took a while for him to realize she was reading the same page over and over. That didn't make sense.

"Read faster, Mama."

But Mama didn't answer.

"Mama. Mama. Read faster, please."

It was as if Mama couldn't hear him, and no matter how many times he asked, she didn't respond. He was beginning to get scared. Something was wrong with Mama. He let go of his teddy bear as he turned to face her.

Then his heart thumped. He wasn't sitting in Mama's lap, after all. It was the monster. He had him. And he was smiling. When Bobby tried to get out of his lap, the monster started to laugh. Bobby struggled, kicking and screaming to get free. The burned skin on the monster's body started coming off in pieces, like leaves falling off a tree, revealing bloody flesh and bones, and the monster just kept laughing.

"Help, Daddy, help!"

Then the monster stopped smiling and pointed at Bobby. "You don't belong to your daddy anymore. You belong to me."

"No!" Bobby said, and then he screamed.

The scream was so startling, Newt nearly

ran off the road. Frantic to right the truck before he lost control and rolled it, he fought the skid with every skill he had. When he finally steered the truck to the side of the road and hit the brakes, he was shaking.

"Son of a holy bitch!" he yelled, as he slammed the shift into Park.

His heart was pounding, and his hands were shaking so bad he couldn't even grip the wheel. He stared down at the kid who was still asleep in the floor of the truck and then laid a hand on his chest just to make sure his heart was still pumping.

"What the fuck?"

It was obvious the kid was dreaming. His eyelids were fluttering, and his body was jerking.

"Chill out, damn it," Newt muttered, but he didn't say it too loud. He didn't want the kid to wake up and start causing trouble before he had some food and drink to placate him.

Still rattled by the shock, he glanced in his side-view mirror to make sure the road was clear behind him, then pulled back out onto the highway. According to a sign a mile back, there was a gas station a few miles ahead.

He drove with one eye on the highway and

the other on the kid, making sure there were no more surprises. When he finally saw the gas station, he signaled a lane change, then moved over. A moment later the semi that had been on his tail whizzed past, making the plastic garbage bags in the truck bed rattle like the flapping of a thousand birds on the wing.

He glanced into the rearview mirror, making sure none of his belongings had blown out, then flipped on the turn signal again, slowed enough to take the turn and pulled off the highway into the parking lot of the gas station. There was a small café next door and a half dozen semitrucks parked off to the side. If truckers ate there, it was a given that they served good food in healthy portions.

His belly growled again, and the thought of settling down to a big bowl of gumbo, or maybe a shrimp po'boy, made his mouth water. But he didn't dare leave the kid alone in the truck, and he couldn't take him inside. Which meant he was going to have to settle for whatever he could buy inside the station.

He pulled up to a pump and killed the engine, but he didn't get out until he'd scanned the area, making sure no one was around to notice a pickup loaded with trash bags. Deciding it was safe, he got out, scanned his credit card into the gas pump, then proceeded to fill up.

Once the tank was full, he got in, drove past the pumps up to the front of the station and parked. He glanced down, then reached over and carefully pulled the corner of the bedspread up over the kid's head, completely concealing him from sight. Should anyone be nosy enough to look in as they walked past, they would see nothing of interest. He knew he was taking a risk, but he needed food and drink, and he needed to pee.

He hurried inside, pausing long enough to locate the restrooms, then headed there without looking around. He'd learned a long time ago that not making eye contact was one of the simplest ways to stay unobserved.

He stepped quickly into the bathroom and was out within a couple of minutes. Then he headed straight for the coolers in the back, grabbed some bottled water and a six-pack of cold Pepsi-Colas, before moving to the deli counter near the register.

The clerk was a middle-aged woman with bad skin and even worse teeth. "What'll it be?" she asked.

Newt pointed to some precooked corn

dogs and burritos.

"Gimme four corn dogs and a couple of those burritos. Oh. And maybe some of those potato wedges. To go."

While she was sacking up his order, he added a bag of cookies, a bag of chips and a couple of Snickers bars. It had been a while since he'd had himself a Snickers, and he was craving one big-time.

He kept glancing toward the truck while he waited for the clerk to total up his purchases.

"Could you hurry that up?" he asked. "I got somewhere to be."

The clerk looked him up and down but didn't comment.

Newt silently cursed himself. What the hell had made him say that? Now she was gonna remember him. Fuck.

"That'll be twenty-three dollars and forty cents," she said.

Newt slid a five and a twenty across the counter, pocketed the change she gave back and headed out the door with his food.

A car pulled up behind him, then stopped, as he was getting into the truck.

"Now what?" he muttered.

When he saw a Parish Police emblem on the door, he nearly fainted. What had made them suspicious enough to look for him?

Someone must have seen him leaving the trailer carrying the boy. But how had they found him so fast?

"Oh, God . . . oh, no. Oh, shit, shit, shit."

Just as he was about to get out with his hands up, a woman walked out of the gas station, walked right past him on the driver's side and got into the cruiser. A moment later the car pulled away, leaving Newt weak and shaking behind the wheel.

"Oh, crap. That was close," he said, and then quickly started the engine and drove away.

FIFTEEN

Mabel Pryor had lived in lot seven of Walker's Trailer Park ever since her divorce more than fifteen years earlier. She used to work the night shift at the nursing home, but she'd retired a little over a year ago and had been trying to get her body clock adjusted to daylight living ever since.

To do so, she spent as much time outside in the sunshine as she could tolerate, but in the heat of a summer day, she generally opted for the cool comfort of her trailer, her knitting in her lap and the television talking constantly in the background.

Today, though, regular programming continued to be interrupted by an Amber Alert regarding Bordelaise's own Bobby Earle. Mabel knew the Earles and was heartsick over what had happened. She hadn't been able to concentrate on much of anything for worrying about the boy, and

had been in and out of her trailer all morning.

She'd watched her neighbor's yard getting cleared of storm debris, watched Sam and Freddy stacking up firewood and hauling off brush, and she was still outside when they drove away with the last load.

She'd gone back into her trailer soon after, but when she happened to look out to see Newt Collins hurrying back and forth from his trailer carrying electronic equipment and garbage bags, it didn't take her long to figure out he was moving. She snorted beneath her breath, thinking to herself that he was probably running out on the rent he owed Sam. She watched him as he made trip after trip, right down to the last time when he dumped that load into the cab of his truck instead of the truck bed. It wasn't until he left the park that she went back to her knitting.

When she saw the Amber Alert again, she thought of all the people she knew who drove blue trucks, even that worthless Newt Collins, and shook her head, thinking if they didn't have any more than that to go on, the little boy would never be found.

It was a couple of hours later when she saw two Bordelaise police cruisers pull into the trailer park. They were driving without

lights or sirens, so she thought nothing of it, until they came to a stop at lot four.

At that point Mabel's curiosity got the better of her. She dumped her knitting on the floor and rushed to the window. When she saw a blue pickup pull in behind the police cruisers and recognized J.R. and Katie Earle, her heart skipped a beat. It was their little boy who was missing!

And then it hit her again that Newt drove a blue truck — just like the one mentioned on the Amber Alert. Surely there wasn't a connection. Surely.

She moved closer to the window to watch.

Chief Porter was the first one out of the cruiser. He turned immediately and pointed at J.R. and Katie.

"Stay back."

Katie stopped, but J.R. didn't. He kept walking toward the trailer. At that point Katie wasn't about to stay put and hurried to catch up.

"Well, hell," Hershel said, and quickly took the lead. "Check the back," he said to his men, and Carter split off from the group and disappeared around the corner.

The sound of their footsteps echoed on the wooden deck as they approached the front door. Out of habit, Hershel brushed

335

his hand across the butt of his pistol, checking to make sure it was there, then knocked.

No one answered.

He raised his fist and pounded on the door again.

"Bordelaise Police. Open the door, Mr. Collins."

Silence.

"Want me to kick it in, Chief?" Lee asked.

"No. Wait. I'll —"

At that moment, they heard a man's voice, shouting from across the way.

"Hey! Hey! What's going on here?" It was Sam Walker, the owner of the park, hurrying toward the trailer. "What's happening?" he asked, as he started up the steps.

"We need to talk to Mr. Collins," Hershel said.

Sam shrugged. "His truck is gone, so he's probably gone, too. Said something earlier about needing to be somewhere this afternoon, I think. Can't blame him. He's been stranded here all week. . . . Ever since the tornado, actually. Me and my boy, Freddy, just got the debris cleared away from his truck this morning."

J.R. groaned. If they had figured this out yesterday, Newt Collins would still have been here — maybe with Bobby.

Hershel understood J.R.'s frustration, but

they still didn't know if this was the man they were looking for.

"I need to ask you a couple of questions," he said to Sam.

Sam shrugged. "Shoot."

"Have you seen any kids around the park in the past week?"

Sam frowned. "None that don't belong. As for Newt, he's been nearly bedfast the last week from his injuries. I felt sort of guilty he got hurt at all, because I'm the one who came and got him. All the men here went downtown to help out with search and rescue. Newt fell into some kind of chemicals at the lumberyard and burned himself down the front pretty bad. He's spent most of the week naked." He glanced at Katie and shrugged. "Sorry, ma'am. Just stating the facts. He was too sore to wear clothes, you understand. I took him to the doctor and such."

Katie clutched J.R.'s hand. She wanted to look inside. She needed to know for herself that her baby wasn't there and — please, God — had never been there.

Hershel's hopes fell. Still, he needed to eliminate this man before moving on with the search.

"Here's the deal, Sam. Newt isn't here, but I need to look inside his trailer."

Sam frowned. "I don't know. It don't seem right to —"

"We're looking for my boy," J.R. said. "Newt Collins fits the description of the man who took him."

Hershel frowned. This was getting out of hand, just like he'd feared it might. "That's not for —"

But J.R. wasn't about to be quiet. "This is my son we're talking about. Sam, either open the door or I'll open it for you."

Sam's eyes bugged. "I heard about that Amber Alert a while ago. Are you saying Newt's the man who took your boy?"

"We don't know, but since he fits the general description, we need to eliminate him to be able to move on," Hershel said.

Sam took a ring of keys out of his pocket, found what he was looking for and promptly opened the door.

"He's pretty messy," he said, as he walked inside with them. "But he always pays his rent on time."

Except for the filth, at first glance nothing seemed strange. Then suddenly J.R. pointed to the corner of the room.

"The television is gone."

Lee turned toward the kitchen area. "And the counters are a mess, except for this area here. It's about the size of a microwave. I'd

say that was missing, too."

J.R. bolted for the back of the trailer before Hershel could stop him, with Katie right behind.

"Shit," the chief muttered, and hurried down the hall.

"Don't touch anything!" he yelled, and then came to a stop in the bedroom doorway.

J.R. was kneeling beside the bed, looking at the pieces of rope lying on the floor. Katie's hands were over her mouth, but they didn't muffle the keening sound coming up her throat.

"There's blood on those ropes," J.R. said, and then stood. "There's also blood on the sheets on this bed."

"I told you he got hurt," Sam said.

"That might explain the blood on the sheets, but not on the ropes," Hershel snapped. And then he noticed something tied to the headboard. He lifted it with the barrel of his gun, then cursed. Women's nylons. They were bloody, too. "What the hell?"

He moved to the closet. It was empty, as was the dresser. His heart sank as he turned to face the room.

"Someone was tied to this bed by their hands and feet," Tullius said, as he pulled more nylons from beneath the end of the bed, then stretched them across the mattress. "Someone who wasn't very tall."

J.R.'s stomach rolled, imagining his little boy tied spread-eagle to this bed. Imagining the horrors he must have gone through.

Katie sobbed.

J.R. grabbed her.

"What happened here?" Katie whispered. "What happened to our baby?"

J.R. could only shake his head as Katie hid her face against his chest.

Hershel was sick to his stomach. "Lee. Get Carter in here. I want this place dusted for fingerprints and all this taken into evidence."

Lee headed out of the room on the double.

Sam was in shock.

"I didn't know! I swear . . . I had no idea."

"Everybody out!" Hershel said.

"Come on, baby . . . I've seen enough," J.R. said.

Katie looked up at J.R., and then started to sob harder. He put his arm around her and led her out of the trailer, but when they started down the steps, he felt her sliding out of his grasp.

"Katie!" he cried, but she didn't hear him. She'd already fainted.

J.R. caught her before she fell, scooped

340

her up into his arms and rushed her toward their truck.

Just as he was sliding Katie onto the seat, Mabel came running.

Hershel was already down the steps and heading for his cruiser when he saw Mabel Pryor bolt out of her trailer. At that point, he realized, he might just have himself a witness.

"Is she all right?" Mabel cried, as she reached J.R.'s truck. "I saw her fall."

"She fainted," J.R. said.

"It's about your boy, isn't it?" Mabel said. "I saw the Amber Alert. You went inside Newt's trailer. He drives a blue truck. I heard the news. I pay attention to stuff."

J.R. inhaled sharply and then turned to face her.

"What did you see?"

At that point, Hershel stepped into the conversation.

"J.R., I know where you're coming from, but you have to let me do my job."

"I'm not stopping you," J.R. said. "But just know you're not stopping me, either."

At that point, they heard the truck door open.

"J.R.?"

It was Katie, pale and shaky, but climbing out.

He ran to her, and helped her down.

"Easy, honey. You could still be a little unsteady on your feet."

"I'm sorry. I just —"

"Damn it, Katie. Do not apologize," J.R. said. "I felt like puking up my guts and wished I could pass out. Your reaction was normal."

"What's happening?" she asked.

"We're hoping Mrs. Pryor might know something about that," J.R. said.

"Mabel?" Katie said.

"Hello, Katie. I'm real sorry about your little boy."

"What do you know?" Katie asked. "Did you see my baby?"

Hershel sighed. "I'm asking the questions," he muttered, then turned his attention back to Mabel.

"What do you know about Newt Collins?"

"He's weird," Mabel said.

"That's not illegal," Hershel said.

"I used to work nights, remember?"

Hershel nodded. "Newt was always roaming around town, especially at night. I saw him plenty of times when I was leaving for my midnight shift."

J.R. felt sick, thinking of this sexual predator peeking into windows, prowling the

342

streets of their little town looking for victims.

"Did you see Newt today?" Hershel asked.

Mabel nodded. "He loaded up his TV and microwave in the back of his truck, then piled a whole lot of garbage bags on top and took off — probably owing Sam a month's rent."

"What time?" Hershel asked.

"I don't know. . . . A little after ten, I think."

"Oh, God," J.R. said. He still felt like puking, thinking of how close — how desperately close — they'd been to stopping him before he got away.

"Did you see him with a little boy?" Hershel asked.

"No," Mabel said. "Just all those garbage bags. Oh. And that rug. At least, it looked like a rug. It was rolled up like one of Pinky's burritos from the Get and Go. It was the only thing Newt put up front with him. Everything else was in the truck bed."

"Bobby," J.R. said. "That had to be Bobby!"

"We don't know that for sure," Hershel said.

J.R. stared at Hershel, then turned to Katie. "Get in the truck, Katie."

She didn't need to know why. She just

headed for the truck on the run, jumped in and slammed the door shut, even as the chief was yelling, "J.R.! Wait!"

J.R. pulled his cell phone out of his pocket and kept on walking. By the time he got behind the wheel, he had Brent Macklan on the line.

"J.R.! Glad you finally checked in. We've been worried. Is your family all okay?"

"No. I need a favor."

"Anything," Brent said.

"My son has been kidnapped."

Brent Macklan's stomach fell. "Oh, my God. What's the ransom? Whatever you need, just ask."

"No ransom. The man who took him is a convicted child molester."

"Sweet Lord," Brent said. "What can I do?"

"I need one of the company choppers to come and get me. The man has at least a three-hour head start. We don't know where he went, but we know what he's driving. I need to do something. I can't just sit and wait."

"Are you in Bordelaise?"

"Yes."

"I have a chopper less than thirty minutes away. It's yours. Where can he land?"

"There's a helipad behind the hospital on

the west edge of town. I'll be waiting. And, boss . . . thank you."

"No thanks needed. Just find your boy," Brent said. "I'll say prayers."

"Thanks," J.R. said, and then started the truck.

"What are you going to do?" Katie asked.

"Get in the air. I can't stand by and wait. I have to go, Katie. I just have to."

"I'll go with you," she said.

"No. I need you to go back to the police station. Stay by Vera and the radio. We can't use cell phones in the air, but if you hear anything that might tell us which direction they went, you have to convince her to let me know."

Katie nodded. "I won't flake out again. I promise."

"I know that," J.R. said, and headed for the helipad.

As soon as they arrived, he turned to Katie, cupped his hand against the back of her head and pulled her to him.

Their lips met in a hard, desperate kiss. When he pulled back, his eyes were bright with unshed tears.

"I *will* find him, baby. I promise. I won't come back without him."

Too moved to speak, Katie could only nod.

"I'm getting out now," J.R. said. "The chopper should be here within a few minutes. You drive back to the station and stay close to the radio. Whatever traffic you hear related to Bobby, I need to know."

She nodded again. "Be careful."

"I will."

He had started to get out when she grabbed his hand.

"Wait."

"What is it, honey?"

"I love you, J.R. Remember that. No . . . matter what, I love you."

His vision blurred as tears welled and spilled down his face.

"Ah, Jesus . . . I love you, too, Katie bug. Stay strong for me and for Bobby, you hear?"

"I hear," she said softly.

"Now go. I don't want the chief to know what I'm doing until we're already in the air."

Katie watched him walk away, then put the truck in gear and drove away without looking back.

J.R. paced around the helipad like a caged tiger, constantly scanning the skies. About fifteen minutes later he began hearing the chopper before he actually saw it. When it finally appeared on the horizon, like a big black bug, coming closer and closer, he stopped pacing.

He didn't know how the next few hours were going to play out, or what he would find at the end of their journey, but there was one certainty in his head. Newt Collins was, for all intents and purposes, a dead man.

Bobby woke up before he opened his eyes. The first thing he thought was that his hands and feet were no longer tied and he was not in that bed. When he heard the familiar sound of a car engine and realized he was moving, his heart skipped a beat. How would Daddy find him if they were no longer in Bordelaise?

In a panic, he kicked back the covers and sat up.

"Well, now! Look who woke up!" Newt said, and smiled widely.

"Where are we?" Bobby asked.

"We're going on vacation," Newt said. "And I'll bet you're hungry as a little bear. See that sack? There's corn dogs and burritos inside. Grab yourself one and chow down, boy. It'll make you grow big and tall like me."

Bobby saw the sack and the food inside. He didn't want to be hungry, but he was.

Still, he hesitated. Everything the man gave him was suspect. He didn't want to be sleepy again.

"It's okay," Newt said. "See, it's still all wrapped up from the store just like I bought it. Have one."

Bobby eyed the man behind the wheel, then the sack again. A few moments later, he reached in and pulled out a corn dog. When he started to climb up into the seat to eat it, Newt stopped him.

"Whoa, whoa! Why don't you just eat down there? That way, if you make crumbs, it won't matter, okay?"

Bobby shrugged then peeled back the paper wrapping and took his first bite. The crust was soft and the weiner was cold. It didn't taste as good as a hot one, but he was too hungry to argue. He wouldn't let himself think of how good his mama used to make his food. Mama was in heaven. He didn't want to think about never seeing Mama again and took another bite.

"How about some chips?" Newt asked, and offered the open bag.

Bobby frowned.

Newt stuffed his hand inside, pulled out a handful and started eating them as he drove.

When Bobby realized Newt was eating them, he took some, too, knowing the bad man wouldn't eat sleepy chips, because he had to drive.

Newt waited until he knew the kid was bound to be thirsty before he offered him something to drink.

"There's Pepsi in a can and water in a bottle. Help yourself," he said.

Bobby eyed the drinks. None of them had been opened. They should be safe, as well. He chose water, but then couldn't open it.

"Here, let Uncle Newt help you with that," Newt said, and quickly broke the seal, then handed it back for Bobby to open.

Bobby took a small sip, then let the water go down his throat, waiting to see if he tasted that bitter aftertaste. When he didn't, he took a bigger drink, then settled back and finished off his corn dog, trying not to think that they were getting farther and farther away from Bordelaise.

SIXTEEN

Taking Interstate 49 was proving to be a good choice, Newt thought, as the miles between them and Bordelaise continued to lengthen.

Bobby was sitting quietly on the floor of the truck, eating his food. Newt was truly sorry that he'd had to resort to force with the kid, and even sorrier that Bobby was sporting two black eyes and a swollen nose. Newt considered himself a kind man, albeit a kind man with a quirk. He got a kick out of watching the little boy enjoy something he'd provided without fighting or complaining. It gave him a sense of empowerment.

Getting burned had been a setback to their new relationship, but he hadn't lost his touch. He knew how to get around kids' inhibitions, and food and kindness were the easiest and most obvious methods.

"Want a cookie, kid?" Newt asked, as Bobby washed down the last of his chips with a drink of cold water. "They're in the sack by me. Help yourself."

When Bobby started to get up to reach the sack, Newt yelled before he thought.

"No, no, stay down, stay down! The crumbs, remember?"

He tossed the pack of cookies toward Bobby before returning his attention to driving, but Bobby just shoved the cookies away, then sat with his arms folded over his chest and a nervous expression on his face.

Newt cursed beneath his breath, then reminded himself that it would be better when they got someplace new. When they were truly "on their own," with no place for the kid to run to.

"I need to go to the bathroom," Bobby suddenly announced.

Newt frowned.

"I don't have time to stop now." He pointed to a used coffee cup rolling around on the floorboards. "Pee in that cup."

"I don't need to pee. I need to do number two," Bobby said.

"Son of a bitch," Newt muttered. "Can't you hold it?"

"Not for long," Bobby said. "I need to go. Bad."

"Great," Newt muttered. "Just great. Well, you're gonna have to hold it for a couple of miles until we get to the next gas station. I saw a sign a while back. We should be coming up on one anytime."

Bobby nodded, but he continued to fidget until he had Newt convinced that unless he stopped soon, he would have to smell shit all the way to Texas. When he finally saw the oil company sign looming high over the small red-roofed building, he was actually relieved, even though it meant showing the kid in public.

He pulled off the highway and came to a stop to the right of the store, then pointed a finger at Bobby.

"When we go inside, you don't ask for anything. You don't talk to anybody. You just hold my hand and keep walking, do you understand?"

"But —"

"No buts. And don't make me have to whup your ass!"

Bobby cowered as Newt got out. When he didn't immediately follow, Newt paused, then looked back.

"Well, are you comin' or not?"

Bobby lurched up from the floor of the truck and climbed out quickly, before the monster could change his mind. He was in such a hurry to get to the bathroom that when Newt grabbed him by the hand and started dragging him toward the store, he didn't even bother to fight back.

Evaline Corwin had worked for the Gas and Grub for more than eight years. During that time she'd been robbed twice, shot at once by an ex-husband who was now serving time in Angola Prison and seen both her sons shipped off to war in Iraq. She was a tough, no-nonsense woman with a weathered expression and a soft heart for kids, which was why her motherly instincts went on alert when she saw the middle-aged man with a barrel chest dragging a little boy into the store. Even though all six gas pumps were busy outside and customers were lined up inside to pay, she paid more attention to the newcomers than normal. And after she spotted the child's black eyes and swollen nose, her instincts moved up a notch. She knew kids often hurt themselves and, having raised two boys, was well aware that there were many ways besides abuse for a kid's eyes to turn black. Still, the sight made her watch the unlikely pair more closely than she normally might have.

When she saw them heading toward the back of the store in a hurry, she guessed they were heading to the bathrooms. Nothing unusual about that.

"Hey, Evaline, are you gonna take my money, or is this stuff free today?"

The question shifted her attention to the trucker in front of her.

"Nothing is free these days, Marty. That'll be twenty-two fifty."

"Dang, woman. You're getting all my money," he teased.

She pointed to his burgeoning belly. "I'm not the one eating meatball subs and Pay-Day candy bars by the sackful."

The trucker laughed. "You're startin' to sound like my wife. See you next time around, Evaline."

"See you, Marty," she said, as he paid up and left.

After that she moved on to the next customer, and then the next, and by the time the last customer in line had paid up and left, the man and the kid were coming back through the store.

"Hey, guys!" she called, as they walked past the counter. "How's it going?"

Newt nodded. "Good, good. Take care," he said, and kept on walking.

She wouldn't have thought anything more of it, but then the little boy's gaze locked with hers. Breath caught in the back of her throat. The plea in his eyes was heartbreaking. She didn't know what it meant, but she knew, with every fiber of her being, that the kid was in trouble.

"Hey, kid . . . looks like you had a run of bad luck there. How about an ice cream bar?"

Bobby nodded.

Newt frowned. "He can't have sweets. He's diabetic," he snapped, and kept on walking.

"Sorry, I didn't mean anything —"

They were out the door before Evaline could blink.

She watched them load up into the truck and frowned. Obviously on the move. Looked like everything they owned was packed in garbage bags in the back of that blue truck.

When they backed up and drove off, she wrote down the tag number. She didn't know why, but it felt like the thing to do.

A short while later another spate of customers outside and in had finally driven away. She turned her attention to the TV mounted in the wall behind her just as the broadcast was suddenly interrupted by a serious of beeps.

When she realized it was an Amber Alert, her mood shifted to wondering why God let bad people anywhere near a kid. It wasn't until they flashed a picture of the missing child on the screen that she began to really pay attention. It looked a whole lot like the kid who had just been here, although it was difficult to be certain, because of the kid's swollen nose and black eyes. Then she heard them mention a blue truck with a lot of garbage bags in the bed, and her heartbeat accelerated. That sounded exactly like the truck in which they'd driven away. Then they gave the license number, and she picked up the scrap of paper where she'd written down that tag number. All the blood left her face, and she reached for the phone.

Katie had taken up residence in the police department, at J.R.'s request. When the Macklan Brothers chopper entered Bordelaise airspace, Hershel had immediately realized what was happening and why J.R. wasn't with her. He needed to be in control of the situation, but he understood J.R.'s panic. Hershel had immediately requested the assistance of the Louisiana Highway Patrol, but he was still waiting for acknowledgment that they would dispatch their copter to aid in the search. In the meantime, Newton Collins was getting farther and farther away. It was a worst-case scenario, and the chief was over a barrel. He could hardly demand J.R. cease and desist when time was of the essence.

Per the chief's request, Carter was running a credit-card check on Newton Collins. If he'd used one in the past few hours, it could give them an idea of where he was going.

In the middle of Hershel's dilemma, Carter suddenly burst into his office.

"Chief! Newton Collins used his credit card to buy gas at Hank's gas station this morning a little after 10:00 a.m., then at a place out on 49 a couple hours later."

Katie had been trying to stay quiet, but when she'd seen Carter running back to the chief's office, she'd followed. And when she heard this, she interrupted.

"Hank's is just off Highway 190 on the west side of Bordelaise. That has to mean he went west, right?"

Hershel shoved a hand through his hair. "Yeah, but then he took Interstate 49, which means he could have gone north or south from there. We have to find out where that second station is."

Katie grabbed Hershel's arm. "You have to let J.R. know. You have to, Chief! If we lose this man today, I may never see my little boy again!"

Hershel knew she was right. "Vera! Find that chopper pilot. Give them the information. Tell J.R. that we'll find out where on 49 he bought gas and feed him info as it comes in. But tell him not to take action himself. Tell him if he spots them, just let us know. We'll take them down from the ground."

"Yes, sir," Vera said, as she turned toward the dispatch center.

"Thank you, Chief. Thank you," Katie breathed.

Hershel sighed, then nodded. "Yeah, sure."

Cody Sands had been flying choppers for Macklan Brothers Oil for nearly ten years. He had a son from a previous marriage who lived in L.A., and he saw him — maybe — three or four times a year. Definitely not often enough.

When he'd gotten the call to divert to Bordelaise and then learned the reason why, he'd been in shock. He knew J. R. Earle. He'd seen him with his son more than once. The thought of that little dark-haired kid at the mercy of a sexual predator was horrifying. By the time he picked J.R. up and got back in the air, he was almost as focused on the chase as J.R. was.

They didn't talk much. There wasn't much to say. And then the Bordelaise dispatcher found him.

Vera quickly relayed the information that Newt Collins had purchased gas from a station off of Interstate 49, north of where it intersected with Highway 190, west of Bordelaise.

J.R. headed the chopper north.

By now it was nearing four hours since Newt Collins had made his escape from Bordelaise, and he was feeling pretty cocky. He'd gotten out without a hitch, and the kid seemed to be cooperating better than he'd expected, even though he'd been unable to slip another dose of sleep meds into him.

He'd learned the hard way that pushing an issue only made the kid bullheaded, so for the time being he'd backed off. And when Bobby Earle asked to sit up on the seat, claiming his legs were hurting from sitting cross-legged on the floor for so long, Newt, thinking they were most likely out of immediate danger, had waved him up. Now the kid was buckled in the seat beside him, with the package of cookies in his lap.

"Don't eat too many of those," Newt warned. "You don't wanna make yourself sick."

Bobby reluctantly set the package aside,

then drank the last of his water and tossed the empty bottle onto the floorboard.

Newt glanced up at the rearview mirror, saw nothing out of the ordinary and then concentrated on the road ahead.

The phone had been ringing with regularity since the Amber Alert had gone out. But after Hershel had updated the report with more information, including Newton Collins's tag number, the garbage bags in his truck and his physical appearance, the calls had increased. Others were going into the state police HQ where the alert had been issued, and they sent the information down to Bordelaise.

Vera took down all the information as it came in, although she could tell from most of the calls that they were going to wind up being useless. So far, no one had reported what she would call a verifiable sighting. Either they'd seen a man and a kid in a blue truck but with no garbage bags, or they'd seen a family pulling a trailer full of furniture and garbage bags, or something in between. And none of them had given the correct license tag number.

When the phone rang again, Katie spun toward the desk where Vera was sitting and held her breath as she listened, just like she did every time.

"Bordelaise Police Department," Vera said.

"Um, hello. My name is Evaline Corwin. I work at the Gas and Grub off Interstate 49. That's between Bunkie and Alexandria. I'm calling about that Amber Alert. I just saw that little boy."

Vera grabbed her pen. "Yes, ma'am. Can you be more specific?" she asked, sure this was going to be another false alarm.

"Um, yeah. Sure. They were in a blue truck with a bunch of garbage bags in the truck bed . . . like they were moving or something, you know? They came in to use the restrooms."

Vera's heart skipped a beat. "Did you get a good look at the driver?"

"Yeah. He was white . . . middle-aged, with a potbelly and a weak chin. He was wearing shorts and a tee. The little boy had on a red-and-blue-striped shirt and blue jeans."

Vera stifled a gasp. "Did you get a good look at his face?" she asked.

"Yes, ma'am. That's what bothered me most."

"What do you mean?" Vera asked.

"Both his eyes were black. His nose was swollen, and his upper lip was puffy. He looked like the kid on the news, just all beat up."

"Sweet Lord," Vera muttered.

Katie was standing behind Vera, watching her taking down the information, and when she saw the physical description of the little boy, her stomach lurched. If this was Bobby, what in God's name had he been enduring?

"Anything else?" Vera asked.

"Yes. Because the little guy looked like he might have been abused, I took down the tag number. And then I saw the Amber Alert, and —"

"Can you give me that tag number?" Vera asked, her adrenaline pumping.

When Evaline rattled off the number, Vera stifled a shout. This was it. Their first big break. Now they knew for sure that Bobby Earle was still alive! She felt Katie's fingers gripping her shoulders and knew she'd gotten the message, as well.

"How long ago was it when they stopped at your store?" Vera asked.

Evaline glanced at the clock. "Oh, I'd say fifteen minutes ago . . . give or take a few."

"Thank you for calling in," Vera said. "May I have your name and number for the record?"

Evaline rattled them off.

"Thank you for the call. You may literally

be a lifesaver," Vera said, and disconnected.

"Why did you write down black eyes and bruises? What does that mean?" Katie tried to keep the fear from her tone, but she knew she wasn't doing a very good job.

"The caller said the little boy she saw had black eyes, and a swollen nose and lip."

Katie felt sick all over again. "But it was them, right? Is that the tag number for Newt Collins's car?"

Vera smiled. "Yes. It was them."

"Oh, Lord, oh, Lord . . . Bobby is alive." Katie breathed, and then she started to cry. "Call J.R. . . . you have to tell J.R."

"I need to notify the chief first. I can't take control of this. He's in charge." Vera spun her chair toward the dispatch center and reached for the phone.

Hershel was already on his way back to headquarters from a quick trip out for food when he got Vera's call. He could tell by the quiver in her voice that something big had happened.

"Porter here. What's up?"

Ever careful of civilians with scanners, she kept her information vague.

"We got a hit," she said briefly.

Hershel's heart skipped a beat. "A good one?"

363

"Yes, sir."

"Notify the highway patrol, then the chopper. I'm on my way back."

Anxious to hear details, Hershel took a shortcut through an alley and accelerated on the other side, running with lights and sirens all the way to headquarters.

Cody and J.R. had been so focused on watching the highways for blue trucks that when the radio squawked again, they both jumped. When Cody answered the call sign, he felt J.R.'s attention shift.

J.R. could hear everything in his earphones that the pilot could hear. When he recognized Vera's voice, his first thought was, Please, let this be good news.

"We got a call from a clerk at a gas station off Interstate 49, between Bunkie and Alexandria. She reported seeing a man and boy matching the descriptions of Bobby Earle and Newton Collins. They were in a blue late-model truck with a whole lot of garbage bags in the bed. The tag number she gave matches Collins's tag."

"How long ago?" Cody asked.

"Around fifteen minutes," Vera said. "The highway patrol has been notified. What's your twenty?"

"Maybe thirty minutes behind them,"

Cody said, then added, "But not for long. Over and out."

He glanced at J.R. "Are you up for a ride?"

"Just get me there," J.R. said. "I don't give a damn how low or how fast you have to go to do it."

Cody grinned. "That's what I wanted to hear."

Newt had pulled over at a rest stop off the interstate to take a piss. He was feeling so cocky about his escape that he even let Bobby out to pee, showing him how to stand close to the pickup so passersby couldn't see them, and cautioning him about staying close so he didn't get run over. He had Bobby so nervous, he knew he wouldn't run.

By the time they were through and back on the road, Bobby was getting sleepy.

"If you're tired, just lay your head down here next to me," Newt said, and patted the seat beside his leg.

Bobby eyed the white hairy legs with the healing burns on the thighs and shook his head.

"I'm not sleepy," he argued, and reached for the cookies instead.

Newt shrugged. Whatever. If the kid gave himself a bellyache, it was no skin off his nose. He didn't care what he did as long as he stayed still and stayed quiet.

Newt cast a quick look in the rearview mirror. Satisfied that there was nothing behind them but normal traffic, he switched on the radio, searched for a country music station and then settled back against the seat.

The air conditioner kept his discomfort to a minimum, and before long he was eating cookies with Bobby Earle.

"Hey, kid . . . can you open up one of those Pepsi-Colas for me?"

Bobby reached into the sack and pulled out a can.

"It's not cold," he said.

"Don't matter to me," Newt said. "Just pop the top easy like . . . just in case it wants to spew."

Bobby popped the top.

The can fizzed, then spewed.

Newt cursed.

Bobby laughed out loud.

It was the shock of the little boy's laughter that turned Newt's thoughts to lust. His grin was more like a leer as he took the sticky can out of the kid's hand. "Thought that was funny, did you?"

Bobby seemed as startled by his laughter as Newt had been. Even though the bad

366

man was smiling, he ducked his head and wouldn't look up or answer.

Newt shrugged and downed a swig.

Yep. He knew what he was doing. All he needed with this kid was some time.

SEVENTEEN

The black Macklan Brothers chopper was flying so low and so fast that the ground below was a blur. When J.R. suddenly spotted the Shell Oil sign on a pole high above the roof of a small building, he pointed.

"Gas and Grub! That's it! That's the place where the call came from!" he shouted.

Cody Sands nodded, then pointed to his watch.

"Five minutes. We should catch up to them shortly. Keep watch!"

J.R. gave him a thumbs-up and looked back down.

All of a sudden, a blur of flashing blue lights appeared on the highway up ahead. Two dark blue Chevy Caprices were merging onto the interstate from a frontage road. When he saw the gold stripes and the Louisiana state outline emblazoned at an angle on the doors, he knew the cars were Louisiana Highway Patrol.

"Cops!" Cody said.

J.R. nodded. He just hoped to God they were after Newt Collins and not on their way to some wreck.

Long moments passed with J.R. frantically scanning the highway below for sight of a blue truck, while the highway patrol cars sped up the highway, their lights and sirens still flashing.

Cars quickly gave way, pulling over into the slow lane or even onto the shoulder to let them pass.

J.R.'s heart was pounding as the chopper quickly overtook them, then passed them from above.

"Unless the truck pulled off, we should be coming up on them any minute," Cody said, as they quickly left the patrol cars behind.

Only a couple of minutes later J.R. spotted a blue truck on the highway below. The bed was loaded with black plastic garbage bags packed full to bursting.

"There!" he shouted.

Cody reached for the radio, keyed in on the police frequency and started to broadcast what they'd seen.

Within moments the airwaves were alive with traffic from below. The troopers acknowledged the sighting and ordered them to maintain visual contact without interfering.

"Is Bobby in there?" J.R. shouted.

"Can't tell," Cody answered.

"Get lower!" J.R. begged.

"Can't!" Cody said, pointing to the electric wires.

J.R. groaned.

Seconds later the highway patrol cars caught up with the truck.

Then they watched in horror as the truck accelerated, fishtailed, then sped forward at an alarming rate.

The race was on.

Newt was downing the last of his Pepsi when he caught a glimpse of flashing lights. He glanced up in the rearview mirror just as a Louisiana Highway Patrol car swerved out from behind a semi and headed toward him.

Startled, he coughed, then choked, spewing hot Pepsi through his nose.

Seeing pop spew out of Newt's big nose looked funny to Bobby, who snickered, then covered his mouth and ducked his head, afraid he would be in trouble again.

This time there was nothing about Bobby Earle's mirth that was amusing to Newt. His lust level was in the dirt. There were myriad reasons why the highway patrol might be running with lights and sirens, including a wreck up ahead, but something told Newt that they were after him.

"Oh, shit! Oh, no! Oh, hell!" He moaned, then stomped the accelerator.

His tires squealed. The truck lurched and then fishtailed as the engine revved.

Bobby's smile disappeared. He grabbed hold of the armrest with one hand and the edge of the seat with the other, and started to yell.

"Slow down, mister. Slow down!" he cried.

"Shut up! Shut the fuck up!" Newt screamed, and swerved around a car pulling a camper, then back in front of a minivan. He caught a glimpse of panic on the driver's face as he flew past and wondered if his own expression was as frantic.

As they swerved back into the fast lane, the seat belt yanked hard against Bobby's throat, cutting off his air supply and almost strangling him. Panicked, he unbuckled it before he thought, and within seconds slid to the floor, bumping his head against the dash.

"Damn it, kid! Stay down! *Stay down!*" Newt yelled, and dodged into the right-hand lane, cutting off an eighteen-wheeler, then swerved onto the side of the road, where he began passing vehicles from the shoulder.

"Damn it!" J.R. shouted, and flinched as the truck flew in front of the semi, then swerved to the shoulder of the road, before passing everything on its left. "Can you see Bobby? I need to know if he's still got my boy."

Cody glanced down. There was a mile of space between a cell phone tower and another span of electric lines. It would be tricky getting down and getting out before flying into the wires, but it was a risk he was willing to take.

"Look hard!" he yelled. "We've only got time for one pass."

With that, he shoved the stick forward, sending the chopper into a shallow dive.

J.R. leaned forward, bracing his hands against the dash, and fixed his gaze on the cab of the truck.

Closer, closer, they drew until they were almost even with the pickup.

Suddenly a small, dark head popped up in the window. It was a little boy with two black eyes and a swollen nose. When he saw the chopper, he started beating on the window, and even though J.R. couldn't hear him, he could tell the boy was screaming one word over and over and over.

For the space of a heartbeat J.R. couldn't think past the sight of that panicked expression and the battered face. Then he saw the driver grab at Bobby's arm and pull him away from the window. At the same time he saw Bobby take a swing at the driver's face, fighting to get away.

Suddenly the truck skidded sideways.

J.R. moaned. Before he could see what happened next, the chopper suddenly lifted straight up, yanking him back to reality. He watched with his heart in his throat as the truck skidded off the shoulder, down into the grass, and then back up onto the shoulder and straight across two lanes of traffic onto the center median.

"Sweet Jesus . . . no, no, no, no," J.R. prayed, hoping no one would hit them before they came to a stop.

To his relief, they managed to escape being hit, but once the driver regained stability, he took off again.

All J.R. could do was watch helplessly from above as the truck pulled back onto the highway and accelerated wildly, with the Louisiana troopers still in hot pursuit.

J.R. was sick to his stomach. His child was only seconds away from dying. He kept remembering that look on Bobby's face, and while he hadn't heard the word his son had been shouting, he knew what he'd been saying.

Daddy.

He'd been screaming, "Daddy!"

And that was when J.R. lost it.

"Damn it. That's enough. Cody! Get in front of him! We've got to stop that truck before he kills my son."

Cody frowned. It was a risky move. The crazy bastard could just decide to drive straight into the chopper and take everyone, including himself, out. But he, too, had seen the look on that little boy's face and could only imagine what the child must already have suffered.

"Shit, J.R. You're gonna owe me big-time," he muttered.

"Whatever you want, it's yours," J.R. said. "Get about a half mile ahead of him, then turn around and set it down. I'm thinking that son of a bitch won't have the balls to play chicken with a chopper."

As they shot past the truck and the highway patrol cars, it was evident that people in the cars ahead were tuning in to what was happening behind them. They were pulling off the highway at alarming rates, some going into the center median, others taking off into the grass off the shoulder. No one wanted to become involved in the race, much less some fiery crash.

Cody took the chopper up, then swooped, making a perfect U-turn and coming in dead center over the interstate. He could hear chatter from the highway patrol, shouting orders that he blatantly ignored.

J.R. was right. The crazy bastard was going to kill himself and the kid unless someone got them stopped.

"We're going down," he said.

J.R. gritted his teeth. The blue truck was about a half mile in front of them and coming fast.

"God . . . please let this work," he muttered, and braced himself for the sudden jolt.

Newt was bawling and cursing at the top of his voice.

Bobby was on his knees on the seat, looking out through the cracked glass of the back window of the truck. He could see the highway patrol cars. He could see the chopper flying up, up, up, seemingly flying away. He began beating on the glass with the flats of his hands.

"Stop! Stop! Stop!" he screamed. "That was my daddy. You have to stop and let me out! Daddy! Daddy! I want my daddy!"

Newt doubled up his fist and hit the kid on the side of his head, knocking him against the passenger side door, where he slid quietly onto the floorboard.

One of the troopers in pursuit had already seen the boy in the truck and was relaying information that the child was alive when he saw the driver hit the boy with a fist. When the child disappeared, he winced, then stepped on the gas. They had a road-block set up just a mile and a half ahead. If the truck stayed upright just a little while longer, that was where they would stop him.

Then suddenly, the oil company chopper disappeared from his immediate line of sight. Just when he thought they'd gone, he saw it swoop back into sight, make a sharp U-turn over the highway and then set down.

"Oh, shit," he muttered, and reached for the radio.

Except for the radio chatter, the Bordelaise Police Department was as silent as a wake. Sometime after the chase began, the radio chatter between the chopper and the highway patrol had ended. Katie didn't know what had happened to Cody and J.R., and was desperate to learn if Bobby was even inside the truck. Everyone was just standing around the front desk, listening to the troopers relaying information back and forth to headquarters.

For Katie, it was like hearing her worst nightmare coming true. She knew the chief was in the room, as were Lee and Carter, but no one talked. No one moved.

She hovered beside Vera, praying to hear something positive.

Then all of a sudden a trooper began broadcasting the words she'd been praying to hear.

"The boy's inside. I have a visual on the boy."

When it became apparent that Bobby was alive, she screamed for joy, but the joy quickly dispersed at the next piece of information.

"Suspect is moving at one hundred and seven miles an hour. Request confirmation that roadblock is in place."

When she realized Bobby was inside a truck hurtling down a busy interstate at a speed of more than a hundred miles an hour, she nearly lost it.

"They have to stop him! Why don't they stop him?"

Vera grabbed Katie's hand and gave it a quick squeeze, but Katie couldn't bear to hear any more. She wanted this to stop, but she couldn't move away. Instead, she hovered with her hands over her mouth and her heart in her throat, silently praying for both Bobby and J.R., because she no longer knew where her husband was.

Then out of the blue, she heard one of the troopers shout, "The chopper is going down!"

She nearly fainted.

"Oh, my God, oh, my God . . . this isn't happening," she moaned, and turned away from the radio with her hands over her ears.

Suddenly Lee Tullius was grabbing her by the arms and yanking her hands away from her face.

"It didn't crash, Katie! It didn't crash. The chopper is setting down on the interstate. It's a good thing. They're trying to force Newt to stop before he wrecks."

She couldn't think past the words *didn't crash.* By the time she managed to refocus on the radio chatter, all she could hear was someone shouting, "Get down! Get down!" and then what sounded like gunshots.

Katie blanched.

"Are they alive? Did they crash? Dear God . . . what's happening to my family?"

Newt was in the worst place he'd ever been in his life. Not during his longest stretch in prison had he ever been this scared. He was going so fast — faster than he'd ever driven in his life. He didn't know why they were still upright, or why he hadn't crashed a dozen times over. The tires on his truck were emitting a high-pitched whine, and the instruments on his dash were going crazy. The truck engine was overheated. The oil light was on, and he could smell smoke. Something was on fire. Was it going to blow? Was that how he was going to die — blown to kingdom come all over Interstate 49?

He glanced down at the speedometer. It was topped out at one hundred and ten miles an hour. It wouldn't take much to cause a wreck. All he would have to do was tap the brakes and turn the wheel, and the sucker would roll like a burrito, scattering him and everything he owned all over a solid acre and then some.

But did he have the guts to do it? He didn't know. What he did know was that he didn't want to go back to prison, and especially in Louisiana. The state prison in Angola had a rep he didn't want to test.

He glanced down at the kid on the floorboard. He wasn't moving. If the little bastard had gone and broken his neck, then they would get him for more than kidnapping. He would go down for murder.

He sobbed. If only he could turn back the clock. If only he'd driven away when the storm sirens started blowing. He'd spent so many years living under the radar of the law. He'd taken pride in getting lost in the system. And then he'd fixated on this kid and screwed himself straight back into hell.

His fingers ached. The steering wheel was vibrating beneath the palms of his hands. Vehicles ahead of him were taking to the ditches on either side of the road. The Louisiana Highway Patrol was hot on his heels. All he had to do was tap the brake and turn the steering wheel just a little. At one hundred miles an hour, it would be over in seconds.

But could he do it?

Should he do it?

He took a deep breath. Just as he started to lift his foot off the accelerator, the kid stirred.

Newt glanced down, then flinched.

A tiny stream of blood was running from Bobby Earle's hairline past his two black eyes and down the bridge of that swollen little nose. And in a moment of blinding clarity, he couldn't believe what he had done.

It was time to end this.

He looked up, but instead of a clean

stretch of blacktop rolling out before him, a big black helicopter was coming straight at him.

He screamed.

One look at those massive, spinning rotors and he knew he didn't have the guts to be sliced and diced on his way to hell.

"Son of a bitch!" he cried, took his foot off the accelerator, counted to ten, hoping it would slow the truck down enough to keep from rolling, then hit the brakes.

The truck started sliding. The hood popped up, then broke off, flying over the cab and then the back of the truck bed to go bouncing end over end down the interstate. Steam and smoke began pouring from the engine as he rode the brakes.

A tire blew, sending the truck into a spin.

Newt took his foot off the brake and hung on to the wheel for dear life, managing to steer out of the spin and onto the grass of the center median, where the truck finally came to a shuddering stop.

He reached down and turned off the key.

Smoke was boiling into the cab. He could feel the heat on his legs.

He opened the door and started to jump out, then thought of the kid and looked back.

Bobby Earle was climbing up onto the seat

with a panicked expression on his face.

"Grab my hand!" Newt yelled.

Bobby didn't hesitate. He reached out.

Newt grabbed him by the wrist, yanking him out of the truck, and then they started running — away from the truck and the fire, away from the chopper and its crazy spinning blades. Just running.

Just running.

Because there was nothing else left to do, and he was still afraid to stop.

J.R. knew when smoke began coming out from under the truck that his son's life was hanging by a thread. He saw the driver hit the brakes, watched the hood pop off the truck and fly over the cab and then nearly died of fright when the truck blew a tire and spun out of control.

"Put it down! Put it down!" he screamed.

He was out of the chopper before it fully landed and was running down the middle of the interstate toward the truck when he saw the driver jump out, dragging Bobby with him.

He didn't see the highway patrol cars coming to a sliding halt from the other direction, or know that both troopers were also out of their cars and running, too.

All he could see was his little boy in the

clutches of a devil.

A shot rang out. Then another.

The troopers were shouting, "Get down! Get down!"

Newt heard the shots, and then the troopers' orders, and stumbled. Breaking stride was like a slap in the face. All of a sudden he was done. He turned loose of the kid and threw his hands in the air. He was turning around to face the cops when something hit him from behind.

The pain from the blow radiated from his back to his head, then down to his feet. It felt as if he'd been cut in half. Then there was a blow to his head, followed by another, then another, and then blows to his stomach, his face, and all the while he kept screaming, "I didn't touch him! I didn't touch him!"

Suddenly, in the middle of chaos, his gaze connected with his assailant and he found himself looking straight up into J. R. Earle's eyes. It was like looking at an adult version of the kid, only there was so much hate in this man's eyes. J.R.'s fingers curled around his throat, and Newt knew he was about to die.

"I didn't touch him," Newt croaked.

The man's eyes were black with rage. His

nostrils flared from the exertion. But it was the soft, deadly whisper in Newt's ear that sent him over the edge. "If you don't die now, the day you get out of prison I will kill you."

Then those fingers tightened around his neck and everything went black.

Bobby didn't know what was happening. He'd seen Daddy, and then Daddy was gone. He'd seen the police cars behind them, but then they disappeared when he got knocked into the floor. When he woke up again, smoke was coming inside the truck, and the monster was screaming and yelling. All of a sudden they were out and running, and he kept trying to pull free, but the monster wouldn't let go.

They were running, running, so fast — too fast. Bobby couldn't keep up. His legs were hurting, his chest was burning, and he needed to stop, but there was no breath left in his lungs to cry out for help.

Then all of a sudden he was free-falling, flying through the air. He landed hard on his side, knocking the breath from his body. He tried to get up, but he couldn't move. He tried to cry out, but he had no breath left to voice his panic.

Then he heard two loud pops and someone yelling.

And then all he knew was that when he took his first breath, it was in his daddy's arms.

J.R. was crying. "You're okay, little guy. Daddy's got you. Daddy's got you. You're safe, son. You're safe."

Bobby took a deep breath, then threw his arms around Daddy. His body was shaking so hard he couldn't speak, so he hid his face against Daddy's neck and started to sob.

J.R. turned in a circle with his child in his arms, then started walking toward the chopper. All he could think about was getting back to Katie.

Before he'd gone twenty feet, one of the troopers stopped him.

"Sir. You need to come with us."

J.R. shook his head. "I need to take him home."

"Mr. Earle . . . You are Mr. Earle, right?"

J.R. nodded.

"Your son was the victim of a kidnapping. He was the subject of an Amber Alert. He needs immediate medical attention. There are channels we have to go through to make sure he's taken care of properly. As much as we might want to, we can't just let you walk away with him."

J.R.'s shoulders slumped. He understood what they were saying, but by car, it was such a long way back. He looked down at his son, still wearing the same clothes he'd been snatched in, dirty and beaten, sobbing and shaking like a leaf in a windstorm.

"Don't make us ride that three hours home in a car . . . not when there's a chopper standing by," he begged.

"There's a highway patrol chopper on the way. Get in the car with us. When we meet it, we'll make the transfer. Okay?"

J.R.'s voice broke. "It seems we don't have an option," he said. "Just let me tell my pilot so he can return to base."

The trooper pointed. "Looks like he's coming to you. And by the way, when you talk to him, tell him that was one fine piece of flying he did today."

J.R. nodded. "Just give me a minute," he said, then stopped. "Has somebody notified the Bordelaise police? I want my wife, Katie, to know our son is alive and safe."

"Already done, sir," the trooper said, then nodded toward Cody, who was almost on them. "Make it quick. We need to get your boy medical attention as soon as possible."

J.R. turned around just as Cody Sands arrived. There were tears in his eyes and a big smile on his face.

"This is probably going to be one of the best days of my life," Cody said, and then clapped J.R. on the shoulder.

"Thank you, Cody. I owe you. Big-time. The troopers think you're quite a cowboy."

Cody grinned even wider.

"We're going to have to go with the police, but when you get back in the air, would you let Brent know we're okay and thank him for me?" J.R. asked.

"You know it," Cody said, and then gently brushed the palm of his hand across Bobby's head. "Really glad to see you again, little guy. Your daddy's a hero. Don't you ever forget that."

There was a lump in Cody's throat and a smile on his face as he turned and walked away.

J.R. shifted Bobby into a firmer grasp, then patted him gently.

"Come on, son. Let's go home. Mama's waiting."

He felt Bobby flinch, then gasp as he lifted his head. For the first time in days, they were face-to-face, eye to eye. It was all J.R. could do to look and not weep.

Bobby's voice was still shaking, but his gaze was steady.

"Mama is dead."

J.R. was shocked. "No, no, son, she's not.

387

Why would you think that?"

Bobby's voice began to shake. "The monster told me Mama was dead."

J.R.'s heart sank; then he cursed silently. "That's a lie," he said sharply. "That's a lie. Mama is not dead. She's been scared half out of her mind. We both have. We've been looking and looking for you."

"Mama didn't die in the tornado?"

"No. Your mama is just fine," J.R. said. "We've been so worried, trying every way we knew how to find you."

Bobby's chin quivered, but he managed a nod. "I knew it," he said softly. "I told the monster, but he wouldn't listen. I told him he needed to call you. To tell you where I was, but he just kept putting bad stuff in my water to make me sleepy and tying me to the bed."

J.R. cupped the back of his little boy's head and then closed his eyes. He couldn't talk. He couldn't think. There was nothing to say that would ever make what this child had endured all right.

"Are you two ready?"

J.R. turned.

The trooper was waiting.

J.R. tightened his hold on his son and started walking toward the car.

EIGHTEEN

"Suspect is in custody. Child is safe. Father and son being transported to hospital in Baton Rouge. Request Bordelaise Police Department advise the mother."

Shouts erupted inside the Bordelaise Police Department. Lee and Carter gave each other a high five, then gave the chief a big pat on the back.

Vera threw her hands up in the air and did a little happy dance around her chair, shouting, "Praise the Lord . . . praise the Lord!" at the top of her voice.

Katie was numb. The relief of knowing both Bobby and J.R. were alive and on their way back to her was overwhelming. She could hear the revelry in the room but couldn't focus enough to share in it.

Her legs were shaking and her hands were trembling when she backed into a chair and then sat down with a thump.

"Thank you, Jesus," Katie whispered, then

leaned back and took a deep breath.

Before she had time to relax, the phone rang. She looked up, watching as Vera answered, wrote down some information, then handed it to the chief.

When Hershel turned to look for her, she was on her feet in seconds.

"Is something wrong?"

"No, ma'am. This is just information about the hospital where they're taking your boy."

"I've got to get there. I have to be waiting when they arrive." Then she turned in a circle, looking around the lobby.

"Has anyone seen my purse?"

Vera picked it up from behind her desk.

"Here it is, honey."

Katie ran to get it, dug out the keys to the truck and was about to head out the door when Hershel stopped her.

"Wait a minute, Katie girl. You're in no condition to make that drive on your own. Lee. Carter. One of you drive her truck, the other one take her to the hospital in your cruiser, and don't dawdle. Run hot all the way to Baton Rouge if you have to."

Lee held up his hand. "She's riding with me, Chief. We started this journey together. I'd be honored if she'd let me help her end it."

Katie turned. "We did?"

Lee nodded. "I'll tell you all about it on the way to Baton Rouge. If you need to powder your nose and fuss a bit, go do it now. I've been waiting for a reason to use the lights and sirens for something other than a disaster. This is going to be one heck of a ride."

Katie handed her keys to Carter, then flew off down the hall to the bathroom. When she came back, Lee was waiting for her at the door.

"We have to go by Penny Bates's house and get Oliver," Katie said.

"Who's Oliver?" Lee asked.

"Bobby's teddy bear. He slept with it every night of his life, and it was one of the few things that made it through the storm. The days when I thought that was all I had left of him were the worst days of my life. Now, I can't wait to see his face when I put it back in his arms."

Lee nodded. "That sounds like a plan," he said.

Within minutes, she was in his cruiser and on her way to Penny's. After a quick stop to give Penny the good news, and get Bobby's bear and some clean clothes, they headed out of town.

As promised, Lee turned on the lights and

siren as they sped through town, which brought everyone shopping or working on Main Street to the windows to take a look.

It didn't take long for word to get around.

Not only had Bobby Earle been found, but he had been rescued by his daddy and the Louisiana Highway Patrol.

The drive to Baton Rouge passed in a blur for Katie. After hearing Lee's story of how he'd found her at her house and then taken her to the hospital, Katie hadn't been able to shake a growing sense of urgency. She clutched the teddy bear tight against her chest and kept focusing on the facts.

Her son was alive. She wouldn't think about what had happened to him. That would be for later. Right now, it was enough that J.R. was bringing him home.

Carter had reached the hospital in Baton Rouge first, learned that local news crews had caught wind of the rescue and called Lee to give them a heads-up.

When Lee and Katie pulled into the drive leading up to the emergency entrance, they could see the news vans with their satellite dishes parked nearby and a gaggle of news crews waiting near the entrance.

"Oh, no," Katie muttered, when she saw the gathering crowd.

"Don't worry," Lee said, as he wheeled past them and stopped in front of the entrance. "There's Carter. He'll get you inside without a fuss. We'll put your things in the truck and bring you the keys later. In the meantime, I'll take care of this crowd, don't you worry. Heck. You might even see me on the evening news." Then he grinned.

Katie laid her hand on Lee's arm.

"I will never be able to thank all of you enough for what you did for us."

Lee shook his head. "It's thanks enough knowing your little guy is coming home."

"Yes," Katie said, and then tightened her grip on Oliver and her purse.

"Go on!" he urged.

She opened the door and sprinted toward the hospital as the crowd surged toward her. Even as Carter grabbed her arm and ushered her through the entrance, she could hear Lee Tullius's voice, rising above the crowd.

The first thirty minutes after she'd gotten to the hospital were a whirlwind of identifying herself to the people in charge and then getting a pass to the roof of the hospital so she could accompany the staff who'd meet the chopper.

Lee found her, told her where to find her

truck, handed her the keys and then headed out the door with an apology. The chief had given them a call, and they were needed back in town. From what Chief Porter had said, he thought something was about to a break in regard to the missing prisoners.

Katie waited anxiously, glad to have Oliver for company, and when they finally got word that the chopper was inbound, the team headed for the roof with Katie right behind them. At that point she was riding a high, knowing she was only minutes away from seeing her son.

As they exited the building, she glanced up. The late-afternoon sun was moving slowly toward the west. The sky was clear, without a cloud in sight. This high above the city, the air seemed cleaner — even lighter — muffling the noise from the streets below.

Suddenly, she heard one of the nurses shout and point.

"There it comes!"

They'd made the transfer from the patrol car to the police chopper within fifteen minutes.

"We're heading to a hospital in Baton Rouge," the pilot told J.R. "Your wife has been notified. She'll be meeting you there."

Once J.R. got Bobby inside the chopper, he tried to buckle him into the seat beside him. But the little boy began to shake his head and cry, begging to sit in Daddy's lap.

The pilot turned to look over the back of his seat and started to argue. "Sir, he needs to be —"

"It's okay, son," J.R. said. "You can sit in my lap. We'll make it work."

He lifted Bobby into his lap, fastened the seat belt around the both of them, then wrapped his arms around his little boy and pulled him close.

The pilot gave them a thumbs-up, and within minutes they were airborne.

J.R. could feel the tension easing from Bobby's shoulders. He watched as his son's eyelids grew heavy, and when he finally fell asleep, he was still clutching the front of J.R.'s shirt.

J.R. knew his son was dreaming. His little body jerked and twitched as he slept, and his eyelids were fluttering, as if he was trying to wake up. J.R. could only imagine the hell he was reliving and wondered if he would ever be okay again. He saw the healing rope burns on Bobby's wrists, and then the ones on his ankles, and wished Newt Collins to hell again.

Twice Bobby cried out, and both times

J.R. kept saying over and over, "You're okay. You're okay. Daddy's got you. Daddy's got you."

He watched Bobby's eyes open just a crack, as if assuring himself he wasn't dreaming, and then he fell back to sleep.

By the time the pilot announced they were about to land at the helipad behind the hospital, J.R. was stone-faced. He didn't know for sure how Newton Collins's fate was going to play out, but he knew that he would do whatever it took to make good on his promise.

If Newton Collins was ever released from prison again, it would be his first and last day of freedom. If the justice system turned him loose after what he'd done to Bobby, J.R. would track him down and kill him, and never lose a minute of sleep over the decision.

A few moments later the chopper began to descend. J.R. glanced out the window. There was a group of people standing on the roof of the hospital near the doorway. Even from several hundred feet up in the air, he saw Katie. The wind from the rotors was beginning to stir the air below. Her long legs were braced against the gusts, and her dark hair was being lifted and whipped in a crazy fashion, but she seemed impervious to the disturbance. Her expression was fixed, her posture steadfast.

Finally his family was once again intact.

Then his vision blurred, and after that everything began happening in rapid-fire sequence.

Katie clutched Oliver with one hand, while shading her eyes against the glare with the other. The familiar whup-whup sound of the chopper's rotors grew louder as it drew closer.

One moment the chopper was just a blur, and then every detail was clear and perfect. She could even see the pilot's face, but though she struggled to look past him, the interior was too dark for her to make out any passengers.

The wind from the rotors was fierce, whipping her hair back and forth into her eyes, but she didn't move, didn't care. She was too focused on seeing J.R. and Bobby.

Then the chopper was down.

"Wait here!" an intern said, and the crew rushed forward pushing a gurney.

Katie groaned. Wait? How could she wait? Didn't they understand that her little boy had, almost miraculously, been raised from the dead?

She shifted from foot to foot with the bear

clutched beneath her chin, agonizing for her first glimpse. And then they opened the chopper door, and she saw J.R. bracing himself to step down. When she realized he was carrying Bobby, her heart leaped.

Despite her orders to wait, she couldn't. She started moving toward the chopper with her gaze fixed on the sleeping little boy.

Then they were taking Bobby out of J.R.'s arms, and she saw him stir, then wake, then begin to panic. When she heard him scream, Katie started to run.

J.R.'s eyes had been on Katie the moment the door was opened, but then Bobby had begun to rouse, and his focus quickly shifted back to him. As they emerged from the chopper into the waiting hands of a hospital team, things began to spin out of J.R.'s control.

Someone took Bobby out of his arms and laid him on the gurney. The moment he lost touch with J.R., Bobby woke. He took one look at the strangers around him and started to scream.

J.R. moved back into Bobby's line of sight as the hospital staff started pushing him away from the chopper.

"It's okay, buddy. It's okay. Daddy's here. We're at the hospital. These people are going to check you over . . . make sure you're okay."

"Don't touch me! Don't touch me! I wanna go home!" Bobby wailed.

J.R.'s gut knotted. There was no way to make this easier.

Then he heard Katie's voice and looked up.

She was coming toward them on the run. Behind him, the chopper took off into the air, whipping the wind even higher and harder, but it didn't slow Katie down.

"Bobby! Look, buddy . . . it's Mama! Mama's coming, and she's got Oliver."

Bobby sat up on the gurney and then rolled over on his knees, even as they were trying to subdue him.

Katie was crying Bobby's name, and then suddenly she was there.

Bobby leaped from the gurney into his mother's arms and began sobbing as if his heart had broken. "He kept saying . . . The monster said you were dead. He said you were *dead.*"

Katie gasped, caught the look in J.R.'s eyes and knew she had yet to hear the worst. Then she quickly looked away. Right now, nothing mattered but the warmth of her son's little body against hers and his arms wrapped tight around her neck.

"Well, that bad old monster lied, didn't he, honey?" she said, and then smothered his face with kisses.

At that point the gravity of what this child had endured brought everything to a halt. Nurses hardened to the grimmest of life's tragedies were in tears. The doctor stepped back, allowing the family their moment, knowing that what was taking place now was more powerful than any medicine.

Finally Katie set Bobby down on the gurney, then managed a teary smile as she looked him in the face. It took every ounce of control she had to speak calmly.

"How did you get your black eyes and puffy nose, honey?"

Bobby put a hand on his nose, then the back of his head, and felt the knot.

"I got tied to the bed every day. Once I almost got away. I was all the way out the door, and then the bad man hit me in the back of the head with something and made me fall down. When I woke up, my nose and my lip were bleeding. It still hurts, Mama."

"Son of a bitch," a nurse said softly.

The doctor put his hand against the back of Bobby's head, gently feeling the knot and a half-healed cut on his scalp.

"We better get you inside, little guy. And

while we're going, why don't you tell me how you almost got away? I'll bet you were running really fast."

Bobby looked nervous, until Katie plopped Oliver down in his lap.

"You better lie down so Oliver doesn't fall off," she said softly.

Bobby reluctantly stretched out on the gurney, then inhaled deeply as he stuffed the bear beneath his chin.

"Oliver smells good, Mama."

Katie smiled. "He got a bath after he went through the tornado."

"I need a bath, too," Bobby said. "I didn't take my clothes off. Not even once." Then he frowned. "I didn't want to. Was that okay?"

"Hell, yes, that was okay," J.R. said shortly. "You did everything right, son, and don't ever forget it."

Bobby managed a crooked smile, then hugged the bear a little tighter.

At that point they began moving the gurney toward the hospital, and Katie's gaze went straight to J.R.

"He swore he didn't touch him," J.R. said.

Katie's chin quivered. She tried to speak, but nothing came out but a sob. At that point she walked into J.R.'s embrace and buried her face against his chest.

"I don't care what happened. I just care that I have him back."

"I know, baby," J.R. said softly, then took her by the hand as they ran to catch up. Whatever happened, they would face it together.

EPILOGUE

New Orleans, Christmas Day

Bobby sat in front of their Christmas tree, posing for a picture with his dog, Hero, sprawled across his lap. Just as the flash went off, the half-grown black Lab looked up and licked Bobby under the chin.

Bobby threw back his head and laughed.

"Eww . . . Hero . . . your breath stinks," he said, and then grabbed the dog around the neck and rolled, taking the long-legged puppy with him.

Deliriously happy to be wrestling, the dog nipped and yipped and appeared to be laughing.

"Look at them," J.R. said. "Just alike. Both long-legged boys with a whole lot of growing up yet to do."

Katie scooted onto the arm of the chair where J.R. was sitting, and then laughed when he wrapped his arm around her waist and pulled her into his lap.

Bobby heard the sound and immediately stopped, just to make sure he wasn't missing out on something fun. When he realized it was just Mama and Daddy kissing again, he rolled his eyes and fell backward with a groan.

Hero pounced, and their game continued.

The kiss between J.R. and Katie was sweet, with a promise of more to come.

"Hold that thought for later," J.R. whispered, as Katie leaned back with a sigh.

"Don't worry. That thought's always with me," she said softly.

J.R.'s eyes darkened. "I love you, Katie."

The smile slid off her face. "I love you, too."

Instinctively, they both turned their attention to their son. The past few months had been agonizing, as Bobby had battled what his doctors called post-traumatic stress disorder. His youth was a positive. And the older he got, the more he would be able to understand what had happened, and how fortunate he'd been at what had not.

They'd slept with him between them in their bed until he'd finally accepted that his nightmare was over. And once Hero had come into his life, his nights had turned around. In his mind, with Oliver in his arms and the small black puppy at his side, and all of them no longer living in Bordelaise, he would be safe. The more time that passed, and the larger the dog grew, the more confident Bobby became.

And it wasn't only Bobby who'd faced down a demon and won.

Katie and her son each had their own brand of hell to exorcise. Ironically, New Orleans had turned out to be their refuge and not the hell Katie had expected it to be.

Just lying in J.R.'s arms and watching Bobby and Hero play was its own reward. They'd all learned the hard way that nothing was impossible when you were backed by people you loved.

Just then Bobby stopped, sat up and got quiet.

Hero was still chewing on his shoe, but Bobby didn't seem to notice.

Katie saw him, frowned, then sat back, uncertain what was happening.

"Everything okay, buddy?" J.R. asked.

Bobby was still frowning as he turned to his dad.

"Daddy . . . ?"

"Yes, son?"

"I've been thinking."

Katie's breath caught in the back of her throat. Were they about to experience their first backslide? The psychiatrist had warned them it might happen.

"What about?" J.R. asked.

"My friend Holly."

Katie held her breath. It was the first time he'd mentioned anyone or anything from Bordelaise since the rescue.

"What about her?" Katie asked.

"I miss playing with her. She would like Hero. Do you think we could go visit her someday? And maybe we could take Hero with us?"

Katie exhaled softly. This had to be a good sign.

J.R. smiled. "I'll give her parents a call later. Maybe we can drive up one day during Christmas vacation."

A slow smile broke across Bobby's face. "Yay!" he said, and then rolled back onto Hero and the wrestling began anew.

Katie leaned back in J.R.'s arms with a sigh.

"That was a first," she said softly. "He's never even mentioned Bordelaise since we got him back."

J.R. was smiling as he nuzzled Katie's ear. "Yeah. I think he's gonna grow up just like me."

Katie giggled. "What do you mean?"

"I was always a one-woman man. Looks

like our little guy might be leaning that way, too. He hadn't mentioned a single person from back then, and when he finally does, it's a girl."

Katie smiled.

"But what a girl! If it hadn't been for her, we might never have gotten Bobby back."

"I know," J.R. said, and then kissed the back of her ear.

Katie sighed. "I am so happy."

J.R. stilled, suddenly reminded of how much he had to be grateful for.

"So am I," he said softly.

"So . . . what do you want to do?" she asked.

"Make mad, passionate love to my woman," J.R. growled. "However, that's going to have to wait until later. Right now I guess I'd better go make that call to the Maxwells and see if they're up for a visit later in the week."

"We can drop by and see Penny, too," Katie said. "I owe her a lot."

"Yeah, and we can make sure the contractor has cleaned up the storm debris off the property."

Katie nodded. "I guess it's time we all faced a trip back to Bordelaise."

J.R. hugged her. "We both learned the hard way that places aren't the monsters.

It's the people who live in them who can't always be trusted."

Katie sighed, thinking of the tornado and the damage it had wrought. "Too bad we're such slow learners. It took an act of God to show us the way."

They looked toward their Christmas tree, decorated with colorful lights and sparkling ornaments, and then both of them gasped and then yelled at the same time.

"Bobby! Look out for the tree!"

They were out of the chair and running toward their son just as he and the dog rolled under the tree.

A low-hanging limb poked Hero in the rear, startling him, and he spun toward it with a yelp. As he did, a strand of lights slipped beneath his head and drew taut against his throat. That was all it took to make the dog leap.

"Hero! No!" Bobby cried, but it was too late.

The gangly pup bolted, taking the lights — and the tree — with him.

Down it went, burying Bobby somewhere beneath.

"Help! Mama! Daddy! Get me out of here!" Bobby shrieked.

"Get the dog!" she yelled.

J.R. lunged for the dog and the lights, as

408

Katie began pulling Bobby out from under the tree.

By the time she got him rescued and made sure he wasn't hurt, J.R. was coming back carrying the quivering pup.

"What a mess," he muttered, as he looked at the upended tree, the tumbled ornaments and the lights strung across the floor.

Bobby was verging on tears, clearly thinking he and his best friend were in serious trouble.

Then Katie started laughing.

Bobby froze.

J.R. paused.

Even Hero looked perplexed.

And Katie kept laughing.

And laughing. Until she was on the floor and rolling in the middle of the mess.

J.R. dropped the dog, got down on his knees and took her in his arms.

"You're crazy," he said, and then kissed the side of her cheek.

Katie threw her arms around his neck.

"This night is a miracle, J.R. None of this would be happening if we hadn't gotten our little boy back." Then she made a face and threw a wad of tinsel into his hair.

J.R. grinned, picked a silver ornament off a nearby limb and hung it in her hair.

Hero's tongue dropped out the side of his

mouth. His legs began to quiver. There was rolling going on. He liked to roll.

He glanced up at his master.

Bobby looked at the dog, then at his parents.

Mama was still laughing. He didn't know why, but he wanted in on it, too.

He jumped off the sofa and threw himself into the mix, tossing tinsel and lights up in the air.

"This is fun! Right, Mama?" he yelled.

Katie sat up, wrapped her arms around him and pulled him down with them.

"Yes, little man. This is fun."

At that point, Hero launched himself at them.

They all went down again in a tangle of arms and legs and a long wagging tail. Outside the sky turned dark, but in this house, the room was filled with light and laughter.

Katie Earle had been right.

None of this could have happened if they hadn't been given a miracle. Their family had already been torn apart before the tornado hit. In an odd twist of fate, it was the storm that had put them back together.

We hope you have enjoyed this Large Print book. Other Thorndike, Wheeler, Kennebec, and Chivers Press Large Print books are available at your library or directly from the publishers.

For information about current and upcoming titles, please call or write, without obligation, to:

Publisher
Thorndike Press
295 Kennedy Memorial Drive
Waterville, ME 04901
Tel. (800) 223-1244

or visit our Web site at:

http://gale.cengage.com/thorndike

OR

Chivers Large Print
published by BBC Audiobooks Ltd
St James House, The Square
Lower Bristol Road
Bath BA2 3SB
England
Tel. +44 (0) 800 136919
email: bbcaudiobooks@bbc.co.uk
www.bbcaudiobooks.co.uk

All our Large Print titles are designed for easy reading, and all our books are made to last.